Tanya Huff

Tanya Huff is best known for her Blood novels, about a modern vampire's crime-fighting alliance with a Toronto ex-cop: Blood Price, Blood Trail, Blood Lines, Blood Pact and Blood Debt. She has also written more than fourteen other novels, and her short stories have appeared in numerous fantasy magazines. She currently lives and writes in rural Ontario and is one of Canada's best selling and most beloved speculative fiction authors.

About Tanya Huff's Work

"Ms. Huff is a superlative talent who brings freshness and excellence to all of her work, also adding a depth of characterization that greatly enhances the appeal of her inventive fantasy novels."
                                        - Rave Reviews re: *The Fires's Stone*

"This is fantasy at its finest, full of electrifying tension and wondrous events. Ms. Huff develops both plot and characters with sumptuous elegance, spinning a magical tale of high adventure and glorious triumph." - Rave Reviews re: *The Last Wizard*

"Contemporary urban fantasy at its best."
                        - Locus Magazine re: *Gate of Darkness, Circle of Light*

"The author's delightfully light touch lends a sense of timeliness to this effortlessly told fantasy mystery."
                                    - Library Journal re: *Smoke and Shadows*

"Plot-driven, at a pace worthy of NASCAR, and the characters are well-drawn and compelling. Huff also takes aim with a freshly sharpened stake, skewering conventions with finesse and style. Huff's novel amply demonstrates that genre fiction doesn't have to be junk-food fiction." - The Globe and Mail re: *Smoke and Shadows*

"Ms. Huff is a marvelous talent whose vibrant characterizations and intelligent prose make each and every book a very special reading experience. Bring on the next verse!"
                                    - Romantic Times re: *Sing the Four Quarters*

"Plenty of odd characters and touches of unexpected magic and humor to keep things moving, for a contemporary fantasy that's lots of fun." - Locus re: *Summon the Keeper*

Stealing Magic

A complete collection of short stories
featuring Magdelene, the world's most
powerful (and laziest) wizard and
Terazin, a top-notch thief

by
Tanya Huff

EDGE SCIENCE FICTION AND FANTASY PUBLISHING
AN IMPRINT OF HADES PUBLICATIONS, INC.
CALGARY

Edge Science Fiction and Fantasy Publishing
An Imprint of Hades Publications Inc.
P.O. Box 1714, Calgary, Alberta, T2P 2L7, Canada

In house editing by Kimberly Gammon
Interior design by Brian Hades
Cover Illustrations by David Willicome
ISBN: 978-1-894063-34-0

EDGE Science Fiction and Fantasy Publishing and Hades Publications, Inc.
acknowledges the ongoing support of the Canada Council for the Arts and the
Alberta Foundation for the Arts for our publishing programme.

The Alberta Foundation for the Arts   Alberta COMMUNITY DEVELOPMENT   Canada Council for the Arts   Conseil des Arts du Canada
COMMITTED TO THE DEVELOPMENT OF CULTURE AND THE ARTS

Library and Archives Canada Cataloguing in Publication

Huff, Tanya
Stealing magic / by Tanya Huff. -- Expanded ed.

ISBN-13: 978-1-894063-34-0
ISBN-10: 1-894063-34-1

1. Fantastic fiction, Canadian (English) I. Title.

PS8565.U328S73 2005   C813'.54   C2005-905375-5

FIRST EDITION
(k-20051016)
Printed in Canada
www.edgewebsite.com

Contents

Stealing Magic

Magdelene

The Last Lesson

The lizard peered out from under its layer of dust and seemed to sneer at the girl languidly flicking a cloth around the cluttered room. Safely tucked on a top shelf, it rested far beyond the reach of such a careless cleaning. Although its topaz eyes were dull under years of accumulated grime, and sawdust seeped from a tear in an uplifted front leg, the lizard gave the very definite impression it would rather continue to slowly deteriorate than risk destruction under the grimy rag now being waved about. It almost flinched as a rodent skull, as ancient as itself, was caught up and dashed to the floor.

"Oh, lizard piss," muttered the girl looking down at the scattered ivory shards. She pushed heavy chestnut hair back off her face and kicked a yellowed tooth beneath the edge of a bulging cabinet. "I don't even know why I bother."

"It's no wonder a wizard's apprenticeship is so long," she continued, glaring about the room — the edges of several loose papers curled, and a tarnished silver goblet acquired a tracery of frost — "a good half of it's spent cleaning up after other people." Then her eyes lit on the massive spell book lying closed and locked on its lectern, and she smiled.

She stuffed the cleaning rag between a badly dented brass horn and the jawbone of an ass and sped across the workroom. At the lectern, she ran her fingers lightly over gilded runes, murmured the standard unlocking spell, and watched the worn leather cover of the spell book roll back.

"He doesn't really expect me to get this place clean," she told the prodding of her conscience. "He only wants me to stay busy while he's gone." That the massive book and its ancient contents had been expressly forbidden her, she chose to ignore. Had her master truly wished her not to read the book, surely he'd have used a stronger lock spell. The one on it was absurdly easy to break.

"Besides," she added, tossing her hair back over her shoulders, "he could be closeted with the king for hours. I'm sure he'd want me to study." She flipped the thick parchment pages with little respect for their age and quickly scanned the titles as they passed. A spell for bringing in water? Not likely, bringing in the water ranked amongst the high points of her day. A spell to look as beautiful as the morning? Mornings were made to be slept through. A spell to move carpets through the air? She'd tried that the last time, and as far as she knew, her little rug still rose through the heavens.

Good thing she'd jumped off as it headed for the window. A spell to bring warmth on the coldest of days? Now that was more like it.

Glancing up through the workroom's frost-edged window, she shivered at the bleak view of winter grey sky. At least here in the palace, the windows were glassed. She bent her head to read.

"MAGDELENE!"

When she could breathe again, when her heart had stopped pounding so loudly in her ears, Magdelene slowly turned around.

Adar, the king's wizard, her master, stood just inside the doorway, the color of his face almost matching the deep purple of his robes. "WHAT DO YOU THINK YOU'RE DOING?"

Magdelene dove for her duster and grabbed it just as Adar, moving faster than a man of his apparent age should've been able, got her by the ear. She twisted in his grip and waved the filthy bit of cloth under his nose.

"I've been, ouch, cleaning."

"You've been into the spell book again!"

Well if you knew, why did you ask? Magdelene wondered, but wisely kept the thought to herself. "I didn't do any. I was only reading."

"I thought I told you to stay away from it!" He punctuated each word with a tug on her ear. "I'll say when you're ready." He thrust her away and shook his head. "I should beat you."

Magdelene rubbed her throbbing ear and backed up. "We have a deal," she reminded him.

The wizard's eyebrows rose almost to the edge of his hat. "I know we have a deal," he snarled. "You remind me of it every time I catch you doing some thing I've told you not to." His arms flew wide for dramatic emphasis. "You get beaten less than any wizard's apprentice in the history of the art."

"How would you know about other apprentices?" Magdelene asked before she considered the consequences. "You've been in hiding for years." She yelped as a heavy hand cuffed her soundly and a well-placed foot sent her sprawling toward the door.

"Go!" roared her master. "Get out of my sight before I forget myself!"

"Where should I go?"

"I don't care."

"I could go get water."

"You do that."

As his apprentice caught up her jacket and fled the room, slamming the door behind her, Adar rubbed his face with both hands and attempted to calm down. Teaching a dragon manners would be easier than living with that obnoxious brat. He walked slowly over to the spell book and looked down at the open page. Reading it was she? The words crawled about the parchment in joyous abandon, one in five in a recognizable language. In the six years he'd had the ancient book, he'd deciphered two spells. The lock spell she'd so blithely demolished had been stronger than the one on the king's treasury.

He sighed, plucked a large grey and white cat off his chair, and collapsed into it.

"I don't know why you're looking so depressed," he muttered at the cat, who snorted and walked away. "Your apprentice doesn't walk through your most powerful spells like they aren't there." He snatched off his sagging felt hat, and a surprising amount of scraggly grey hair came with it. Gradually, wrinkles and lines smoothed out and the wizard's true face emerged. Although the king thought his wizard an elderly sage, Adar was barely ten years older than his apprentice.

He swung his feet up on the scarred oak table that dominated the room, and let his head fall back. "Why?" he asked a spider mending her web by the ceiling, "do I bother?"

"You bother," growled a small, harsh voice, "to keep your miserable life."

Adar turned his head just enough to see the glass vial that held his greatest achievement. The tiny demon within glared out at him and flicked impossibly small claws.

"You bother," the demon continued, "because you know full well she'll tell if you don't. The king and your cushy job'd be no protection if your master's old friends find you."

"It was an accident."

"Oh sure, that's why you burned the body, grabbed his spell book, and ran."

"And who asked you, H'sak?" Adar purred, black eyes glinting dangerously. "Remember who put you there."

H'sak shrugged scaled shoulders and leaned against the wall of his prison. "Oh, you've got power, I'll give you that, but it was a lucky shot that put me here and you know it. You'll never do it again."

"I'll never have to."

"Now your apprentice ... if you want to talk about power..."

"I don't." The wizard scooped up Magdelene's discarded cleaning rag and tossed it over the vial. "And I've plans for taking care of her as well. Her and her power."

From under the rag came muffled but malicious laughter. "Better hurry."

Hurry? Adar rose, stretched, and preened a little in front of the large oval mirror leaning upright against a stack of moldering books. Why hurry? He glanced over at Magdelene's bed tucked into a corner of the workroom. *The brat couldn't be more than...* he thought back. She'd been ten when she'd nearly exposed him before the king and all the court at the last Seven Year Festival and that was only... Netherhells! Over four years ago? It couldn't have been. He counted back on his fingers.

Six years ago he'd slain his master to get at the forbidden spell book, a book the old fool was incapable of even opening.

Five years ago he'd used the book to trap the demon and then used the demon to impress the king and become court wizard. A position that not only netted him rooms in the palace with his every material need instantly seen to but was the first step on his road to world domination. He paused and preened again; world domination, how he loved the sound of that.

Four years ago a grimy girl-child had almost snatched paradise away by seeing through his elaborately magicked disguise. A disguise which, until then, had held up against the combined powers of his ex-master's searching friends. He'd struck a bargain with the brat — who fortunately had no idea of her incredible potential — training for her silence. He knew, in time, he'd remove the threat. Knew, in time, he'd use the second spell gleaned from the stolen book.

Over four years... why that would make her...

"Show me Magdelene!" he commanded, and the mirror, like the well-trained wizard's tool it was, cleared to show his apprentice sitting on the well's edge gazing up through her lashes at a brawny guardsman. The demon was right. He'd better hurry.

ぬ ぬ ぬ

Precariously perched on the ice-covered stones of the well, Magdelene considered how much she hated being cold. She hated the woolens she was forced to wear in the winter, she hated the way her hands ached, and she hated the way her nose ran. Given a choice she'd make her home where the only cold came in frosted mugs, and she'd every intention of finishing that spell to bring warmth on the coldest of days. In the meantime, however, she explored a possible alternative source of heat.

"There you go, Magdelene." The young guardsman secured the well handle and reached out to swing in the full bucket. "This'll fill your other pail, and you'll be set."

"Thank you." Magdelene peered up through her lashes and wondered when Pagrick was going to do something besides draw water. She hoped he didn't expect her to make the first move; she hadn't the vaguest idea of how to begin. And a girl could only take so much flexing and sweating and sighing.

Pagrick flexed mighty shoulders, the ripple visible even through his winter furs, wiped the sheen of sweat from a tanned brow, met Magdelene's eyes, and sighed. Magdelene gritted her teeth. Several large icicles broke free from the south tower and crashed to the ground.

Ever vigilant, Pagrick spun about at the noise. His sword, hanging sheathed at his side, caught between Magdelene's legs and tipped her neatly into the well.

Although chunks of ice floated on the surface, the water began to steam when she hit it. For quite possibly the first time in recorded history, the white heat of rage meant exactly that.

ଓ   ଓ   ଓ

Spraying water with every move, Magdelene slammed open the door to the workroom and stamped through the barricade spells. If she hated being cold, there were no words to describe how she felt about being cold and wet. She slammed the door shut again just to hear the noise.

Adar, perched on the edge of the table, was thankful he'd had enough time to recover from his bout of near hysterical laughter and arrange his expression into one more properly sympathetic. Beside him lay his own fleece lined robe. The scene at the well had decided him. He would use the second spell this afternoon, and in a few short hours he'd not only be rid of his apprentice but would have more than enough power to face his master's old friends and anyone else who dared interfere with his plans.

"The great, stupid, clumsy . ." She sniffed and flung her sodden jacket to the floor. "Oh, how I hate him!"

"Enough," Adar said firmly. "Get out of those wet clothes before you catch a chill." He forced a note of gentle concern into his voice.

Magdelene fumbled with her tunic laces, but her fingers were too stiff to untie the wet leather. She started to shake and found, to her surprise, she couldn't stop. She sniffed again, and a tear joined the ice water still dribbling down her face from her hair. She realized the path of the tear was the only warm spot on her body, and as it felt so pleasant, she began to cry in earnest.

The wizard sighed, impatient to begin now he'd made his decision. Finally, he threw the robe over his shoulder, stepped forward, and with his dagger split Magdelene's tunic from collar to hem. Holding the wet wool distastefully in two fingers, he slipped it back and off, to join the jacket on the floor.

Magdelene continued to sob, turning, lifting, and moving obediently as the wizard undressed her. The next thing she knew, she was wrapped in his robe and sitting on her bed, her hands clutching a mug of warm milk. She sniffed once or twice more and stopped crying. There seemed to be nothing remaining to cry about.

That was certainly interesting, she thought, drinking the milk and remembering the touch of warm fingers on breast and hip. *I wonder what happens next*. Surprisingly enough, Adar was thinking pretty much the same thing. He knew what he had to do before he could work the spell, the ancient book had been very specific, but under the layers of wool and leather and cotton, his apprentice was not the grubby child he remembered. Four years, he was forced to conclude, made one netherhell of a difference. He wondered how he'd missed it happening.

For her part, Magdelene had discovered that her teacher was actually quite attractive in a, well, wizardly sort of way. He was no Pagrick, with mighty thews and sun-bronzed curls, and she doubted he could croon a ballad to save his life, but his black hair lay sleek and shining against his head and his black eyes had an intensity that sent new chills up and down her back. Even his silly ambitions — why anyone would want the bother of dominating the world, Magdelene had no idea — took on a slightly majestic hue. When he sat on the bed beside her, she realized, with a sudden stab of excitement, she was finally going to discover what came after the flexing and sweating and sighing. She quickly drank the last of the milk just in case the next step would require both hands free. Unfortunately, she choked and a great deal of warm liquid came back up through her nose.

During the back pounding that followed, things got a bit tangled up. The empty mug fell to the floor, but neither Adar nor Magdelene noticed. The robe soon followed.

H'sak, watching from his prison, almost felt some sympathy for Adar as the wizard struggled valiantly to match the enthusiasm of his apprentice. Almost.

℣ ℣ ℣

When Adar awoke the next morning, it took him a moment to remember where he was. Hardly surprising; once or twice throughout the night he'd forgotten *who* he was. Where were his red velvet bed curtains? What on earth had happened to make his feather mattress so hard and cramped and... Magdelene...

He slid out of bed, not a difficult maneuver as he was barely balanced on the edge of the cot, and looked down at his sleeping apprentice. Slowly he smiled. More slowly still, because he wasn't entirely certain his back was up to it, he straightened to his full height. The prerequisite of the second spell had been met, and as prerequisites went, Adar mused, it beat the netherhells out of sacrificing goats. He began to chant.

"What are you doing?" Magdelene asked sleepily, rising up on one elbow. "You're making an awful lot of noise."

"Noise? Ha!" His eyes widened, and red and gold sparks, the visible manifestation of his power, danced along his outstretched arms. He couldn't resist gloating. "With this spell I take your power just as I took your virginity!"

"Took?" She pushed her hair out of her eyes and yawned. "Who took? I gave it to you."

"Ha!" Adar repeated and spoke the last three words of the spell. In spite of, or perhaps because of, his exertions of the night before, he felt terrific. And once he added Magdelene's power to his own...

Always fascinated by new magic, Magdelene watched with interest as sparks of green and blue began lifting from her and flying to join their red and gold brethren on Adar's arms. Faster and thicker they flew until Adar was near buried in them and beginning to look worried. Then they merged and became a stream of green and blue fire.

The last Magdelene saw of Adar, he was definitely not happy as he disappeared within the flames. For an instant longer, a roaring column of power danced in the centre of the room, the occasional red or gold spark looking lost and alone in the green and the blue, then, almost too fast to follow, it flowed into the only receptacle in the room capable of containing it. It returned to the girl on the bed.

All that remained of Adar was a pile of soft grey ash.

Never at her best first thing in the morning, Magdelene studied the ash for a moment. "Ooops," she said at last. Common sense told her this was not what Adar had intended. Before she could ask what next, the sound of breaking glass made the question unnecessary.

One inch, two, a foot, three, seven... H'sak stretched and his claws scored the ceiling. "FREE!" he roared. "FREE!"

Magdelene looked up, way up, and tried a tentative smile. It wasn't returned. "Oh, help," she sighed and dove off the cot just as eight-inch talons reduced it to kindling.

"Couldn't we talk about this?" she protested, scrambling under the table.

"Talk?" bellowed the demon. He grabbed the table's edge. "All I've done for five years is talk! I wanna kill something!" Muscles bulged under scaled skin, and the massive table flipped up against the wall.

At the last possible instant, Magdelene dove between his legs. "Your death," H'sak bellowed, whirling about, "will restore my standing in the Netherworld!"

"Mine?" Magdelene squealed, and ducked. "Why mine?"

"You saw —" H'sak stopped suddenly and leaned against the wall to get his breath back while his quarry watched him warily. Apparently five years' imprisonment had left him a little out of shape. "You saw," the demon began again, "what your power did to Adar?"

"Yeah." She slid one foot toward the door but stilled when H'sak tensed. "The spell failed."

H'sak roared with laughter. "Failed? It succeeded only too well. He took your power, but the posturing braggart was unable to contain it. The sheer amount of it destroyed him."

"But I got it back."

"You did," the demon agreed. "And his as well. Not," he added, "that you needed it."

"I have Adar's power?"

"You do."

Magdelene checked. There were certainly a number of strange feelings surging about this way and that, but until now, she'd considered them to be related to the rather remarkable activities of the night before and concentrated on staying alive. A closer look showed their true cause. The demon was right.

"Am I going to be in trouble because of this?" she wondered.

"You mean more trouble?" H'sak asked.

"Good point," Magdelene conceded, diving out of the way as the demon took up the chase again.

Five circuits of the room later, and he sagged against the door, gasping.

"But why," Magdelene panted, a little winded herself, "kill me?"

"Prestige," H'sak told her, puffing out his chest so the scales gleamed. "What matter that I was captured and held when I've just killed the most powerful wizard in the world."

"Me?" Her voice was an incredulous squeak.

"You."

"Because of Adar's power?"

"Hah, a drop in the bucket."

"The most powerful wizard in the world." Magdelene savored the words, then her eyes narrowed. "Demons," she accused, "lie. Swear it on the six Demon Princes."

H'sak sighed. "If it makes you happy during the short time you have left to live, I swear it on the six Demon Princes."

The most powerful wizard in the world, Magdelene thought, leaping the demon's grasping arms and scrabbling to the top of a bulging cabinet. *Me. Wow.*

H'sak demolished the cabinet, but his prestige had already climbed onto the laden shelves above it, barely keeping her footing as years of accumulated junk rained down around her. She snatched a leather bag from the air, ducked an overhand slash that nearly scalped her, and threw the contents in the demon's face.

He screamed a physical impossibility, and both hands went to his eyes.

As silently as she could, Magdelene slipped to the floor and began to move toward the door.

H'sak froze, green tears streaming, his head cocked to catch the smallest noise.

Magdelene's bare foot came down on a yellowed rodent's tooth, and with out thinking, she swore.

H'sak swung at the sound.

Magdelene dropped.

H'sak clutched at air.

Magdelene rolled through the pile of ash that had been her master and up against the ruins of her bed.

H'sak nearly embedded the full length of his claws in the floor.

Magdelene dodged a vicious swing from the demon's left hand.

H'sak closed his right.

Magdelene looked down at the scaled fingers that nearly encircled her waist, at the tiny trickles of blood from where the tip of each claw just barely pierced her skin, and sighed. H'sak brought up his other hand and completed the circle. Magdelene now wore a girdle of demon flesh that tightened and hoisted her into the air.

As her feet came off the floor, she kicked once or twice in an experimental sort of way, but the claws dug deeper and so she stopped.

"You're going to take a long time to die," H'sak informed her in conversational tones, blinking the last of the powder from his eyes.

"If it's all the same to you," Magdelene replied, just as politely, scrabbling behind her for something, anything, to hit him with, "I'd rather not."

The demon licked his lips.

Magdelene's fingers closed on the edge of something cold and smooth.

"I think" — H'sak almost purred with anticipation — "I'll start at the top and work my way down. This should, after all, be an event. Perhaps I'll begin by sucking the fluid from your eyes."

"Oh yeah, well suck this!" Magdelene screamed, and slammed Adar's mirror down on the ridge of bone between the demon's ears, hoping to startle him enough for her to squirm free.

It was difficult to know who was more startled, the demon or Magdelene herself, when the mirror, with a loud slurp, responded to the wizard's order and did exactly as it was told.

Breathing heavily, Magdelene stared at the mirror lying face down on the floor then squatted beside it. She pushed at it with the tip of one finger. It skidded a few inches. Moving slowly, ready to leap back at any further display of initiative, she flipped it over.

Receiving no further instructions, the mirror held what it had swallowed.

Trapped within the glass, H'sak roared in silent rage, fists uplifted to pound against his new prison.

Pounding?

Magdelene shook her head. No, that wasn't coming from the mirror.

"Open this door! Open I say in the name of the king!"

She looked at the door. She looked at the mirror. She looked at the demon marks around her waist. She looked up to the heavens. "Why me?" she wailed.

The pounding continued.

"Stuff a sock in it!" she screamed, just a little on edge. "I'm coming!"

Digging through the wreckage, looking for clothes, the most powerful wizard in the world — newly named — considered her options. The king was going to be royally angry; wizards were rare, and she'd just killed his. There was bound to be unpleasantness, and Magdelene hated unpleasantness. She picked up the old stuffed lizard, which had somehow survived intact, and placed it carefully on the room's one remaining shelf. As far as she could see, there was only one way out: abject surrender. Perhaps groveling. She dragged Adar's robe free and put it on.

At the door, she paused.

"It wasn't really your fault," she reminded herself firmly, and opened it.

Pagrick, just about to demand entry for the second time, snapped his mouth shut at the sudden view of destruction within the room, and let the butt of his spear drop slowly to the ground.

"We heard noises," began the king from behind his guardsman.

Magdelene bowed awkwardly; she hadn't expected the king himself. "There, uh, was a slight accident."

The king leaned forward and took a quick look around. "A slight accident? Child, if this is your idea of a slight accident, I'd hate to see what you consider a disaster. What happened?"

"Well..." Magdelene shot a look back over her shoulder. H'sak certainly had made a mess of the room. "The demon did it."

"The demon?"

"Yes, Sire. While he was chasing me, he — "

"The demon got loose?"

Pagrick's spear came up as he prepared to defend his king.

"Yes, Sire. But it's all right, I took care of him and — "

"You?" His Majesty looked skeptical. His guardsman merely looked adoring.

Magdelene bristled a little. "Yes, me." She stood aside. There, leaning against the wall, was the mirror. Within the mirror was H'sak. "I trapped him within the mirror and —"

"How?"

"Well, I don't exactly know." Her brow wrinkled. "It was an accident."

"Another accident," said the king. "You appear to have had a busy morning."

"You could say that; yes, Sire."

"Where was your master through all of this?" He took another look around the room. "Where is Adar?"

Magdelene's mouth opened and closed a few times, but nothing came out. Finally, she held out her arm. On the sleeve of Adar's robe was a fine sprinkling of pale grey ash.

The royal brows rose. "Adar's robe," he prompted.

"No, Sire." She indicated the ash. "Adar." A lesser man, on hearing his court wizard, his ace in the hole, had become nothing more than a laundry problem, would have taken his anger out on the bearer of the news. The king, stronger than that, said only, "One last accident?"

"The first actually." She sighed. "It's kind of a long story. Which," she added, "would go a lot faster if you stopped interrupting, Sire."

"Your pardon." He leaned up against the doorframe, crossed his arms over his chest, and gave every indication of settling in for a long stay. "Tell," he commanded.

So she did.

"The most powerful wizard in the world..." the king said speculatively as she finished. He studied the demon in the mirror. "So, where do you go from here?"

Magdelene swallowed hard. "You aren't going to detain me? For, uh, what happened to Adar? To replace him?"

"Detain you? How could I?"

The most powerful wizard in the world thought about that for a moment. "Oh. Yeah." This, she decided, was going to take some getting used to.

"And besides," the king added, "I have the safety of my people to think of." With the toe of one boot, he nudged something, shattered beyond recognition, back into the room. "You seem to attract an unusual number of... accidents. I'm reasonably certain it's easier to replace a wizard than a country. I suggest you head toward less-populated areas. Perhaps south."

South. The pique she'd felt at not being wanted — quite different from not being detained — vanished. South. To never have a runny nose again...

"And what's more," His Majesty continued, breaking into her reverie, "if you take your friend there with you, I'll see what I can do to ease your way. Just in case he gets free again" — his mouth twitched — "accidentally, of course. Better he's with you than me."

Magdelene dropped a deep curtsey. South. The world was her oyster and she the pearl in it. "Your wish, Sire, is my command."

"How fortunate for us both," replied the king and turned to leave. Pagrick smiled down at her as he made ready to follow his liege, and Magdelene remembered one last bit of unfinished business. Adar's end had been poetic justice of a sort, done in by his own ambition, but she'd always be grateful for the last thing he'd taught her before he died.

"Oh, Sire," she called. The king paused. "Could I, uh, borrow Guardsman Pagrick for a time?" Pagrick flexed, sweated, and sighed all in the space of about two seconds. "I'd like to, uh, clean up the workroom before I go."

Be It Ever So Humble

"So, got any dirt on this place?" Magdelene asked the gold and black lizard sunning itself on a nearby rock.

The lizard, looking more like a beautifully crafted piece of jewelry than a living creature, merely flicked its inner eyelid closed and pretended to be asleep. Children with rocks or nets it had to do something about. Young women in donkey carts who asked stupid questions could safely be ignored.

Magdelene studied the little village nestled along the curve of its natural harbor and chewed reflectively on a strand of chestnut hair. It looked like a nice place but, as much as she wanted to settle down, as tired as she was of constantly packing up and moving on, she knew better than to get her hopes up.

In a dozen years of travelling, she'd learned that the most jewel-like villages, in the most bucolic settings, often had the quaintest customs. Customs like welcoming wandering wizards with an axe, or attempting to convince wandering wizards to stay by outfitting them with manacles and chains, or by suggesting the tarring and feathering of wandering wizards with no better reason than the small matter of a straying husband or two. For the most part, Magdelene had found these customs no more than a minor inconvenience although, had she know the man was married, she would never have suggested they...

She grinned at the memory. He'd proven a lot more flexible than she'd anticipated.

"Well, H'sak?" She spit out the hair and glanced back at the large mirror propped up behind the seat of the cart. "Shall we check it out?"

H'sak, trapped in the mirror, made no answer. Magdelene wasn't entirely certain the demon was aware of what went on outside his prison but, travelling alone, she'd fallen into the habit of talking to him and figured, just in case he ever got out, it couldn't hurt if he had memories of pleasant, albeit one-sided, conversations. Not, she supposed, that a bit of chat would make up for her trapping him in the mirror in the first place.

Stretching back, she pulled an old cloak down over the glass — no point in upsetting potential neighbours right off — then gathered up the reins and slapped them lightly on the donkey's rump. The donkey, who had worked out an understanding with the wizard early on, took another few mouthfuls of the coarse grass lining the track and slowly started down the hill to the village.

At the first house, Magdelene stopped the cart and sat quietly studying the scene. A few chickens scratched in the sandy dirt that served the village as a main street and a black sow sprawled in the only visible bit of shade, her litter suckling noisily. A lullaby, softly sung, drifted through one of the open windows and from the beach came the screams of and laughter of children at play. Just the sort of lazy ambience she appreciated.

"Who are you?"

Languidly, for it was far too hot to be startled, Magdelene turned. A boy, nine or ten years old, naked except for a shell threaded on a frayed piece of gut, peered up at her from under a heavy shock of dusty black hair. Although he showed no signs of malnutrition or neglect, his left arm hung withered and useless by his side.

"My name is Magdelene." She pushed her hair back off her face. "Who are you?"

"Juan." He edged a little closer. "You a trader?"

"No. I'm a wizard." Over the years, she'd discovered life worked out better if she didn't try to hide that. It made explanations so much easier when things started happening. And things always did.

The boy looked her up and down and tossed his head. "Ha!" he scoffed. "Tell us another one. Wizards got grey hair and warts. You're not old enough to be a wizard."

"I'm twenty-seven," she told him a little indignantly. He was a fine one to talk about not old enough...

"Oh." Juan considered it and apparently decided twenty-seven was sufficiently ancient even without the grey hair and warts. "What about your clothes then? Wizards wear robes and stuff. Everyone knows that."

He had a point. Wizards did wear robes and stuff; usually of a dark, heavy, and imposing fabric; always hot, scratchy, and uncomfortable. Magdelene, who preferred to be comfortable, never bothered.

"I'm the most powerful wizard in the world," she explained as a rivulet of sweat ran under her bright blue breastband, "so I wear what I want."

"Yeah, sure," he snorted. "Prove it."

"All right." She gathered up the multicolored folds of her skirt, jumped down off the cart, and held out her hand. "Give me your arm and I'll fix it."

"Oh no." He backed up a pace and turned, protecting the withered arm behind the rest of his body. "You ain't proving it on me. Find something else."

"Like what?"

Juan thought about it a moment. "Could you send my sister some place far away?" he asked hopefully.

Magdelene thought about that in turn. It didn't seem worth antagonising the village just to prove a point to one grubby child. "I could, but I don't think I should."

The boy sighed. The kind of sigh that said he knew what the answer would be but thought there could be no harm in asking.

They stood together in silence for a moment, Magdelene leaning against the back of her cart — perfectly content to do nothing — and Juan digging his toe into the sand. The donkey, who could smell water, decided enough was enough and started towards the centre of the village. He was hot, he was thirsty, and he was going to do something about it.

As her backrest jerked forward, Magdelene hit the ground with an unwizardlike thud. Closer proximity proved the sand was not as soft as it looked. "Lizard piss," she muttered, rubbing at a stone-bruise. When she looked up, Juan had disappeared.

She shrugged philosophically and, following along behind the donkey, amused herself by pulling back an image of Juan as an adult. Long and lean and sleekly muscled, it was a future worth sticking around for. At some point between now and then, she appeared to have convinced him to let her fix his arm. It looked like she'd be staying, at least for a while.

An impatient bray demanded her attention and she allowed the image to slip back to its own time; they'd arrived at the well.

When the trough was full, and the donkey had bent his head to drink, Magdelene, pulled by the realization she was no longer alone, slowly turned. All around the edges of the square, stood the children of the village, staring at her with wide dark eyes.

"Yes?" she asked.

The children merely continued to stare.

Demons, she decided, were easier to deal with. At least you always knew what demons wanted.

"Magdelene-lady!"

The children stared on as Magdelene gratefully noted Juan approaching with a adult in tow. The old man had been bent and twisted by the weight of his years, his fingers warped into shapes more like driftwood than flesh. His skin had been tanned by sun and wind and salt into creased leather and any hair he'd had was long gone. He followed Juan with the rolling gait of a life spent at sea and his jaws worked to the rhythm of his walking.

"Whacha doing sitting around like a pile of fish guts?" he growled at the children as he stopped an arm's length from Magdelene and glared about. "Untie her beast, put him to pasture, and get that wagon in the shade."

The children hesitated.

"You are staying a bit?" he asked, his growl softening, his dark eyes meeting hers.

Magdelene smiled her second best smile — she couldn't be certain his heart would be up to her best — and said, "Yes." She wanted very much to stay for a bit. Maybe this time things would work out.

The old man nodded and waved both twisted hands. "You heard her. Get!"

They got, Juan with the rest, and Magdelene watched bemused as her donkey was lead away and her cart was pulled carefully to rest under a stand of palm.

"Boy says you told him you're a wizard."

"That's right."

"Don't have much need for a wizard here. Wizards make you soft and then the sea takes you. We prefer to do things for ourselves."

"So do I," Magdelene told him, leaning back against the damp stones. "Prefer to have people do things for themselves, that is." She grinned. She liked this old man and sensed in him a kindred spirit. "To be honest, I like people to do things for me as well."

He returned the grin and his eyes twinkled as he looked her up and down. "Ah, child," he cackled, "what I could do for you if I were only fifty years younger."

"Would you like to be?" she asked, rather hoping he would.

He laughed, then he realized she was serious. "You could do that?"

"Yes."

His gaze turned inward and Magdelene could feel the strength of the memories he sifted. After a moment, he sighed and shook his head. "Foolish wishes, child. I've earned my age and I'll wear it with honor."

Magdelene hid her disappointment. Personally, she couldn't see the honor in blurred eyesight, aching bones, and swollen, painful joints but if that was his choice...

There were sixteen buildings in the village, eight goats, eleven pigs, twenty-one chickens, and fourteen boats. No one had ever managed an accurate count of the cats.

"Six families came here three generations ago," Carlos, the old man, explained as they stood on the beach watching boats made tiny by distance slide up and down the rolling waves. Through his eyes, Magdelene saw the harbor as it had been, sparkling untouched in the sun, never sailed, never fished, theirs. "I'm the last of the first. I've outlived two wives and most of my children as well."

"Do you mind?" Magdelene asked, knowing she was likely to see entire civilizations rise and fall in her lifetime and not entirely certain how she felt about it.

"Well..." He considered the question for a moment. "I'll live 'til I die. Nothing else I can do."

"You didn't answer my question."

He patted her cheek. "I know."

ଔ ଔ ଔ

That night, in the crowded main room of the headman's house, Carlos presented Magdelene to the adults of the village. "...and she'd like to stay on a bit."

"A wizard," the headman ruminated. "That's something we don't see everyday."

Magdelene missed much of the discussion that followed as she was busy trying to make eye contact with a very attractive young man standing by one of the deep windows. She gave up when she realized that he was trying to make eye contact with a very attractive young man standing by the door.

"...although frankly, we'd rather you were a trader."

"The traders are late this year?" Magdelene guessed, hoping she hadn't missed anything important.

"Aye. They've always come with the kayle."

Just in time, she remembered that kayle were fish.

"Surely you saw them on the road?" a young woman asked hopefully.

"No." Magdelene frowned as she thought back over the last few weeks of travel. "I didn't." The emptiness of the trail hadn't seemed strange to her at the time. It did now.

"I don't suppose you can conjure one?" asked a middle-aged woman dryly, tamping down her pipe.

The room rippled with laughter.

"I could," Magdelene admitted.

The room fell silent.

Magdelene cleared her throat. She might as well get it over with. "I'm the most powerful wizard in the world," she began.

The middle-aged woman snorted. "Says who?"

"Well, uh..."

"Doesn't matter. Would this conjured trader do us any good?"

"Probably not." A trader conjured suddenly into the village would be more likely to trade in strong hysterics than anything useful.

"I thought as much." The woman expertly lit her pipe with a spill from the lamp. "What in Neto's breath are we wasting our time here for, that's what I want to know? We've kayle to bring in at dawn and I hear my bed calling."

"I though you might like to know that a stranger, a wizard, has come to the village," Carlos told her tartly.

She snorted again. "All right. Now we know." She pointed the stem of her pipe at Magdelene and demanded, "You planning on causing any trouble?"

"Of course not," Magdelene declared emphatically. She never planned on causing any trouble.

"Will you keep your nose out of what doesn't concern you?"

She had to think about that for a moment, wondering how broad a definition could be put on what didn't concern her. "I'll try."

"See that you do."

"So I can stay for a while?"

"For a while." Her head wreathed in smoke, the woman rose. "That's that then," she said shortly, and left.

The headman sighed and raised both hands in a gesture of defeat. "You heard her. You can go."

As people began to leave, Magdelene leaned over and whispered to Carlos, "Why does he let her get away with that?"

Carlos snickered, his palm lying warm and dry on Magdelene's arm. "Force of habit," he said in his normal speaking voice. "She's his older sister, raised him after their mother drowned. Refused to be headwoman, said she didn't have the time, but she runs every meeting he calls."

The headman smiled, for Carlos' speech had risen clearly over the noise of the departing villagers. "Look at it this way, grandfather; the village gets two fish on one piece of bait. I do all the work and Yolanda does all the talking." He stood, stretched, and turned to Magdelene. "Have you got a bed, Wizard?"

Studying the muscles of his torso, still corded and firm for all his forty odd years, Magdelene considered several replies. All of which she discarded after catching a speaking glance from the headman's wife.

"While the weather holds," she sighed, "I'm perfectly comfortable under my cart."

ର ର ର

"And I am perfectly comfortable," she sighed again a half hour later, plumping up the pillows on her huge feather bed, "but I wouldn't mind some company." As if in answer to her request, the canvas flaps hanging from the sides of the cart parted and Juan poked in his head. "I was thinking," she muttered to whatever gods were listening, "of company a little older."

Juan blinked, shook his head, and gazed around curiously. "How'd you get all this stuff under here?" he demanded.

"I told you," Magdelene poured herself a glass of chilled grape juice, "I'm the most powerful wizard in the world." She dabbed at the spreading purple stain on the front of her tunic. "Can I fix your arm now?"

He'd didn't answer, just crawled forward and found himself in a large room that held — besides the bed — a wardrobe, an overstuffed armchair, and huge book bound in red leather lying closed on a wooden stand. "Where's the wagon?"

Magdelene pointed at the ceiling, impressed by his attitude. She'd had one or two supposed adults fall gibbering to the carpet.

Juan looked up. Dark red runes had been scrawled across the rough boards of the ceiling. "What's that writing on there?"

"The spell that allows this room to exist."

"Oh." He had little or no interest in spells. "Got any more juice?"

She handed him a full glass and watched him putter about, poking his nose into everything. Setting his glass down on the book, he pulled open the wardrobe door.

"What's that?"

"It's a demon trapped in a mirror, what's it look like?" She'd hung the mirror of the inside of the door that afternoon, figuring H'sak was safer there than in the wagon.

"How long's he been in there?"

"Twelve years."

"How long you gonna keep him in there?"

"Until I let him out."

An answer that would have infuriated an adult, suited Juan fine. He took one last admiring look at H'sak, finished his juice, and handed Magdelene the empty glass. "I better get home."

"Juan."

About to step through the canvas walls, he glanced back over his shoulder.

"You still haven't told me if I can fix your arm."

His gaze slid over to the demon and then back to the wizard. He shrugged. "Maybe later," he said, and left.

CR CR CR

Magdelene spent most of the next three days with Carlos. The children treated her like an exotic curiosity and she tried to live up to their expectations. The adults treated her with a wary suspicion and she tried not to live up to theirs. Carlos treated her like a friend.

The oldest in the village by a good twenty years, his eyes sometimes twinkled and sparkled and looked no older than Juan's. Sometimes they burned with more mature fires and she longed to give him back his youth if only for a few hours behind the dunes. Sometimes they appeared deeper and blacker and wiser than the night sky. Sometimes they just looked old. Marvelling, she realized that he remembered all the ages he had been and more, that they were with him still, making a home, not a prison, of his age. This was his strength and Magdelene placed the lesson it taught her carefully away with her other precious things.

She began to hope the village had a place for her.

On the morning of the fourth day, they'd gathered about the well — the wizard and the few adults who remained ashore due to age or disability — when the high pitched shriek of a child jerked all heads around.

"Riders!"

Screaming out the news of their discovery, Juan and three of the other children burst into the centre of the village. The chickens panicked, screeched, and scattered. The adults tried to make sense out of the cacophony.

"One at a time!" The baker finally managed to make himself heard. "Juan, what happened?"

"Riders, Uncle!" Juan told him, bouncing in his excitement. "Five of them. On horses. Coming here!"

"Are you sure?"

"Yes! We were going up the track to look for gooseberries..." The other three children nodded vigorously in agreement. "...and we met them coming down."

"They aren't traders?"

Juan sighed in exaggerated exasperation. "Uncle, I seen traders before. And these aren't..." He noticed the baker was no longer looking at him, noticed no one was looking at him, so he let the last word trail off and he turned.

They rode slowly, with a ponderous certainty more threatening than a wild charge. Voluminous robes in tans and browns hid all but their eyes and each wore a long, curved blade. They stopped, the line of horses reflecting the line of the well, and the rider in the centre let the fabric drop from his face.

Nice, thought Magdelene, continuing to stroke the black and white cat sprawled across her lap. *Good cheek bones, flashing eyes, full lips*, and, she realized, shoulders drooping a little in disappointment, *about as congenial as H'sak*.

"We have come," said the rider, "for the kayle."

Carlos stepped forward, his hand on Juan's shoulder — both to support himself and to keep the boy from doing anything rash. "What do you have to trade?" he asked levelly.

"Your lives," replied the rider and his hand dropped to the hilt of his sword.

Magdelene rolled her eyes. She'd never much cared for melodrama.

"If you take the kayle, we will have nothing when the traders come."

"The traders will not come. The Warlord rules here."

"I don't recall being conquered," Carlos snapped, temper showing at last.

The rider smiled, showing perfect teeth and no sense of humor. "You are being conquered now." The line of horses took a single step in intimidating unison.

Juan's one hand curled into a fist.

Magdelene stood, dumping the indignant cat to the ground.

"Just one minute," she began.

"SILENCE WOMAN!" the rider thundered.

"Stuff a sock in it." She brushed cat hair off her skirt. "You're not impressing anyone."

For just an instant, acute puzzlement replaced the rider's belligerent expression. A people in the process of being terrorized simply did not behave in this fashion. With a perceivable effort, he regained his scowl and drew his sword. To either side, his men did the same.

"Kill them all," he said.

The horses leapt forward and vanished.

The saddles and the riders hung in the air for one long second then crashed to the ground, raising great clouds of dust and more panicked squawking from the chickens.

"And as you want the kayle so badly," Magdelene said.

Steel swords became silver fish making desperate attempts to get free of the grip on their tails.

The children laughed and pointed.

When they found they couldn't release the fish, the riders began to panic.

"When you get back to your warlord," Magdelene told them, smiling pleasantly, "you'll be able to let go. If I can make a suggestion, don't waste any time. Very shortly those fish are not going to be the best of travelling companions."

Throwing garbage and clots of dirt, the children chased the riders from the village.

Magdelene turned and saw four of the five adults regarding her with awe. Carlos merely looked thoughtful.

"With luck, they'll convince their warlord that this village is more trouble than its worth," Magdelene explained reassuringly, rubbing at the beads of sweat between her breasts. "Unless he has a wizard of his own, he'll only be beaten again if he comes back." She didn't add that even if he did have a wizard, he'd still be beaten — it sounded too much like bragging. Even though it was true.

"And without luck?" Carlos prodded.

Magdelene sighed. "Without luck, I'll just have to convince him myself. But I hope he does the sensible thing."

Carlos snorted. "Men who style themselves `The Warlord' seldom do the sensible thing."

"Men in general seldom do the sensible thing." Magdelene winked at the baker who had, after all, only lost one leg at sea. "Fortunately, they have other uses."

Carlos cackled wildly. The baker blushed.

                              CR CR CR

"...although you did say you'd keep out of what didn't concern you."

"My home concerns me."

Yolanda peered at Magdelene through a cloud of pipe smoke. "Home is it? I thought you were just staying for a while?"

"The village needs me."

"We neither need nor want you taking care of us," the older woman growled.

"Good. Because I wasn't planning to." Even through the smoke, she could see Yolanda's eyes narrow. The five empty saddles had been piled by the well when the fishing fleet returned. "I'll be like the seawall. Just another buffer against the storms." She spread her arms. "Without me, the persecutions your people left could well follow them."

"This warlord could send others," Carlos pointed out, pulling himself to his feet on the wizard's shoulder. "We have no way to defend ourselves."

"I can be your defenses," Magdelene insisted.

Yolanda's teeth ground against her pipe stem. "You could use your power to enslave us."

"I could... but why would I bother?."

She sounded so sincerely puzzled that Carlos began to laugh. "She's right," he cackled. "The only thing she'd rather do than lie in the sun is..." Just what exactly Magdelene would rather do than lie in the sun got lost in a violent coughing fit but more than one stupid grin was hastily hidden.

"I thought I'd build a house on the headland," Magdelene said firmly, shooting Carlos a look that almost set him off again. "If no one has any objection."

"Humph." Yolanda's snort brought with it another cloud of smoke. Magdelene couldn't be sure, but she thought there was a smile behind it. "Well, if grandfather is so certain, I've no objection."

The headman sighed. "Does anyone else wish to offer an objection?" he asked mildly. Yolanda glared at the assembled villagers who wisely remained silent. "In that case," he inclined his head graciously, "you may build as you wish, Lady-wizard."

cs cs cs

Magdelene studied the designs she'd drawn on the bare rock of the headland then checked them against the originals in the book. Although her hair and bright yellow shift blew wildly about in the wind, the pages of the spellbook remained still and not one grain of the fine white sand she'd used for the parameters of her house shifted. The moment Juan returned from the beach she'd be able to finish. She could have just lifted the last bit of sand she needed but the boy had wanted to help. If she let him hang around, she figured she'd eventually do something he considered worthy and he'd let her fix his arm.

She turned her face to the sun, eyes half closed in blissful anticipation of actually having a place of her own. No more travelling and no more adventures. Adventures were highly overrated as far as Magdelene was concerned as they usually included uncomfortable sleeping arrangements, primitive or nonexistent toilet facilities, and someone — or someones — in direct and often violent opposition.

"Magdelene!"

Jolted out of her reverie, she squinted at the tiny figure scrambling up the steep path from the beach. It wasn't Juan for the child had two healthy arms he... no, she ... flailed about for balance.

"The riders," the little girl panted as Magdelene reached down to pull her the last few feet. "They've come back."

So, the warlord hadn't taken the hint. "Don't worry about it," the wizard advised, holding a hankie to a nose obediently blown. "That's what I'm here for."

"But they've got Juan!"

"What?!" Magdelene spun around and stared down at the village, the distant scene snapping suddenly into clarity at the touch of her will. Not the same riders, but the same type, their robes of tan and brown billowing in the wind. A full two dozen men faced the well this time, a red pennant snapping about over their heads as if trying to leap from the lance tip. One horse stood a little forward and Juan had been thrown across the pommel of its saddle, his good arm twisted cruelly back.

She could see the villagers gathering — the kayle run had stopped and the seas had been too high to put out for a less certain catch. Carlos — the headman and Yolanda at his back — stepped out of the crowd and spoke. Magdelene could see his lips move although the wind whipped away the words. Juan began to struggle and squirm.

The rider's grip shifted and it didn't take a wizard's ears to hear the high-pitched scream that rose on the wind.

"Magdelene!" The little girl tugged on the wizard's shift. "You gotta do something!"

Juan went limp.

Magdelene's fingers closed on the child's shoulder and the next instant the two of them stood by the well. The child tore herself out of Magdelene's hold and dashed to her mother.

"Did you see, Mama? Did you see? We went poof!"

Alone now, between the villagers and the riders, Magdelene took a deep breath, clamped her teeth, and forced the wobbling world to steady. The last time she'd used the transit spell, she'd puked her guts out upon arrival. This time she couldn't give in to the nausea; retching at the warlord's feet might be unpleasant but it could hardly be considered intimidating. When she regained her ability to focus, most of the riders still wore expressions of combined fear and disbelief.

Only the man who held Juan looked unaffected.

He smiled down at her. "You must be the wizard," he said.

She returned the smile with equal sincerity. "And you must be the warlord."

"I got your message. I'm here to give you my answer. And," his eyes narrowed, "I wouldn't suggest a repeat of the last incident, not while I have the boy."

Magdelene wasn't particularly worried. She could send the warlord and his men back where they came from without disturbing a hair on Juan's head. The problem was, they'd only come back. If she played to the Warlord's ego, she might be able to negotiate a more permanent solution. "What do you want?"

"You." His smile broadened, the scar that split one side of his mouth twisting his face unevenly.

Magdelene's brows reached for her hairline. "I beg your pardon?"

"I have decided I could use a wizard." He waved his free hand expansively. "You are to put yourself under my command."

Pompous bloody twit. He actually sounded as if she should be thrilled with the opportunity. She folded her arms and glared up at him. "Why would I want to do that?" she demanded.

"If you don't, I will kill the boy."

"And if I do?"

"I will spare both the boy and the village."

"Magdelene..." Carlos' voice sounded strained, all the laughter gone from it.

"It's all right, Carlos," Magdelene muttered out of the corner of her mouth. "I've got things under control." Or she would have shortly. A man who expected his mere presence to overwhelm all opposition could be dealt with.

"While I appreciate your very generous offer," she told him, preparing to launch a special effects extravaganza that would convince him to never tangle with her village again. "I'm afraid I shall have to decline."

His smile never wavered. "Pity," he said. Throwing one arm about the boy's upper body, he grabbed the small head and twisted.

The crack sounded very loud.

Juan's body slid to the ground to lie in a crumpled heap, the head bent around at an impossible angle.

Magdelene's mouth worked but no sound emerged. She hadn't really believed he would do that. Behind her, she heard a wail of grief from Juan's mother.

The warlord's men moved forward until they surrounded the villagers with a wall of steel.

"Now," said the warlord, still smiling, "what have you to say to my most generous offer?"

The smile slipped as Magdelene raised her head and met his eyes.

"Die," she told him.

He didn't have time to look surprised. His eyes rolled up, his mouth went slack, and he collapsed forward over the pommel. Startled by this new limp weight, the horse tossed its head and shied sideways, dumping the warlord's body to the sand beside the small heap of bones and flesh that had been Juan.

In silence that followed, the breathing of the surrounding horses sounded unnaturally loud. Their riders made no sound at all, each hoping desperately that the wizard would not now turn her attention to him.

The silence grew and stretched, broken only by the sobbing of Juan's mother. Pushing her hair back off her face with a trembling hand, Magdelene knelt by the boy's body. She straightened his tangled limbs and gently turned his head until it sat naturally once again.

"Lady-wizard..." It was the first time Carlos hadn't used her name. "...this isn't to say you haven't done what you felt you had to in removing this man from the world, but..."

He fell silent as Magdelene took Juan's cold little hand in her's and called his name.

The slight chest began to rise and fall. Juan hiccupped and opened his eyes.

"I wasn't here," he said, scratching his nose.

"That's right." Magdelene was a firm believer in telling children the truth. "You were dead."

"Oh." He thought about that for a moment. "It sure was boring."

She moved out of the way as his family rushed forward to claim him. He squirmed, looked disgusted, and tried to avoid the sloppiest displays of affection.

"Mama, stop it."

"Lady-wizard?"

Magdelene turned to face the villagers. They'd ask her to leave now. Or they'd deify her. Things wouldn't be the same. She stifled a near hysterical giggle. People so often over-reacted to the raising of the dead.

"If you can bring back Juan," the headman told her quietly, "you must bring back the warlord and right the wrong you've done."

"Wrong?"

"We don't believe in the taking of life." He glanced down at the warlord's body and his lip curled. "As much as we may recognise the emotion that prompts it." Behind him, the villagers stared at her, no two expressions the same.

She heaved a sigh of relief. If that was all they wanted, they were taking it rather well. Maybe she could still salvage the situation. "But what of that lot?" Magdelene shot a glance back over her shoulder at the warlord's men who tried very hard to appear harmless and insignificant. "Cut the head off a snake and the snake dies. If I rejoin the head then the snake lives and eats the heads of others and..." She frowned, lost in the metaphor, and sighed again. "Look, I don't think it's a good idea."

"If you want to make this your home," Yolanda told her bluntly, as unaffected by miracles as she was by most things, "you must respect our beliefs."

"But he deserved to die."

A couple of the villagers nodded in agreement. Yolanda stood firm. "You have no more right to decide that about him than he did about Juan. If you wish us to respect you, you must respect us."

Was it as easy as that? Magdelene wrapped her arms about herself and thought it over.

"Does your warlord have a name?" she asked the riders at last.

They looked at each other and then down at the body of their leader.

"Anwar, Lady-wizard," ventured the young man who held the lance with the warlord's pennant. She smiled her thanks and he began breathing again.

Squatting by the warlord's body, Magdelene took his hand in hers and called. She didn't bother to make him more comfortable first.

This time, she wouldn't underestimate him.

His eyes opened. He looked around, slowly untangled himself, and sat up. "Bleshnaggle?" he asked, grabbing for a blowing strand of Magdelene's hair.

She pulled it out of his hand and stood. The warlord pouted for a second then discovered his boots. He gazed at them in fascination, babbling nonsense words and patting at the air with limp hands.

Everyone, the villagers and the riders, took a step forward.

"What happened?" Yolanda asked finally.

Magdelene watched the warlord trying to catch the billowing end of his own robe. "Death seems to have unsettled him a bit," she said.

"But Juan was fine."

The wizard shrugged. "Children are a lot more adaptable about..."

"Would you make up your mind!" The dark-haired, pale-skinned young woman appeared suddenly beside the warlord, hands on hip and eyes flashing. Her black robes hung straight to the sand, unaffected by any breeze. "What are we playing, musical souls? First I've got 'em, then I don't. You're not supposed to do that!" She spotted Juan worming his way to the front of the crowd. "Hi, kid."

Juan's mother grabbed his ear and yanked him behind her, cutting off his cheerful greeting. As far as she could see, there was no one there and her baby had been involved with quite enough strangeness for one afternoon.

"Death?" Magdelene hazarded.

Everyone, the riders and the villagers, took a step back. At this point, they were willing to take the wizard's word for it.

"Good guess," Death snapped. "Now, do you want to explain what's going on around here."

"It's a long story."

"Look, lady," Death began, a little more calmly.

"Magdelene."

"Okay. Magdelene. Look, Magdelene, I haven't got time for a long story, I've got places to go, people to see. Let's make a deal — you can keep the kid but tall, dark, and violent comes with me." She pointed a long, pale finger down at the warlord. Both her ebony brows rose as he pulled off a boot and began filling it with sand. "Now look what you've done!" she wailed, causing every living creature in earshot to break into a cold sweat. "You've broken him!"

"Sorry." Magdelene spread her hands.

"No, you're not." Death tapped one foot against the sand. "Okay. I'm sure we can work this out like sensible women. You can keep him, just give me one of them." She swept her gaze over the riders.

One sensitive young man fainted, falling forward in the saddle, arms dangling limply down each side of his horse's neck.

"Sorry," Magdelene said again, lifting her shoulders in a rueful shrug. "They're not mine to give. Why don't you just take one?"

Three saddles were suddenly wet.

"I don't work that way." Death shook her head. "I can't take someone if it isn't their time."

"Lady?"

Both Death and the wizard turned.

Carlos stepped forward, one twisted hand held out before him.

Death's expression softened and she smiled. She had a beautiful smile. "Don't I know you?" she asked softly.

"You should," Carlos told her. "I've been expecting you for some time."

Her voice became a caress. "Forgive me for taking so long."

When she took his hand, he sighed and all the aches and pains of his age seemed to drop off him. He stood straight for a moment, his face serene, then he crumbled to the ground.

All eyes were on the body of the old man. Only Magdelene saw the young one, tall and strong, who still held Death's hand. Lips trembling, she gave him her best smile. He returned it. And was gone.

Magdelene stood quietly, tears on her cheeks, while the villagers lovingly carried Carlos' body away. She stood quietly while the warlord's men managed to get their leader onto his horse and she didn't move as they headed out of the village. She stood quietly until a small hand slipped into hers.

"I've got the rest of the sand," Juan told her, a bulging pouch hung round his neck. "Can we go finish your house now?"

She looked down and lightly touched his hair. "They want me to stay?"

He shrugged, unsure who they were. "No one wants you to go."

Hand in hand, they climbed the path to the headland.

"Are you going to stay here forever?" Juan asked.

Magdelene met the anxious look in his black eyes and grinned. "How old are you, Juan?"

"Nine."

The image of the young man she'd pulled from the future stood behind the child and winked. She shooed it back where it belonged. "I'll be around long enough."

Juan nodded, satisfied.

"So... I took you back from Death today. Can I fix your arm now?"

He tossed his head. "I'm still thinkin' about it."

The most powerful wizard in the world stared down at him in astonishment then started to laugh. "You," she declared, "are one hard kid to impress."

Mirror, Mirror, On The Lam

The turquoise house on the headland had stood empty for some weeks. The wind off the sea whistled forlornly through the second floor cupola, tried each of the shuttered windows in turn, and finally, in a fit of pique, tossed a piece of forgotten garden furniture into what appeared to be a halfhearted attempt at a shrubbery.

The green and gold lizard crouched under a wilting bayberry scrambled to safety just in time. Racing counterclockwise up the nearest palm, it stopped suddenly, lifted its head, and tested the air.

Someone was coming.

ᔕ ᔕ ᔕ

Ciro had left his donkey and cart carefully hidden at the foot of the hill. Although he doubted that any of the inhabitants of the nearby fishing village would venture so far from the cove, he never took risks he could avoid. As his dear old white-haired mother had told him, right before her public and very well-attended execution, chance favours the pessimist.

He'd have preferred a faster form of transportation but, since his current employer had been somewhat vague on the size of the object he was to acquire, he'd erred on the side of caution. If he couldn't deliver, he wouldn't get paid.

For safety's sake, he avoided paths and moved, where he could, from one patch of rock to the next. As he approached the house, the vegetation grew more lush, easier to hide behind if harder to move through. At the edge of the garden, he paused and studied the structure, a little taken aback by the extraordinary color. It was smaller than he'd expected but perhaps the most powerful wizard in the world had no need for ostentatious display.

To his surprise, the kitchen door was not only unlocked but, if the crystal his employer had given him was to be trusted, also unwarded. As he crossed the kitchen floor, Ciro sincerely hoped that the shadows dancing in the corners owed more to the way the louvered shutters filtered light than to anything the wizard may have left behind.

Stepping out into a large square hall, he found himself facing three identical doors. As he moved forward, eyes half closed against the brilliant sunshine blazing through the circular skylight, the kitchen door closed behind him.

Four identical doors.

The door on his right lead to a bedroom. The bed — a huge, northern style four-poster that overwhelmed the southern decor — had been left unmade. Ciro pulled a sandal from the closest pile of clothing and used it to block the door open before he stepped cautiously forward.

The door closed.

No need to panic, he told himself. You can always go out the window.

A cloak, in a particularly vibrant shade of orange, had been draped over the large oval mirror. Standing safely to one side, he tugged at the cloth and took a quick look into the glass as it fell. A man of average height, his light brown hair and beard a little darker than his skin and a little lighter than his eyes, looked back at him. He frowned and his reflection echoed the movement. Either he'd lost weight or the mirror made him look thinner.

It was the only mirror in the room.

The door proved to be unlocked. It opened when he lifted the latch and, as he stepped back into the hall, it closed behind him.

Continuing to his right, Ciro opened the next door and found himself staring into the kitchen.

This time, he closed the door on his own.

The door to his left should now lead to the bedroom but he was no longer willing to take that for granted. He checked the crystal. The wizardry moving the house about was not directed at him — a mixed blessing at best. For lack of a better plan, he continued moving to the right.

A spare room. An unmade bed and empty wardrobe. One mirror; not very large and not what he was searching for.

The kitchen again. With luck, the shadows had changed only because the light had.

A spiral staircase leading up to the cupola, a small square room containing only a pile of multi-colored cushions. Peering though one of the louvered shutters that made up the bulk of the walls, Ciro found himself staring out at a view from some fifty feet above the house. Without actually lifting his feet from the floor, the thief backed up and made his way carefully down the short — the far too short — flight of stairs.

The wizard's bedroom.

A bathing room. A dolphin mosaic decorated the tiles surrounding the sunken tub. The drying cloths were large, thick, and soft. From the variety of soaps and lotions, it was obvious that the wizard was no ascetic. There was no mirror.

He hadn't found a workshop yet but figured that he would in time. He'd never known a wizard who wasn't happiest puttering about with foul smelling potions and exploding incantations.

The kitchen.

The staircase.

The bedroom.

A sitting room. Big brightly colored cushions were piled high on round bamboo chairs. A carafe, two glasses, and a pile of withered orange peels had been left on a low table. On one wall, floor to ceiling shelves had been messily stuffed with scrolls and books and the occasional wax tablet. There were more shelves on the opposite wall but they were less regular. Most held a variety of ornaments ranging, in Ciro's professional opinion, from the incredibly tacky to the uniquely priceless. Out of habit, he tucked a few of the later in his pockets.

In the exact centre of the wall was an open section. In it, covered in a black cloth, was an oval object about two feet across at its widest and three long. Holding his breath, Ciro flipped the cloth to one side.

Even knowing what to expect, he almost jumped back.

The demon trapped in the mirror snarled in fixed impotence as it had for decades.

Ciro smiled, re-wrapped the mirror in the cloth, tucked the bundle under his arm, unlatched one of the large windows, and stepped out into the garden, politely closing and relatching the window behind him.

He never noticed the watching lizard.

ᘓ ᘓ ᘓ

"Well Emili, did you miss me?"

The tiny grey cat cradled in the Magdelene's arms, hunkered down and growled.

"Because you're too old to leave by yourself, that's why. You're lucky Veelma was willing to take care of you."

The path from the beach to the top of the headland was both steep and rocky although generations of use had worn off the more treacherous edges. As the wizard climbed in breathless silence, the cat kept up a constant litany of complaint, squirming free with a final wail the moment the summit was reached and disappearing under a tangle of vegetation the moment after.

"I know exactly how you feel," Magdelene muttered, sagging against the end of the sea wall and pushing a heavy fall of damp chestnut hair back off her face. "There's no place like home."

Magdelene seldom travelled. It needed far more exertion than she was usually willing to expend and experience had taught her that the easier she made it for herself, the more exertion it invariably required. This particular trip had been precipitated by an extremely attractive young man who'd come a very long way to request her assistance — and had cleverly exploited one of her weaknesses by making the request on his knees. He'd almost made it worth her while.

Reluctantly rousing herself, she crossed to the kitchen door, latched it open and went inside. The wind followed her, only to be chased back outside where it belonged.

Sometime later, cleaned, changed, and holding a tall glass of iced fruit juice, Magdelene entered the sitting room and rolled her eyes dramatically when the opened shutters exposed a fine patina of dust.

"I've got to get another housekeeper," she muttered, dragging a finger along the edge of a shelf and frowning at the resulting cap of grey fuzz. The problem was, every time she got used to a housekeeper, they died. Antuca had been with her the longest and the fifty years they'd shared would make it even harder to replace her.

"On the other hand," Magdelene told herself philosophically, "someone has to do the cooking." Taking a long swallow of the juice, she crossed to the other side of the room. "Well, H'sak, did you..."

The section of wall was empty. Even the black cloth she'd thrown over the mirror before she'd left had been taken.

"Oh, lizard piss," said the most powerful wizard in the world.

ଔ ଔ ଔ

The Five Cities were five essentially independent municipal areas set around a huge shallow lake. Reasoning they had more in common with each other than with the countries at their backs, they'd formed a loose alliance that had held for centuries. The Great Lake was the area's largest resource and the agreement allowed them to exploit it equally. Overly ambitious city governors were traditionally replaced with more pragmatic individuals practically before the body had cooled.

Two weeks to the day after the thief had stolen the mirror, and twenty minutes after she'd dropped the cat back at Veelma's, Magdelene appeared in Talzabad-har, the Third City, clutching a black velvet pillow in both hands. Gratefully discovering that the contents of her stomach had travelled with her, she released the breath she'd been holding and took a quick look around.

The picture embroidered on the pillow over the barely legible words "A Souvenir of Scenic Talzabad-har" had been more or less accurate. The small stone shrine, five pillars holding apart a floor and a roof, had been rendered admirably true to life. Unable to anchor the transit spell in a place she'd never seen, Magdelene had taken a huge chance using the pillow for a reference. Fortunately, it appeared to have paid off.

Unfortunately, the shrine was not standing in isolation on a gentle green hill as portrayed but in the centre of a crowded market square and the clap of displaced air that had heralded Magdelene's appearance had attracted the attention of almost everyone present. Fidgeting under the weight of an expectant silence, Magdelene looked out at half a hundred curious eyes.

Then a voice declaimed, "She has returned!" and everyone fell to their knees, hands over their faces, foreheads pressed against the ground.

Obviously, it was a case of mistaken identity. Magdelene, who had no time to be worshipped — although she had nothing actually against it — ran for an alley on the north side of the square.

Someone peeked.

"She goes!"

Experience having taught her how quickly a crowd can become a mob, Magdelene ran faster. Ducking into the mouth of the alley, she tossed the pillow back over her shoulder.

"A relic!"

"I saw it first!"

The sounds of a fight replaced the sounds of pursuit and Magdelene used the time gained to cover the length of the alley, round a corner, and run smack into a religious procession. By the time the first of her pursuers had come into sight, she'd borrowed a tambourine and an orange veil and was dancing away down the road, indistinguishable from any other acolyte.

At the first cross street, she returned her disguise, re-gretfully declined an invitation to lunch, and went looking for a member of the city guard.

CR CR CR

"Excuse me, Sergeant?" When he glanced down, dark eyes stern and uncompromising under the edge of his helm, Magdelene gave him an encouraging smile. "I was won-dering, who would you consider the best thief in the Five Cities?"

"Ciro Rasvona." His dark gaze grew a little confused, as though he wasn't entirely certain why he'd answered so readily.

"And where would I find him?"

The sergeant snorted. "If I knew that, I'd find him there myself."

"Maybe later," the wizard promised. "I meant, which of the Five Cities does he use as his base?"

"This one."

"This one? My, my." Magdelene was a big believer in luck — luck, coincidence and just generally having life arrange itself in her favour. It made everything much less work and she was a really big believer in that.

"If there's nothing else I can do for you..."

"Maybe later," she promised again and reluctantly let him walk on.

CR CR CR

Ciro Rasvona had an average set of rooms in an average neighbourhood under another, average name. His neighbours, when they thought of him at all, assumed he worked for the city government, a belief he fostered by living as outwardly boring a life as possible. He met his clients in public places and he brought neither friends nor lovers home.

His own mother hadn't known where he lived. This was fortunate since, during the trial, she'd cheerfully impli-cated everyone she knew in the hopes of clemency.

All things considered then, Ciro was astonished when he opened his door and saw an attractive woman in foreign clothes sitting in his favourite chair absently fondling his rosewood flute. Leaving the door open in the unlikely event she turned out to be a constable and he had to make a run for it, he took a step forward, smiled pleasantly and said, "Excuse me. Do I know you?"

Behind him, the door closed.

Heart pounding, he whirled around, yanked it open, and ran back into his rooms, ending up considerably closer to the woman in the chair before he could stop.

"I've come for the mirror," Magdelene told him.

His jaw dropped. "You...? You're...?"

"The most powerful wizard in the world," Magdelene finished when it seemed as though he wouldn't be able to get it out.

"But you're ... I mean..." He swallowed and waved one hand between them for no good reason. "You, uh, you don't look like a wizard."

"Yeah, yeah, I know. No pointy hat, no robe, no staff." Magdelene sighed. "If I had a grain of sand for every time I've heard that, I'd have a beach. But we're not here to talk about me." She leaned forward. "Let's talk about the mirror."

"I don't have it."

"You've sold it already?"

"Not exactly." When her grey eyes narrowed, he felt compelled to add, "I was hired to steal it."

"For who?"

"My clients don't tell me their names."

"Oh please."

Ciro supposed he might be reading a little too much into the way the wizard's hand closed around the shaft of his flute but it sure looked uncomfortably like a warning to him. "All right, I know who he is. But I can't give you his name," he added hurriedly. "I took an oath."

"You also took my mirror."

"It was a blood oath."

"A blood oath?" Magdelene repeated. When he nodded, she sighed and massaged the bridge of her nose. The thief had turned out to be attractive, in an unprincipled sort of a way, with good teeth, broad shoulders, and lovely strong looking hands. And he played the flute. In a just world, she would have found him, retrieved her mirror, and suggested a way he could begin making amends. But he didn't have the mirror and a blood oath, unbreakable by death, or even Death, put a distinct crimp in her plans.

Then, suddenly, she had an idea. "Could I hire you to steal the mirror back?"

Ciro shook his head, a little surprised that he wanted the answer to be different. "I'd never be able to get it."

"You got it from me."

"Your pardon, Lady Wizard, but your door wasn't even locked. You relied too much on your reputation to protect you forgetting that a reputation can also attract unwanted attention."

"Like yours?" Magdelene muttered.

He bowed. "Like mine."

In the silence that followed, Magdelene considered her options and found herself a little short. Magical artifacts were essentially null and void as far wizardry was concerned and she couldn't force the thief to tell her where it was. Tossing the flute onto the table, she stood. "Looks like I'll have to do this the hard way."

Suddenly drenched in sweat, Ciro took a step back. "Lady Wizard, I beg you..."

"Relax. I haven't time to deal with you right now." She paused, one hand on the door and half turned to face him. "But I know you, Ciro Rasvona." Her voice lingered over his name, sending not entirely unpleasant chills up and down his spine. "When this is over, I can always find you again."

A thief had no need for a conscience but a remarkably well developed sense of self preservation made a handy substitute. "I could show you where the mirror is. Actually taking you there wasn't covered by the oath," he explained when both her brows rose. As they slowly began to lower again, he smiled nervously. "I, uh, guess I should've mentioned that before."

CR CR CR

Wondering what had happened to his policy of never taking risks he could avoid — She'd been about to leave, you yutz! — Ciro lead the way down the stairs and out onto the street, exchanging a silent bow with a neighbour in front of the building. When that neighbour raised a scandalized middle-class brow at the sight of his companion, he took her elbow and began hurrying her toward one of the hub streets, aware of eyes watching from curtained windows.

"Did you really want to spend the rest of your life as a cockroach?" Magdelene asked conversationally.

"Sorry." Praying he was imagining the tingle in his fingers, he released her arm. "It's just that I've worked very hard at remaining unnoticeable and you're attracting attention."

A little surprised, Magdelene tossed her hair back off her face and turned to stare at him. "I'm not doing anything."

Ciro sighed. "You don't have to."

"They're not used to seeing wizards around here?"

She was wearing an orange, calf-length skirt, red leather sandals, and a purple, sleeveless vest held closed with bright yellow frogging. "Yeah. That's it."

"I guess you should've considered the consequences before you stole my mirror."

"I took every precaution. You shouldn't have been able to track me."

"I didn't. You're dangling a Five Cities talisman from your left ear so I came directly here."

Unable to stop himself, Ciro clutched at the earring. So much for that protective crystal he'd been carrying. "You had a spell on the house to capture my image."

"No. I had a lizard."

CR CR CR

Both sides of the hub street were lined with shops, merchandise spilling out onto the cobblestones. Magdelene shook her head as she followed the thief through the glittering displays. "This is really unfair," she muttered. "First time I make it to one of the Five Cities and I'm here on business."

Ciro deftly snagged an exotic bloom from a hanging basket, tossing the vender a copper coin in almost the same motion. "Perhaps when you've brought your business to a close," he said, presenting the flower with a flourish, "I can show you around."

"Are you sucking up?"

"Is it working?"

"Not yet."

"Should I keep trying?"

"Couldn't hurt." He really did have a very charming smile Magdelene decided, tucking the blossom into her hair, and she'd never been very good at holding a grudge. "Is the mirror in the city?"

"I can't tell you that, Lady Wizard."

"Call me Magdelene." Titles implied a dignity she certainly wouldn't bother living up to. Stepping over a pile of mollusk shells, their pearly interiors gleaming in the sunlight, she rearranged the question. "Are we staying in the city?"

"Yes."

"Good. I might just find H'sak in ti..."

"It is Her!"

"Oh nuts." Grabbing Ciro's arm, she ducked into the nearest shop."

"What's going on?"

"I'll explain later"

"How may I help you, Gracious Lady?"

Magdelene flashed the shop keeper a somewhat pre-occupied smile. "Does this place have a back door?"

"But of course," he nodded toward a beaded curtain nearly hidden behind bolts of brightly colored fabric. "And on your way through, perhaps I can interest you in this lovely damask? Sale priced at only two dramils a measure. I offer a fine exchange rate on coin not of the Five Cities and I deliver."

The most powerful wizard in the world hesitated then sighed and shook her head. "Unfortunately, we're in a bit of a hurry."

"Because of the demon?" Ciro asked in an undertone as she pushed him through the curtain.

From outside the shop came an excited babble of voices, growing louder.

"Yeah. Him too."

ભ ભ ભ

"You appeared in the Hersota's shrine?" Ciro tapped his forehead twice with the first three fingers of his right hand — just in case. "No wonder you caused so much excitement. Her return has been prophesied by three separate sects."

"I didn't know it was her shrine, did I? It was just the only reference point I had in any of the Five Cities." She peered around the corner then led the way back onto the hub street some blocks from where they'd left it. "So, what was the Hersota like?"

"According to her believers, she was a stern and un-forgiving demiurge who preached that hard work and chastity were the only ways to enlightenment."

Magdelene stared at him in astonishment. "And they want her to come back?"

"I never said that I was waiting for her."

He sounded so affronted that Magdelene chuckled and tucked her hand into the crook of his elbow. There was muscle under the modest sleeve of his cream colored shirt, she noted with approval and when he shot her a question-ing glance, she answered it with her second best smile.

Her fingers were warm even through the cloth and for a moment her smile drove the thought of unimportant bodily functions, like breathing, right out of Ciro's mind. He'd felt safer while she'd been threatening him. "I uh, stole your mirror," he said. It seemed important that she remember that.

Magdelene waved the reminder off. "Now you're help-ing me find it."

"I broke into your home."

"I should've locked the door."

Wondering if he might not be better off finding a mem-ber of the City Guard and turning himself in, Ciro escorted

the wizard out into the Hub and around the civic fountain. "We're here."

"This is the government building."

"That's right."

"The mirror's in there?"

"I can't tell you that."

"I guess it is then."

The government had outgrown its building a number
of times adding larger and equally unattractive structures
as needed. The result looked pretty much exactly like what
it was, architecture by committee — or more precisely, a
series of committees.

Shaking her head, Magdelene released Ciro's arm. "This
is the ugliest pile of rock I've ever seen," she told him,
walking toward it. "And I saw Yamdazador before the
desert sands engulfed it."

Around the Great Lake, time had downgraded that
ancient city's sudden and inexplicable disappearance from
legend to parental warning; "I swear by all the gods, if you
don't stop stuffing beans up your brother's nose I'm sending you to Yamdazador."

Running to catch up, Ciro gasped, "You were at
Yamdazador?"

"I don't care what you heard, it wasn't my fault."

After a moment, he decided he didn't really want to
know.

"So, now you're here, what's your plan?" he asked as
they reached the stairs.

"My plan?" Pausing by the entrance a more practical
administration had cut into the huge, brass double doors,
Magdelene turned to face the thief. "I plan on getting my
mirror back before H'sak is either purposefully or inad-
vertently released and then I plan on making your client
very, very sorry he ever hired you."

Ciro winced. "Good plan."

"I thought so. Let's get going"

It took a moment for the words to sink in and when they
did, he actually felt the blood drain from his face. It was
an unpleasant feeling. "You want me to go with you."

"I might need your help."

"But I already told you, I won't be able to get near the mirror; it'll be too well guarded."

"You can't get near it on your own but you don't know what you're capable of when you're with me." She winked and led the way inside.

While his mind was still busy trying to plan an escape route, his body happily followed. *Oh sure*, he told it, as they crossed the atrium. *One lousy double entendre and you're willing to walk into the lion's den.* "Magdelene, this is a big place and I can't lead you any closer. If you can't scan for it, you'll never find the mirror."

"Of course I will, this is a government building isn't it?" Slipping deftly between the constant stream of robbed officials crossing and re-crossing the atrium, Magdelene made her way to the desk at the centre of all the activity. "Excuse me, could you please tell me if any of the senior officials has recently put him or herself incommunicado? Still in the building but not to be disturbed under any circumstances?"

The clerk glanced up from the continual flow of parchment, papyrus and wax tablets crossing his desk, pale features twisted into a impatient scowl. "Who are you?"

"If you must know, I'm the most powerful wizard in the world."

He leaned out far enough out to get a good look at her. "I find that highly unlikely," he sniffed.

ભ ભ ભ

"Why would he just give you that information?" Ciro demanded as they hurried through the halls.

"Successful government employees survive by recognizing power and responding to it."

"You mean kissing up to it."

"If you like."

According to the clerk, Governor Andropof had spent the day conducting research in the old library and was so insistent on not being disturbed that he'd put guards on all the entrances. "He was in there this morning when I got to work and he hasn't been out since. Please stop melting my wax. His assistant took him lunch, cold fish cakes and steamed dulse, but I don't know if he ate it."

Which was a little more information than Magdelene had required but, happily, it had segued into directions. "Go through that door, second right, past Roads and Public Works, up the stairs, go right again, it's at the end of the long hall and I'd be very grateful, Lady Wizard, if you could return my export documents to a recognizable language."

"Wait a minute! You can't go in there!"

About to follow Ciro into one of the older parts of the building, Magdelene turned to see a clerk, identical but for gender to the clerk in the atrium, hurrying toward them.

"Tourists," she forced the word through stiff lips, "are only permitted in the designated areas."

"I'm on my way to see the governor."

"Have you got an appointment?"

"Have you got a desire to have a demon eat your liver?" Her tone made it clear that this was not a rhetorical question.

CR CR CR

"Another successful government employee?" Ciro asked as they trotted up the forbidden flight of stairs.

Magdelene nodded. "I'm quite impressed by the state of your civil service; no wonder Talzabad-har runs so smoothly. I am a little disappointed in the governor though."

"You're disappointed in the governor? Why?"

"Why? He hired a thief and he's planning to use a demon for political gain."

Ciro turned to stare at her in amazement, tripped over the top step and would've fallen had she not caught him. "Magdelene, he's a politician!"

"And?"

"You don't get out much, do you? This is normal behavior for a politician. In fact," he added as she set him back on his feet, "by Five Cities standards, he's a bit of an underachiever."

"I've never understood this obsessive power seeking thing," Magdelene mused as they turned the last corner and started down a long, narrow hall, barely lit by tiny windows up under the ceiling.

"That's because you've got as much of it as you could ever want." Ciro waved toward the pair of city guards standing shoulder to shoulder in front of a square, iron bound door. "This looks like the place. What are we going to do about them?"

"Not a problem."

"I was hoping you'd say that." Thankful that the light was so bad, the thief kept his head down as they approached. The last thing he needed was some bright boy in the guards remembering his face. He needn't have worried, they were both watching Magdelene.

"Hi. Is this where the Governor is?"

"Yes ma'am," said the taller of the two.

"But we can't let you go in," added his companion.

She smiled sympathetically up at them. "It sure must be boring guarding this old door. You look like you could use a nap."

There's just something about men in uniform. Attempting to put her finger on just what that something was, she watched the two topple over in a tangle of tanned, muscular legs and short uniform kilts. *Oh yeah, now I remember...*

The door wasn't warded but it was locked. Blowing it off its hinges in a blast of eldritch fire, announcing her presence, as it were, with authority, had its merits but she didn't want to startle the governor into doing something he'd regret. He'd only regret it for about fifteen or twenty seconds depending on which end H'sak started with but since she'd then be the one who had to deal with the demon there'd probably be less trauma all around if she merely...

"Magdelene?" Ciro straightened, slipped his lock pick back into the seam of his trousers, and pulled the door open a fingerwidth. "We can go in now."

The door opened onto a second floor balcony about eight feet long by six feet wide in one end of a large rectangular room. To both the left and the right, curved stairs led down to the floor. The library shelves had been emptied of books and any lingering odours of paper and dust had surrendered to the swirling clouds of smoke that rose from a dozen incense burners. Motioning for Ciro to be quiet, Magdelene crept forward, peered over the balcony railing, and stiffened.

In the centre of the floor was a multicolored pentagram. In the centre of the pentagram, suspended horizontally some four feet above the ground was an unconscious, seven foot tall, green-scaled demon. Standing beside the demon, was a short, slight, balding man wearing what were traditionally thought of as wizard's robes.

As Magdelene's jaw dropped, he raised his arms into the air with a flourish worthy of a stage magician. In his right hand he held a dagger and in his left, an ebony bowl. Something green and moist coated the edge of the dagger blade.

"Oh shit!"

Governor Andropof's head jerked up and around toward the balcony. "Whoever you are, you're too late!" Laughing manically, he bent to hold the bowl under the demon's throat and vanished.

The chime of the dagger hitting the floor hadn't quite faded when Magdelene reached the edge of the pentagram, Ciro, fighting every instinct, close behind her.

"Where's the governor?" he panted.

"The middle of the Great Lake."

"What's he doing there?"

"Probably treading water." Circling the pentagram, Magdelene frowned down at the design.

"Why would he send himself...?"

"He didn't. I did. In another minute he'd have completed the sacrifice and we don't want that."

"We don't?"

"Trust me." Inspecting the last of the five points, she nodded in satisfaction and stepped over to H'sak's side.

"Magdelene!" Ciro spun around searching, unsuccessfully, for something to hide behind

"Relax. This is an exact copy of one of the great pentagrams from The Booke of Demonkind." She had to admit that the governor had done impressive research for, as far as Magdelene knew, there were only two copies of that book still in existence and she had one of them — it had been rather drastically overdue when the library'd burned down, so she'd kept it. "Unfortunately, the author had a tendency to chose art over craft and all of her illustrations are completely inaccurate — but then what else can you expect from someone who spells book with an 'e'?"

"Well, if the pentagram isn't holding the demon, what is?" He couldn't prevent his voice from rising rather dramatically on the last word although, when he noticed he was doing it, he did manage to stop wringing his hands.

"This."

This, was a glowing length of delicate silver chain.

"That's the Blazing Chain of Halla Hunta," the wizard explained as Ciro cautiously approached, drawn by the glint of a precious metal.

"Halla who?"

"Ancient warrior; nice buns, no manners. He had the chain forged, link by link, in volcanic fire, specifically to hold demons. It's why I didn't realize H'sak was out of the mirror; the chain's working the same way."

"Is it holding him up as well?" Ciro wondered, leaning closer.

"No. There's a Lombardi Floating Disc under his head and another under his feet and I'd love to know how Governor Andropof's got a pair away from Vince. You didn't...?"

"No."

"Then it looks like you weren't the only thief he employed." Her eyes narrowed as she bent and scooped the dagger off the floor. "This is the Fell Dagger of Connackron, also called Demonsbane. And this..." With her free hand, she removed a cross section of bone from a hollow between the short horns extending out of the demon's forehead. "...is a piece of the thigh bone of Mighty Manderkew. You haven't seen the sacrificial bowl from the destroyed Temple of the Darkest Night have you?"

"It's under..." Ciro waved a hand more or less up and down the length of H'sak's body. "...him."

"Could you get it?"

Common sense suggested he point blank refuse to crawl under an unconscious demon confined by no more than two ounces of silver chain and held off the floor in the centre of an inoperative pentagram by artifacts he couldn't see. Unfortunately, common sense got over-ruled by a desire not to look like a wuss in front of an attractive woman. It didn't help that green slime had dripped all over the floor from a wound in the demon's throat.

When he emerged, bowl clasped between sweaty hands, Magdelene took a quick look inside it, sighed with relief, and shook her head. "I don't know whether to be impressed or appalled. Governor Andropof must've been gathering this crap for years."

"Not quite." Recognition steadying his nerves, Ciro managed a matter-of-fact tone. "I stole this last summer from an inn in the Fourth City. They were using it as a serving bowl."

"They have much business?"

"Actually, no."

"Can't say as I'm surprised."

"Was the governor a wizard then?"

"No. Just a cheap opportunist. The power's intrinsic to the artifacts. Demon blood shed with this knife into that bowl will open the way for one of the Demon Princes to leave the Netherhells. Once he gets here, the piece of thigh bone's a promissory note."

Mouth suddenly dry, Ciro stared into the bowl.

"Relax, I stopped him in time and H'sak's almost healed." Magdelene rapped the demon almost fondly on the chest with the knuckles of the hand holding the bone. "Of course, after the note's redeemed there'd be a Demon Prince loose in the world."

"He wouldn't just go home?"

"Not likely; demons gain rank through slaughter."

"I didn't know that," he said, wishing he'd never had the opportunity to find out. "Now what?"

"Now, I think you'd better hold these for me." She held out the dagger and the bone. "H'sak seems to be waking up."

"I thought the chain was holding him?!"

"It is. But he was unconscious because he'd had his throat slit." A waggle of the dagger she was still holding out towards him, directed Ciro's attention to the demon blood staining the blade. "It takes a lot to kill the demon-kind and unsuccessful attempts make them cranky. Now, if you don't mind, I may need both hands free."

On cue, H'sak's lips drew back off his teeth. A shudder ran the length of his body like a small wave.

"Both hands free," Ciro repeated. "Good idea." Sacrificial bowl from the destroyed Temple of the Darkest Night in his left hand, the Fell Dagger of Connackron and the thigh bone of Mighty Manderkew in his right, he backed out of the pentagram and continued moving back until his shoulder blades hit the wall.

Magdelene glanced up at the impact. "What are you doing all the way over there?"

"I'm a thief," Ciro reminded her. "I'm not good at confrontation."

"Whatever. Just hang onto that stuff until I get time to destroy it."

"Couldn't you just, you know, poof? Like the governor?"

"The governor wasn't a magical artifact. Wizardry doesn't affect them, it's why I had to come after the mirror myself."

"Then how?"

"I was thinking of using a hammer. Now, if you don't mind..." She turned her attention back to the demon.

Ciro watched the eight inch claws flexing at the end of arms that no longer looked quite so limp and decided that being able to raise even one hand in his own defense was better than nothing at all. He dropped the bone and the dagger into the bowl.

A barely viscous drop of demon blood rolled off the blade.

H'sak jerked. His eyes blazed red. "The way is open!"

In the silence that followed, Ciro was pretty sure he heard his heart stop beating.

"You know," Magdelene told him, "I had pretty much decided that bringing me here and opening the door made up for stealing my mirror."

The demon turned toward her. "You!"

"Who else?"

"There was a man... Oh wait," he snorted, "if there was a man I should've expected you to show up."

"You're in no position to make smart ass comments. A Prince approaches, compelled to answer a summons from the mortal world and your blood was the instrument of his summoning. He's going to be royally pissed."

H'sak struggled impotently within the chain. "Your death will follow mine, Wizard," he growled. "And I will die happy knowing you are about to be torn limb from limb!"

"Suppose neither of us has to die?"

Ciro, who'd been watching a speck of darkness grow to the size of a dinner plate, cleared his throat as a cold wind began to blow from the centre of it. "Uh, Magdelene, you'd better hurry."

"H'sak?"

"You're the most powerful wizard in the world," he sniffed, "you close the way."

"I can't close the way against the Prince's power."

"So?"

"So this is no time to sulk about being stuck in that mirror!"

The demon's lips drew back, exposing a double row of fangs. "I've been forced to endure your singing for almost two hundred years. I think this is a fine time to sulk."

"Suit yourself. Ciro, find the mirror, it has to be in the library." She smiled down at the demon as the thief began to search. "I'm thinking of studying opera."

H'sak cringed. "You win. What's the plan?"

"I release you from the chain so I can use it on his Highness and you don't attack me from behind until I've finished with him."

"And what if he finishes you?"

"Then at least you're facing him on your feet."

"Deal."

Grasping one end of the chain, Magdelene began to unwind it.

With one eye on the circle of darkness, now the size of a wagon wheel, Ciro sidled toward the pentagram. "I found the mirror," he muttered, lips close to Magdelene's ear. "It's in pieces."

She leaned closer. "Don't tell H'sak."

"Hadn't planned on it." He took a deep breath and lightly gripped her shoulders. "Magdelene, in case I don't get a chance to say this later, I'm sorry I took your mirror. I'm sorry about putting the bloody dagger in the bowl."

He looked so miserable she couldn't stay angry. Her expression softened. "I'd better send you away."

"Like the governor?"

"Only drier."

"No." The rising wind from the dark gate whipped her hair into her face. He caught a strand and tucked it gently behind her ear. "I'm responsible for this, it's only fair I stay."

Eyes half lidded, Magdelene sighed. "I only regret that..."

"Wizard! You haven't got time!" H'sak kicked his feet, jerking the chain still in Magdelene's hand. "And don't raise those eyebrows at me! You know what you haven't got time for! After two hundred years," he muttered as she took a quick look at the nearly open gate and began to frantically unwind the chain, "you'd think that the novelty would've worn off."

Free, the demon rolled off the Lombardi Discs as the darkness fully dilated. Hooking his claws in the back of Ciro's shirt, he yanked the thief to the far side of the room and dropped him. "The man is out of the way," he hissed as a pale figure began to take shape in the gateway. "You'll only get one chance. Don't screw it up."

In answer, Magdelene leaned into the wind, and snapped the chain out to its full length. Wrapped around H'sak, the links had only gleamed but now, they blazed. She waited, eyes locked on the materializing Prince, noting the full thick fall of golden hair, the broad shoulders, the rippled stomach, the slender waist, the...

"What are you doing?!" H'sak shrieked. "Waiting to see the whites of his eyes?!"

"Not quite," Magdelene murmured, and flicked the chain forward.

The Prince howled with laughter as the delicate links traced a spiral around him from neck to knees. "Foolish little wizard, you can not hold..." His eyes widened, showing only onyx from lid to lid. "This is impossible! This toy is intended to contain the lessor demons!" He writhed in place. "I am a prince!"

Trying very hard not to be distracted by the writhing, Magdelene held out her arms at shoulder height and brought her palms together. The gate began to close.

He stopped struggling. The perfect lines of his face smoothed out as he began to concentrate. The light of the chain began to dim. "You think you have power enough to keep me from this world?" he sneered as link after link went dark. "You think you can defeat m..."

The gate closed.

"Apparently," Magdelene said, twitching her skirt back into place.

Remembering how to use his legs, Ciro leapt to his feet and started forward. "Magdelene, you were magnificen..."

Magdelene turned, knowing exactly what she'd see.

"Now, we make a new bargain," H'sak announced, claws forming a cage around Ciro's head, their tips just barely into the skin of his throat.

Magdelene sighed. "You may find this hard to believe, H'sak, but I'm going to miss you."

The demon frowned. "I have the man."

Folding her arms over the purple vest, she tapped one red leather sandal against the floor.

H'sak withdrew his claws one at a time. Slowly. So that it didn't look as if he were making any sudden moves.

"Thank you."

Ciro's heels thumped back onto the floor and he swayed in the rush of air that filled the space where the demon had been. "Where did you send him?"

"The Netherhells." She pursed her lips sympathetically at the collar of shallow punctures. "I'd have done it years ago but I didn't know the way."

"And now you do?" He glanced over to where the gate had been.

"Now I do."

Ciro managed a shaky smile. "That ought to terrify them."

"I don't see why it should," Magdelene protested. "If they don't bother me, I won't bother them. Shall we gather up the bits and pieces and get out of here?"

The guards were still asleep outside the library door. Magdelene woke them, helped them up onto their feet, and made a suggestion Ciro was rather glad he hadn't heard given the reaction of two strong men.

No one tried to stop them from leaving the building. No one paid them any attention at all until they were past the civic fountain.

"My eyes see Her!"

"Hard work and chastity," sighed the most powerful wizard in the world. "I don't think so." She squeezed Ciro's hand, and disappeared.

A heartbroken wail went up from the crowd. A weeping woman grabbed the thief's arm. "You were with Her! Tell us, tell us, will She return?"

Gently, but firmly, he disentangled himself. And then he smiled. "You can bet on it."

ʕ ʕ ʕ

It took her a week to notice.

Ciro winced at the crack of displaced air and hoped the neighbours weren't home. This was exactly the sort of thing to get a normally quiet man an undeserved reputation. "Good afternoon, Magdelene."

"Don't good afternoon me, Ciro Rasvona, you little shit! You stole the gold hieroglyph of my name!"

He got slowly to his feet and held out his hand, the small gold plaque lying across his palm. "What," he asked, "can I possibly do to make amends?"

Cut off in mid rant, Magdelene looked down at the plaque, up at the thief, and the corners of her mouth turned up into her best smile. "I'll think of something," she promised, stepping forward. "That had better be a lock pick in your trousers, 'cause you don't seem very happy to see me ... oh, wait a minute ... my mistake."

"I also took that big blue pearl," he murmured when he could catch his breath.

"And the crystal gryphon?"

"No, but I'm willing to go back for it..."

Third Time Lucky

The lizard had no idea it was being observed as it lay on top of the low coral wall, its mouth slightly open, its eyes unfocused golden jewels. Its only concern was with the warmth of the spring sun—not that the spring sun was much different from the winter sun.

"The real difference," Magdelene explained every spring to a variety of sweating guests, "is that it goes from being hot to being damned hot."

"How can you stand it?" one visitor had panted, languidly fanning himself with a palm leaf.

Magdelene's grey eyes had crinkled at the corners. "I like it hot." And she'd licked her lips.

The visitor, a handsome young nobleman who'd been sent south by his father until a small social infraction blew over, spent the rest of his life wondering if he'd misunderstood.

The lizard liked it hot as well.

Silk, Magdelene's cat, did not. She was expecting her first litter of kittens and between the extra weight and the heat she was miserable. She did, however, like lizards.

The lizard never knew what hit him. One moment he was peacefully enjoying the sun, the next he was dangling upside down between uncomfortably sharp teeth being carried into the garden where he was suddenly and painfully dropped. He was stunned for a moment, then scuttled as fast as he could for the safety that beckoned from under a broken piece of tile.

He didn't make it.

Twice more he was lifted, carried, and dropped. Finally he turned, raised his head, and hissed at his tormentor.

Which was quite enough for Silk. She lunged with dainty precision, bit the lizard's head off, then made short work of the rest of it.

"Are you sure you should be eating lizards in your condition?" Magdelene asked. The crunching of tiny bones had distracted her attention from her book.

Silk merely licked her lips disdainfully and stalked away, her distended belly swaying from side to side.

Magdelene laughed and returned to the story. It was a boring tale of two men adventuring in the land of the Djinn, but the friend who had brought it to her had gone to a great deal of trouble and books were rare—even with that printing device they had come up with in the east—so she read it.

"Mistress, will you be eating in the garden today?"

"Please, Kali. It'll be happening soon; I want to enjoy the peace while I can."

"Happening again, Mistress?"

"Some people never learn, Kali."

"One can hope, Mistress," Kali sniffed and went back in the house to prepare lunch.

"One always hopes," Magdelene sighed, "but it doesn't seem to do much good."

She had lived in the turquoise house on the hill for as long as anyone in the fishing village that held her closest neighbours could remember. Great-grandmothers had told little children how, when they were young, their great-grandmothers had told them that she had always been there. She had been there so long, in fact, that the villagers took her presence for granted and treated her much the same way as they treated the wind and the coral reef and the sea: with a friendly respect. It had taken them longer to accept Kali and the visible difference of red eyes and ivory horns, but that too had come in time. It had been years since it was considered unusual to see the demon housekeeper in the marketplace arguing over the price of fish. It was, however, still unusual to see her lose the argument.

Occasionally it was useful to have Magdelene for a neighbour.

CR   CR   CR

"Carlos, there's a dragon in the harbor."

The village headman sighed and looked at the three heaps of kindling that had been fishing boats a very short time before. It had been a miracle that all six fishermen had survived. "Yes, M'lady, I know."

"I guess," Magdelene mused, squinting into the wind, her skirt and the two scarves she had wrapped around her breasts snapping and dancing about her, "I should go out and talk to him."

"I'll ready my boat." The headman turned to go but Magdelene held up her hand.

"Don't bother," she said. "Boats are tippy, unstable little things. I'll walk."

And she did. She got wet to about the knees—the swells made for uneven footing—but while the villagers watched in awe, (she'd never done that before) she walked out until she stood, bobbing gently up and down with the waves, about five body-lengths from the dragon.

"Well?" she asked.

"Gertz?" replied the huge silver sea-dragon, extraordinarily puzzled. This was outside his experience as well. He turned his head so he could fix her in one opalescent eye.

Magdelene put her hands on her hips.

"Go on," she said firmly. "Shoo!"

The dragon, recognizing the voice of authority, however casual, suddenly decided there was much better fishing further south, and left.

The villagers cheered as Magdelene stepped back into the sand. She grinned and curtsied, not gracefully but enthusiastically, then waved a hand at the wreckage. Wood, rope, canvas, and the few bits of metal received in trade for fish, shuddered, stirred, then danced themselves back into fishing boats.

Everyone stared in silent surprise. This was more than they'd dared hope for.

"We don't know how to thank you," the headman began, but his wife interrupted.

"Just say it, for Netos' sake," she muttered, knowing her husband's tendency to orate at the slightest provocation. "The Lady knows what she's done, she doesn't need you telling her."

Carlos sighed. "Thank you."

Magdelene twinkled at him. "You're welcome." Then she went home to browbeat Kali into baking something sweet for supper. She hadn't got halfway up the hill before the boats were putting out to replace the morning's lost catch.

ભ ભ ભ

Two days later the soldiers came.

"It is happening, Mistress."

"Yes, Kali, I know."

"What would you have me do?"

"I think," Magdelene shaded her eyes with her hand, "you should make lunch for six. We'll eat in the garden."

The Captain had been sent by his King to bring back the most powerful wizard in the world. What he and the four soldiers he'd brought with him were supposed to do if the wizard refused to cooperate was beyond him. Die, he suspected. The wizard had been ridiculously easy to find; legends—and the memory of some of them caused him to shift uneasily on his saddle—had led him right to her. He wasn't sure what he'd expected but it wasn't a forty-year-old woman with laughing eyes and a sunburned nose who was barely dressed.

"I'm looking," he said stiffly, stopping his small troop at the gate in the coral wall, "for Magdelene, the Wizard."

"You're looking at her." Magdelene liked large, well-muscled men with grizzled beards—even if they were wearing too much clothing—so she gave the Captain her best smile.

The Captain showed no visible reaction but behind him, young Colin smiled back. The most powerful wizard in the world reminded him of his Aunt Maya.

"I am here to take you to Bokta..."

"Where in the Goddess's creation is that?"

"North," he said flatly; worship of the Goddess had been outlawed in Bokta for several dozen years. "Very far north."

"Why does he always go north?" Magdelene asked Silk, who had shown up to see what was going on. "What's wrong with east, or west, or even further south?"

Silk neither knew nor cared; and as she didn't much like horses, she padded off to find some shade.

Magdelene looked up to find the Captain glaring at her and was instantly, although not very sincerely, contrite. "Oh, I'm sorry. You were saying?"

"I am here to take you to Bokta so you may prove yourself to be the most powerful wizard in the world. My King does not believe you are."

"Really? And who told him I wasn't?"

A small smile cracked the Captain's beard. "I believe it was his wizard."

"I'll bet," said Magdelene dryly. "And if I don't come?"

"Then I'm to tell you that the wizard will destroy twenty people daily from the time I return without you until you appear."

Magdelene's eyes went hard. "Will he?"

"Yes."

"That son of a bitch!" She considered that for a moment and grinned ruefully at her choice of phrase. "We can leave tomorrow. I'd travel faster on my own but we'd best follow procedure."

She stepped back and the five men rode into the yard. Suddenly there was no gate in the corral wall.

"Oh, put that away," she chided a nervous soldier, who clutched his sword in an undeniably threatening manner. "If those great big horses of yours can't jump a three-foot wall, even in this heat, you're in trouble. Besides, you couldn't kill me if you wanted to. I've been dead, and it isn't all it's cracked up to be."

The sword remained pointed at her throat.

"Garan!" snapped the Captain.

"But sir..."

"Put it away!"

"Yes, sir."

The Captain swung off his horse. "Then we are your prisoners."

"Don't be ridiculous, you're my guests. Unsaddle your horses and turn them loose over there. They'll be well taken care of." She turned and headed for the garden. "Then you can join me for lunch. I hope you like shrimp." She paused and faced them again, noting with amusement that they were looking slightly stunned. "And please don't draw on my housekeeper; her feelings are easily hurt."

ᘒ ᘒ ᘒ

A small problem arose the next morning.

"You have no horse?" the Captain asked incredulously.

Magdelene shook her head. "I can't ride. No sense of rhythm." She slapped her hands in front of her to illustrate the point. "I go one way, the horse goes another and we meet in the middle. Incredibly uncomfortable way to travel."

As children in Bokta rode before they walked, it hadn't occurred to the Captain that the wizard would not have a horse. Or that she'd be unwilling to get one.

"Never mind," she said comfortingly, "we'll stop by the village on our way and borrow Haylio's donkey and cart."

"Donkey and cart?" repeated the Captain weakly.

"He's not very fast but I can sit in a cart with the best of folk." She waved a hand and the gate reappeared in the wall.

"Mistress—" Kali stood in the garden. "When will you return?"

"How long will it take us to get to this Bokta place?" Magdelene queried the Captain who, in company with his men, was eyeing Kali nervously. Garan had his hand on his sword.

"Uh, about three months."

"Then expect me back in about three months plus a day. After all," she added for her escort's benefit, "I don't intend to take the scenic route back. And you," she wagged a finger at Silk who was lying at Kali's feet. "You take care of yourself, and no more lizards."

Silk inspected a perfectly groomed silver paw and refused to answer.

∞ ∞ ∞

It was a strange cavalcade that moved north along the coast road: five great warhorses carrying overdressed and sweaty soldiers, bracketing a medium-sized donkey pulling a two-wheeled cart and the most powerful wizard in the world.

Magdelene sang loudly and tunelessly as they travelled, her songs usually the type gently bred females were not supposed to know.

"Madam!" The Captain had stood it as long as he was able.

A bawdy lyric, in an impossible key, faded to silence. "Something troubling you?"

"It's that song..."

"Oh? Am I corrupting your men?"

"No, but you're scaring the horses."

For a moment the Captain anticipated being turned into something unpleasant, then Magdelene threw back her head and laughed long and hard.

"Point taken," she gasped when the laughter finally let her talk. "I've no music at all and I know it. Do you sing, Captain?"

"No."

She grinned up at him. "Pity. I'm very," she paused and her smile grew thoughtful as she remembered, "amiable to men who make music."

On his way back to the front of the line the captain almost succeeded in not wondering just how amiable this wizard could be.

∞ ∞ ∞

The soldiers treated Magdelene with a mixture of fear and respect, fear winning most often, for their King's wizard had taught them to dread the breed; all save Colin, who treated her much the same as he treated his Aunt Maya. Magdelene, who had never been anyone's aunt, slipped happily into the role and Colin became the only one of the fair-skinned northerners to stop burning and peeling and burning again.

"Well, I don't care what you say," growled Garan. "Ain't nobody's aunt can grab a fistful of fire, then sit there tossing it from hand to hand."

"I don't think she was aware she was doing it."

"And that makes it better? Hummph."

∽ ∽ ∽

They reached Denada in three and a half weeks. Even forced to the donkey's pace, that was two days faster than it had taken going the other way.

The Captain sighed in relief; he'd about had it with the perpetual heat of the southlands. Even the rain was warm. He spurred his horse towards the city gate.

"Uh, Sir!"

"Now what?" He wheeled around, narrowly missed running down a farmer with a basket of yams on his head, and was soundly cursed. When he reached the cart, Magdelene removed her small bundle of belongings and was kissing the soft grey muzzle of the donkey.

"What are you doing?"

She grinned up at him. "What does it look like? I'm kissing the donkey."

Colin snickered but managed to school his expression before the Captain could look his way.

The Captain sighed. "Metros give me strength," he prayed. "Why are you kissing the donkey?"

"Because I'm sending him home." She flicked the animal between his eyes with the first two fingers of her left hand.

Half a startled bray hung on the air, but the donkey and the cart were gone.

"Can your Aunt Maya do that?" hissed Garan.

Colin had to admit she couldn't.

"Why not send us to Bokta that way," demanded the Captain, walking his horse through the space where the donkey had been, making sure it had truly vanished, "and avoid all this damned travelling."

"I know where I've been," Magdelene replied gravely, "but even I don't know where I'm going to be until I get there." She shouldered her bag and headed for the gate. The Captain and his men could only follow.

The five northern soldiers on their massive war horses made little stir as they moved the width of the city from the gate to the harbor. After all they had been there less than two months before and Denada, a cosmopolitan city with traders arriving daily from exotic places, saved its wonder for the truly unusual. Only a few street whores took any notice of the men, and no one at all noticed the most powerful wizard in the world.

Denada's harbor was huge: twenty ships could tie up, and there was room for another twelve to ride at anchor. Miraculously, the Raven, the ship that had carried the soldiers across the inland sea, was still docked and appeared to have just finished loading.

"Two months!" screamed her master, bounding down the gangway. "Two months I sit here since you leave. First, I must clean smell of abominable animals out of my forward hold though still it smells like a stable then what happens but my steersman — may his liver be eaten by cockroaches — sets sail with a hangover we come up bang on coral and rip off half of keel. It is a miracle — may all the gods in heaven be blessed and I don't doubt they are — that we make it back for repairs. Now at last we are ready to sail." He pounded the Captain's shoulder enthusiastically. "So, what can I do for you?"

"I need passage north for myself, my men and our horses. And for this lady here."

"Aiee, again with the horses!" He didn't give Magdelene, who was dropping stale journey bread into the water to feed the fish, a second glance. "Sill, already I have a hold that smells like a stable. Fourteen gold pieces."

"All right, I..."

"Two," said Magdelene, her eyes glinting dangerously as she dusted crumbs off her hands.

The ship's master stared accusingly at the Captain. "I thought you said she was a lady? Fourteen I say and fourteen it is."

After a spirited discussion, they settled on eight. The Captain paid up, and Magdelene deftly lifted four gold pieces from his pouch.

"Hey!"

"You're still up two," she said sweetly. "While you load the horses, I'm going shopping."

"Don't tell me," muttered Garan, stopping Colin before he could speak. "Your Aunt Maya loves to shop."

Hours passed, the ship was ready to sail on the evening tide and Magdelene had still not returned. Both worried and annoyed, the Captain walked to the end of the docks to look for her. He was considering a trip into the city when she came barreling around a corner, a grimy urchin heavily laden with packages in tow, and crashed into his arms.

"Here, take these." She shoved the parcels at him and tossed the boy a silver piece. "Thanks for the help, kid, now beat it before the mob gets here."

"Where have you been?" demanded the Captain as they trotted towards the ship. "We're ready to leave. Why are we running an..." He stopped. "Mob? What mob?"

Magdelene got him moving again. "I cured a blind beggar. It drew a bit of a crowd. Good thing the kid knew a short cut."

They sprinted up the gangway just as the leading edge of the mob appeared at the end of the docks. A cry went up as Magdelene was spotted.

"Why didn't you do something a little less spectacular," muttered the Captain, tossing the packages over the rail, then vaulting it himself. "Like raising the dead."

"I did that the last time." She accepted his helping hand, having somehow managed to become tangled in a stray line. "This time I was trying to keep a low profile."

"You've been here before then."

"Twice."

"Well, maybe next time you can pass through without starting a riot." He shouted to the ship's master to cast off but it was unnecessary. The instant Magdelene's foot touched the deck, ropes untied themselves and the Raven slipped its mooring just ahead of the first hysterical Denadan.

"Why," asked the Captain, using the toe of his boot on a package in danger of going overboard, "does the most powerful wizard in the world in the have to run from a crowd of shopkeepers and beggars?"

Magdelene collapsed on a bale of rope. "I'll let you in on a secret," she panted. "I'm also the laziest wizard in the world. Running was definitely the least complicated thing to do."

ശ ശ ശ

The trip across the inland sea had never been done faster. The Raven seemed to barely touch the waves and the wind never left her sails.

"I don't like boats," Magdelene explained when the Captain voiced his suspicions about the wind. "They make me sick. It's worse than being pregnant."

He stared at her in surprise. He'd never though of her having a life like other women.

"You had children?"

"Have," she corrected, and it wasn't just the sea that chased the laughter from her eyes. "One. A son. Goddess knows why I ever let his father talk me into it."

"He could make music," the Captain suggested.

Some of the laughter returned. "He could at that."

The ship rolled, and the most powerful wizard in the world turned slightly green.

"Oh, lizard piss!" she muttered and headed for the rail.

ശ ശ ശ

The Raven docked in Finera in eighteen days. The previous record was twenty-seven.

"Anytime you want to travel the seas, Lady Wizard, you are most welcome to sail with me."

Magdelene smiled stiffly at the ship's master, "Next time I travel, I'll walk." She gripped Colin's arm tightly as he helped her down the gangway. "Sometimes I think he situates himself purposefully so that I have to travel by sea."

Colin looked puzzled.

"Never mind, dear. Just get me somewhere that isn't moving."

"Take her to the Laughing Boar," bellowed the Captain over the squeals of the horse being lifted from the hold. "We'll spend the night."

The Laughing Boar was the largest inn in Finera and a favourite with the caravan masters who came into the city to trade with ships from the south. As they crossed the common room, Magdelene counted fifteen different dialects; one of which she was surprised to note, she didn't know. Her room was large and cheerful and so, she observed with satisfaction, was the bed.

"This ought to make him sit up and take notice." She winked at her reflection, now clad in a dangerously low cut green silk gown, and went looking for the Captain.

Later that night he sat on the edge of her bed, suddenly unsure.

"What's wrong?" she asked, gently tweaking a wiry curl.

He caught her hand. "Did you use your magic to bring me here?"

She smiled and there was nothing, and everything, magic in the smile. "Only the magic that women have been using on men since the Goddess created the world."

"Oh." He considered for a moment. "That's all right then." And he lowered himself to her lips.

Next morning, as he left Magdelene's room, the Captain bumped into Colin in the corridor. The young man executed a parade-ground perfect salute and marched briskly off down the hall, his face a study in suppressed laughter.

"Smart-assed kid," muttered the Captain, straightened his tunic, and stomped off to find breakfast.

છ છ છ

"Will we have to camp in this?" Magdelene asked anxiously, watching water stream off the shield she had raised over the entire group. Even Garan was forced to agree there were certain advantages in travelling with a wizard.

"Not for a while," Colin reassured her. "We follow the Great North Road over half the way, and it seems to be lined with inns."

Magdelene eyed the broad back of the Captain. "Good."

CR CR CR

"I'd like to see you claim resemblance to your Aunt Maya now." Garan wiped foam off his mouth onto his sleeve. "She's used her blasted magic to bewitch the Captain."

"That's all you know," Colin chuckled, finishing his own ale. "My family lives in the capital and the Captain has bedded Aunt Maya."

CR CR CR

When they reached the border of Bokta, a full division of the King's Guard awaited them, darkly impressive in their black and silver armour.

"This is the best you could do?" sneered the Guard Captain, staring disdainfully down his narrow nose at Magdelene in her pony cart. "The King and his Wizard are not going to be pleased."

It had been a long trip and Magdelene was not in the best of moods. "How would you like to spend the rest of your life as a tree frog?" she asked conversationally.

The Guard Captain ignored her. "Can't you keep her quiet?" he drawled, ennui dripping from the words.

It was difficult to say who was more surprised, the division of King's Guard or the tree frog clinging to the saddle of the Guard Captain's horse.

"Magdelene," sighed the Captain, "change him back."

"He's a pompous ass," Magdelene protested sulkily.

"Granted, but he's also the King's favourite nephew. Please."

"Oh, all right." She waved her hand. The Guard Captain cheeped once, found himself back in his own body, and fainted. It was a rather subdued trip into the Capital.

CR CR CR

The King's Wizard stirred the entrails of the goat with the tip of his bloody knife. She was here, in the Palace, and when he defeated her he would be the most powerful wizard in the world! Power. He could feel burning through him, lighting fires of destruction that he would release to obliterate this woman, this Magdelene.

He wiped the knife on a skin taken whole off a stillborn babe, twitched his robes into place, and left his sanctum. Behind him, blood began to drip off the table and form a pool on the carpet.

The King was waiting in corridor, nervously pacing up and down. He stopped when the Wizard emerged, and his two men-at-arms thankfully fell into place behind him.

"She's in the Palace. We must hurry or we won't be in the throne room when she arrives."

The Wizard merely nodded curtly. His measured stride didn't change.

"You are sure you can defeat her?" The King, left standing, scrambled to catch up.

"I have studied for over a hundred years. I command the demons of the Netherworld. I control the elements. I can easily defeat one ancient woman."

Magdelene's actual appearance came as a bit of a shock to both men. The crystal had only ever shown her location, never the wizard herself. This was the most powerful wizard in the world? This laughing woman who wasn't even wearing wizardly robes? The King almost chuckled as he took his seat.

ೞ ೞ ೞ

Magdelene approached the throne with the Captain, bowed when he did, and clicked her tongue when she looked up at the King's Wizard. Thick grey hair sprang from a widow's peak and curled on his shoulders, his eyes were sunken black pits, his nails were claws on the end of long and skinny fingers, and his stooped body was covered in a black robe so closely embroidered with cabalistic symbols that from a distance it looked more gold than black.

"If he'd just once realize that self-control comes first," she hissed to the Captain as a herald announced them.

The whispers of the court fell silent as the King's Wizard stepped forward. "I have summoned you to prove your-self," he declared in ponderous tones, blue fire crackling eerily about him.

The Captain shifted his weight so that his cloak fell free of his sword. He had always hated this wizard, this scrawny grey scarecrow of a man, and had it not been for the innocent lives that would have been forfeit he would have never brought Magdelene here to him. At least not after he'd got to know her.

Magdelene successfully fought the urge to giggle. "Interesting outfit, Tristan. Demon-made?"

"My name is Polsarr," snarled the wizard, his lips pulled back over startlingly white teeth.

"Your name," said Magdelene mildly, "is Tristan. I should know, I gave it to you. And now," she turned to the King, "I'd like to be shown to my room, it's been a long trip."

"You are not going anywhere, woman!" bellowed Polsarr. "Until I banish you into darkness!"

"Oh? And would you have everyone say that you defeated the most powerful wizard in the world only because she was exhausted and irritable from four days of bumping over incredibly bad roads?"

The King tugged on Polsarr's sleeve. "We don't want that! There must be no doubt when you win."

Polsarr glowered and muttered but finally had to agree the King was right. "Enjoy your rest," he snarled. "It will be your last." He stalked from the room.

"If he really wants to prove his power," Magdelene muttered to the King, "he should do something about those roads."

The King ignored that. "Captain, take her to the south tower in the east wing. And Captain, you and your men will guard this wizard one more night."

The Captain bowed and backed away. Magdelene gave the King her second best smile and followed.

At the tower — which was as faraway from the rest of the Palace as it was possible to get and still be in the Palace—the Captain dismissed his men.

"Be back at dawn," he told them. "Even if the King's Wizard decides to attack tonight, there's nothing you could do."

Colin raised an eyebrow at the phrasing but he went with the rest.

The tower was deserted and, judging by the unbroken layer of dust, hadn't been used in years. Magdelene waved a hand at her bag and it trailed them up the stairs.

"The man's as big an ass as the King's nephew."

There was no need to ask who she meant.

"He's not much like you."

"Thank you. He's not much like his father either. That man didn't have an ambitious bone in his body." She sighed. "Maybe I should've encouraged the kid's musical talents."

The Captain threw open a door leading to an old-fashioned bedchamber.

"If I remember correctly, this is the only furnished room in the tower."

Magdelene stepped inside, the bag settling to the floor at her feet. "It's not that bad. The bed looks solid enough for one night at least." She grinned over her shoulder at the Captain, only to find him hesitating in the doorway. "What's wrong?"

"I'll stand guard in the hall. You'll need your strength for tomorrow."

"And I want your strength tonight," she told him gently, drawing him into the room and shutting the door.

Some hours later the Captain untangled himself from her embrace and rolled over on his back. "Is there anything," he asked, trying to get his breath back, "that you don't do well?"

Magdelene ran her fingers through the matted hair on his chest. "I'm a lousy mother," she admitted.

ௐ ௐ ௐ

Everyone with a plausible excuse crowded into the throne room the next morning. People were packed so tightly against the walls they had to cooperate with their neighbours in order to breathe. Even the Queen, who hated public functions and wanted only to be left alone, was there. The King was almost quivering with excitement, anticipating when he would control the most powerful wizard in the world. Polsarr stood alone in the centre of the room.

When Magdelene entered, the room released a collective sigh. She had not escaped in the night.

Leaving the Captain and his men by the door, Magdelene walked forward until she stood only three body-lengths from her son.

"Morning, Tristan. Sleep well?"

Polsarr ignored the question. He drew himself up to his full height and declared, "Already I have defeated seven lesser mages."

"Seven," said Magdelene. "Imagine that."

"I banished even the mighty Joshuae to the Netherworlds!" He saw what he thought was worry in Magdelene's eyes and chuckled.

Magdelene wasn't worried. She was annoyed. "You banished Joshuae to the Netherworld? That was remarkably rude; the man is your name-father."

"I HAVE NO NAME-FATHER!"

His outraged volume was impressive.

"Well, you don't now, that's for sure. I only hope he finds his way back."

"I WAS BORN IN THE BELLY OF THE MOUNTAIN AND SPEWED FORTH WITH FIRE AND MOLTEN ROCK!"

Magdelene sighed. "And the time before this you were ripped from the loins of the North Wind. The time before that," her brows wrinkled, "I don't remember the time before that but it was equally ridiculous I'm sure. Now can we get on with this?"

Polsarr shrieked with wordless rage and blue lightning leapt from his fingertips.

Magdelene stood unconcerned and the lightning missed.

A fireball grew in Polsarr's hand. When it reached the size of a wagon wheel he threw it. And then another. And then another.

Magdelene disappeared with the fire. The flames burnt viciously for a moment, then suddenly died down. Although the floor was blackened and warped, Magdelene wasn't even scorched.

Polsarr screamed a hideous incantation, spittle flying from his lips to sizzle on the floor. There was a blinding red flash between the wizards ... and then a demon.

The demon was three times the size of a man, with green scaled skin and burning red eyes. Six-inch tusks drew its mouth back into a snarl and poisons dripped form the scimitar-shaped talons that curved out from both hands and feet. It raised heavily muscled arms, screamed, and lurched towards Magdelene.

Magdelene looked it right in the eye.

The demon stopped screaming.

She folded her arms across her chest and her foot began to tap.

The demon paused and reconsidered. Suddenly recognition dawned. It gave a startled shriek and vanished.

Polsarr began to gather darkness about him but Magdelene raised her hand.

"Enough," she sighed, and snapped her fingers.

When the smoke cleared, the most powerful wizard in the world cradled a baby in her arms. Polsarr's robe lay empty on the floor, and the wizard was nowhere to be seen.

"Here, hold this." She handed the baby to the King. "I want to say good-bye to some people." She walked to the door where the Captain and his men still stood. The silence was overwhelming as the audience tried very hard not to attract the Wizard's attention.

"Colin."

The young man stepped forward, for the first time a little afraid.

"This is for you." She wrestled a silver ring with three blue stones off her finger. "There aren't many wizards left in the world, but should you run foul of one this will protect you." Then she grinned and everything was all right. "Only from wizards though: it won't raise a finger against outraged fathers." She pulled a string of coral beads out of the air and dropped them on his palm. "These are for your Aunt Maya." Reaching up, she pulled his head down until she could whisper in his ear. "Tell her I said..." Magdelene paused, glanced at the Captain, and snickered in a very unwizardlike way. "Never mind, if we're as much alike as you seem to think, she'll come up with it on her own." A kiss on the forehead and she released him. "Come and visit me some time."

"I will."

She moved over to the Captain and took both his hands in hers. "It won't be very safe here for you now. You were responsible for me, and I defeated the King's wizard."

They both turned to look at the King who was holding the baby as if he'd rather be holding the demon.

The Captain smiled down at her. "I was thinking of leaving the King's service anyway."

"That might be a good idea. You can always come and stay with me; young Tristan is going to need a father figure." She gurgled with laughter at the look of terror on his face, kissed him hard enough to carry the feel of his lips away with her, and went to collect her son.

"You really should keep a better eye on him," she said to the Queen, with a nod to the king who was rubbing at the damp spot on his knee.

And then she vanished.

ର ର ର

"Not again, Mistress," sighed Kali as Magdelene handed her the baby.

"Sure looks that way." Magdelene sighed as well, then grinned at a suddenly inspired thought. "See if you can find him a lute!" she called after the demon and went to look for Silk and her kittens.

And Who Is Joah?

The green and gold lizard leapt from his favourite sunning spot and darted for a crevice in the coral wall. Although he moved with panicked speed, another tiny missile bounced off his tail before he reached sanctuary. Once safe, he turned and allowed himself the luxury of an unwinking glare at his attacker.

Magdelene sputtered with laughter and spit another watermelon seed over the wall. "If you'd held still, little one," she admonished, waving a gnawed bit of rind, "I'd never have hit you."

The lizard gave that statement the answer it deserved. Whether she'd meant it or not, he had been hit, and a lizard's dignity is easily wounded. He flicked his tongue at the wizard and then vanished into the dark and secret passageways of the wall.

Magdelene laughed again, tossed the rind on the growing pile to her left, and plucked another slice of fruit from the diminishing pile to her right. It was a beautiful day. Not a cloud blemished the sky, and the heat of the sun lay against her skin like velvet. She stretched luxuriously and considered how wonderful life could be when there was nothing to do but lie in the garden and spit seeds into the ocean.

"You don't look much like a wizard."

At the sound of that clear, young voice, Magdelene unstretched so rapidly she cramped her neck. Fortunately, before she could add to the damage by turning, the owner of the voice came forward to perch on the wall and peer with frank curiosity at the woman in the chair.

She was small, this intruder, and young; probably no more than thirteen years old, still a child but already beginning to show sings of the great beauty that would be hers as an adult. Her skin was the deep, warm brown of liquid chocolate, and her black hair curled tight to her head. The linen shift she wore was torn and travel-stained but still held the hint of bright embroidery beneath the dirt.

The dark skin, even more than the callused and dusty feet, told of the long road from the child's southern home. The most northerly cities of her people were more than six weeks' hard walk away, and her dialect placed her home farther south than that. Her presence in the garden gave rise to an amazing number of questions. Perhaps the most important was how had she done the impossible and entered the garden with neither Magdelene nor Kali, the housekeeper, aware of her.

"I came through the gate," she replied simply when asked.

Magdelene blinked at that. The coral wall didn't usually have a gate. After a moment of mutual staring, she asked, "Who are you?"

"I am Joah."

"And who is Joah?"

"Me." Golden flecks danced in Joah's eyes. "You don't look much like a wizard," she repeated, grinning.

Magdelene couldn't help but grin back. "That depends on what you expect a wizard to look like."

Joah nodded, but her face clearly said she hadn't expected anything like what she'd found: a naked woman, not young, for the untidy mass of red-brown hair was lined with grey, laying in the sun with watermelon juice running between her breasts to pool amid the faint stretch marks on her belly. If she were darker, the girl realized suddenly, she'd look much like Lythia. And no one would ever mistake her father's good-natured and indolent third wife for a wizard.

The two stared at each other for a moment longer, brown eyes curious, grey eyes thoughtful.

"I don't usually have unexpected visitors," Magdelene said at last. She took an absentminded bite from the slice of watermelon she still held. That the child had power was obvious from the moment she'd entered the garden unannounced. That the child had so much power — and Magdelene in all her dealings with wizards had never touched anyone with a higher potential — was another thing entirely. "Well," she finally continued, as Joah seemed content to sit and stare, "now that you are here, what did you plan to do?"

Joah spread her hands. "They say you're the best. I want you to teach me."

"Oh." It lacked a little something as a response, but it was all Magdelene could think of to say. *No* was out of the question. Untrained, Joah would be a hazard to all around her and a temptation to those who would use her for their own ends. Magdelene sighed and said good-bye to lazy afternoons in the garden. It looked like she had an apprentice.

"You might as well have some watermelon." Magdelene sighed again. Even to her own ear that sounded less than welcoming, and the smile that went with it was barely second best. She dragged herself from the chair and walked over to the wall, handing Joah the half-eaten piece of fruit she carried. "I'll show you around as soon as I've washed up." That was a little better. Very little. She hoped the child realized it was nothing personal ...just ... well... an apprentice? Magdelene couldn't remember the last time she'd even considered an apprentice, and suspected it was because she never had. She clambered to the top of the low barricade and launched herself off the cliff in a graceful dive ... which unfortunately flattened out just above the water.

A resounding slap broke the even rhythm of the waves.

"Lizard piss," said the most powerful wizard in the world a moment later. "That hurt."

CR CR CR

"But why doesn't she ever do any magic?" Joah, industriously scraping clean one of Kali's largest mixing bowls, demanded of the demon. "I mean, if you didn't know who she was, she could just be somebody's mother."

"She is."

"That doesn't count." Joah dismissed Magdelene's absent son with a slightly sticky wave of her hand. "The old shaman back in the cohere used to do more hocus-pocus than she does, even if she wouldn't teach me any of it. Do you know what she told me she did this morning? She said she was arguing with the wind god to stop him from destroying the village."

"She was."

"Yeah, right. Even if there is such a god, you just don't go out and argue with him. I mean, you've got to do things first—light fires, wave wands, sacrifice goats."

"Hard on the goats."

"Ok, skip the goats. But you don't just go argue with a god. I mean, it's undignified. I'm finished with this bowl. Can I have that one now?" Bowls were duly exchanged. As to ivory horns and burning red eyes, well, to dark-skinned Joah everyone in this part of the world looked strange. And the demon sure could cook. "Do you know what she's teaching me? She says I have to know myself and keeps asking me who I am. As if I didn't know who I was. I grew up with me. This is new. What flavor are these?"

"Pumpkin."

"What's a pumpkin? Never mind, it doesn't matter as long as it tastes good. She says all power comes from within and that self-discipline is the key to all magic."

"It is."

"Ha," Joah snorted. "You're just saying that because of the chickens. I mean, I'm glad you took care of them while I was busy, but I was going to get to them. I really was." She licked the last bit of batter from her fingers and studied her hands.

"Remember," Magdelene had said, "how your hands looked when you were a baby. Imagine how they'll look when you are old." As she spoke, her hands shifted and changed, fat and dimpled one second, gnarled and spotted the next. "When you can do this, then we'll go on."

Joah's hands had stubbornly stayed the age they were, although to her astonishment she had watched a scrape across her knuckles heal in seconds.

Now, she sat and watched her nails slowly growing and muttered over and over, "I am Joah. I am Joah." A dimple flickered for an instant on her wrist. "I am bored," she said aloud.

"JOAH!" Magdelene's summons, in less than dulcet tones, echoed around the kitchen. "I NEED YOU IN THE TOWER! AND RIGHT AWAY!"

The girl grinned at the demon and swung gracefully off her perch on the high stool. "She needs me in the tower right away," she explained unnecessarily, and skipped from the room.

Kali shook her head, retrieved her bowl, and, although her face had not been built for the expression, looked relieved.

ભ ભ ભ

Magdelene's tower was only one of the peculiarities of the turquoise house on the hill. From the outside, it appeared to be no more than a second-storey cupola. From the inside, the view put the room some fifty feet above the rest of the house. And the room was mostly view; walls provided only an anchorage for the roof and a place to hang the huge window shutters.

It was a little longer than right away before Joah appeared in the tower. She'd run out of the kitchen into a hall she'd never seen before, and it took some time to reorient.

"Why," she demanded, throwing herself down on a pile of cushions, narrowly missing the overweight black cat who had curled up there for a nap, "did you make this place so much bigger on the inside than on the outside?"

Magdelene shrugged. "It left more room for the garden."

"Well, then can't you get it to stop shifting around? I mean, I never know where I am."

The most powerful wizard in the world considered it. The house had been getting more eccentric of late. Visitors often discovered that the shortest distance between two points became the long way around. Eventually, Joah would learn to impose her will on the building; in the meantime, chaos was a handy way of preventing her from discovering there were places she was not permitted to find.

"I can," said Magdelene at last. "But I won't." She dropped to the cushions beside the apprentice. The cat stalked off to find a safer place to sleep. "What do you have to say about this?" She waved a hand at the oval mirror propped by the south windows.

"Wow! Is that ever great!" Joah leaned forward, her eyes wide. "When are you going to teach me to do that?"

The mirror held a bird's-eye view of a running man. Except that it was totally without sound, the two wizards might have been looking out another window.

"When I think you're ready," Magdelene replied firmly. The view moved closer. "Do you know this man?"

Joah nodded, her face splitting in a grin. "Oh, yes. That's Zayd, one of my brothers. I mean, one of my older brothers. He's one of the first six."

"The first six?"

"Father's first wife had six sons, which pretty much secured the heritage, but Father took another four wives anyway. Mother says that was a good thing 'cause it needs five women to get all the work done around the cohere and take care of Father, too."

"Joah, tell me your father isn't the Tamalair."

"Well, I'll tell you if you want me to, but he is." The grin disappeared. "That doesn't matter, does it? You won't send me away."

"Probably not." Magdelene put an arm around the girl and hugged her close. "I've gotten kind of used to having you around. But, if your father is the ruler of Alair, that does explain why this young man is a scant twenty-four hours away and still running hard."

Joah giggled. "Zayd isn't young. He's almost as old as you."

Magdelene laughed and somehow didn't look much older than Joah while she did it. "Impudent child. No one is as old as I am."

Joah stuck out her tongue and Magdelene attacked. Unfortunately, the most powerful wizard in the world was the more ticklish of the two, and Joah soon began to turn the tables.

The shriek of the wind through the room and the crash of the mirror on the tiled floor stilled the laughter. Magdelene stood, pulled Joah up from the cushions, and with a wave of her hand backed the wind out the windows and blocked it's re-entry. They started down at the shards of glass, each fragment holding the entire original image. Magdelene shook her head.

"You broke that mirror," she said firmly out the west window. "The seven-year curse I place on you."

Joah's hand tightened on her teacher's. Just for a heartbeat she saw hanging over the ocean to the west a man's face, huge and ethereal and looking more than a little miffed.

ભ ભ ભ

"Mistress, the —"

"Not now, Kali, whatever it is. That little imp spent the morning badgering me, and I'm exhausted." Magdelene closed her eyes and a breeze came out of nowhere to rock the hammock. "She wanted me to teach her how to shoot lightning bolts from her fingertips. Lightning bolts yet. I finally taught her sparks. I'm sorry, Kali, but she just wore me down."

"Mistress, the way has been opened."

Not even the most powerful wizard in the world can jerk erect in a hammock with impunity.

"I should have strengthened the wards," Magdelene muttered as the demon untangled her. "If the ones around the garden didn't stop her, how could I expect those to?"

"As much my fault as yours, Mistress. I said nothing to you about her rapid control of the house."

Magdelene waved that away. "I knew about it. The child's power is incredible, and she gains control daily."

"Then you think she lives?"

The wizard paused in the doorway and allowed herself a small grin. "I think she's being a royal pain in the ass to somebody else at this very moment. They'll want to use her power, not destroy it. You start cooking, I'll change into something warmer, and then I'll see about kicking some ass myself." She paused and waved a gate into the coral wall. "Big brother's about due. Might as well make it easy for him."

As Magdelene ran into the kitchen some moments later, Joah's older brother entered the garden. Kali turned from the stove, but Magdelene waved her back. She grabbed a couple of muffins and headed for the confrontation.

Zayd stared suspiciously around. The place looked ordinary enough, but he didn't trust wizards. He'd dealt with the shamans of his father's court, and he knew where wizards were concerned things were seldom as they seemed. He had no intention of letting this wizard take him by surprise. He would grab the child and go, and if anyone or anything tried to stop him... He gripped his broad-bladed spear tighter.

He was almost twenty years older than Joah; tall and sleekly muscular. His skin was a little darker and just now glistened in the sunlight. Magdelene watched a rivulet of sweat run over the corded muscles of his stomach to disappear behind his embroidered linen loincloth. She smiled. Even in the midst of disaster, Magdelene could appreciate the finer things in life.

"If you're looking for Joah," she said at last, rolling her eyes as Zayd leapt backward and dropped his spear into a fighting stance, "she isn't here."

"Where is the wizard?" Zayd demanded.

Magdelene polished off a muffin and bowed.

"You?" He recovered faster than most. "What have you done with my sister, Wizard?"

"I haven't done anything with her, but about two hours ago she wandered into the Netherworld." Magdelene stopped his charge, freezing him in a ridiculous and very uncomfortable position. "Now, you can stay like that for a while, or you can believe me when I say I had nothing to do with it and help me go bring her back."

Zayd considered it and found he believed her. Not even a wizard would send another to the realm of the demonkind and then risk her own life with a rescue. "If you're going after her," he said grimly, "I'm going with you." No sooner did the words leave his mouth than the hold on him released and he was face first in the dirt. He scowled up into laughing, grey eyes.

"Sorry," she said, holding out her hand. "I forgot that would happen."

That he didn't believe, and he got to his feet without her help. Still, he realized that a man who attacks the most powerful wizard in the world should expect a little discomfort, and he held no grudge. He brushed himself off and met her eyes squarely. "What I can do, I will. Command me."

Magdelene bit her lip and got her thoughts back to her unfortunate apprentice. "Goddess," she muttered, "you'd be proud of me now." She headed for the house, indicating that Zayd should follow. "First of all, we'll find you some warmer clothes. You'd freeze in what you have on. The Netherworld is always cold, and I think they lower the temperature more for me. They know I hate it and..." She paused at his exclamation. "Oh. That's Kali."

Kali nodded and took a pie from the oven.

Zayd looked from the demon to the table groaning under its load of food. He was willing to accept the demon, most wizards kept a familiar, but he had a little trouble when Magdelene slid into a chair and began to eat.

"My sister lies in the Netherworld and you fill your stomach?"

"Energy," Magdelene explained around half a fish. "Any energy I use in the Netherworld I have to take with me." She slathered a baked yam in butter. "Kali, when you've drained those noodles, take Zayd to Ambro's old room. There're clothes there that should fit him."

Kali faced her mistress in shock. "But Ambro's room is lost."

Magdelene studied the sausage with unnecessary intensity, refusing to meet the demon's eyes. "Third door on the left," she said, memories lifting the corners of her mouth. "Go."

The third door on the left opened into a large, pleasant room, obviously once occupied by a musician. A table, still holding sheets of paper scrawled over with musical notations, stood by the window; the chair pushed back as though the composer had just left. A harp with two broken strings rested against the wall, and a set of cracked pipes peered out from under the unmade bed.

Kali flipped open a small trunk and silently handed Zayd trousers, shirt, and boots. She glared around the room, snorted, began to leave. Then she stopped in the doorway and pinned the warrior with her gaze. "Do you make music?" she hissed.

Zayd took an involuntary step away from the fire in the demon's eyes, but his voice was steady as he answered, "No."

"Good." On any other face, Kali's expression would be called a smile. She closed the door on Zayd's question.

When Zayd returned to the kitchen, Magdelene was just finishing charging her powers. His jaw dropped in astonishment. In the short time he'd been out of the room, enough food for a large family had been devoured by one medium-sized wizard.

"Magic," Magdelene explained, and belched. She stood and stretched, looking Zayd over. The clothes, even the boots, fit perfectly. He held his huge spear in his right hand, and his dagger now hung from a leather belt. Magdelene nodded in satisfaction. Joah's brother was a formidable-looking man. They just might stand a chance. She picked up a large pouch and slung it across her shoulders. "All right then, let's get going."

The hall outside the kitchen was not the one Zayd remembered. This one was large and square and flooded with sunshine from a circular skylight. Each of the four walls held a door. The one they'd passed through, he assumed, led back to the kitchen, but he wasn't willing to bet on it. He jumped as Kali glided up behind him and dropped a serviceable, brown jacket over his shoulders. He shrugged into it, thinking he'd never worn so many clothes in his life.

Almost too fast to follow, the demon twitched a bright orange cape off Magdelene's turquoise and red clothing and replaced it with one of neutral grey. "No need to annoy them unnecessarily, Mistress," she said in reply to the raised eyebrows. Her hands rested for a moment on the wizard's shoulders. "Be careful."

"If I can." Magdelene raised her hand to stop the demon's reply and then continued the gesture, beckoning Zayd. "Let's go."

"Go where?" Zayd spread his hands. "You've drawn no pentagrams, burned no incense, sacrificed no goats. How do you expect us to travel to the Netherworld?"

Magdelene threw open the door she stood beside. "I thought we'd take the stairs."

ೞ ೞ ೞ

The stairs went down a very, very long way. Twice they stopped to rest, and once Magdelene picked a jar of pickles off the shelves that lined the walls, and crunched as they walked. Zayd declined. He'd peered into a jar earlier on and was sure that something had peered back.

And down.

And down.

And down.

At the bottom of the stairs, where the stone walls glistened with a silver slime that was not quite frost, their way was blocked by an immense, brass-bound door. Runes burned into the wood told in horrific detail the tortures that would befall the mortal who dared to pass. Embedded in the stone above the door was the living head of a demon.

As the travelers approached, it drew in its grey and swollen tongue and announced with great spatterings of mucus, "Abandon hope all ye who…" Then through the scum encrusting its eyes, the demon saw who it addressed. "Oh gee, sorry, Magdelene. I didn't realize it was you." And the door swung open on silent hinges.

"Come on." Magdelene grabbed Zayd's arm and pulled. "All he can do is drool on you."

The door closed behind them with the expected hollow boom.

Grey and bleak and cold, prairies of blasted rock stretched as far as the eye could see in all directions.

"Wizard! The door!"

There was no door.

"Don't worry." She gave his arm a comforting squeeze and released it. "The door will be there when we need it. The demonkind are usually very good about getting me out of their domain." And she smiled at a secret thought. It wasn't a very nice smile.

Zayd dropped to one knee and studied the gravel at their feet. "I don't understand it," he muttered as he stood. "She should have left tracks in this."

"The door never opens in the same place twice," Magdelene explained, wrapping her cloak tightly against the biting wind. "The Netherworld follows only its own laws, and sometimes not even those. Joah could've entered ten inches from here or ten miles. Reach inside to the blood tie, and feel which direction we have to go."

"To the what?"

Magdelene brushed his eyes closed with her left hand and with her right turned him slowly around. Her voice dropped so low it became almost more a feeling than a sound. "Find the tie that binds you. Find the cord of your father's blood that links your life to hers. Reach for the part of Joah that is you." When Zayd's body no longer turned under her hands, Magdelene dropped them and stepped back.

Zayd's eyes flew open, searching for the crimson line he knew stretched from his heart to Joah's. The Netherworld lay desolate and empty before him. He took a step and felt a gentle tug on the cord he couldn't see. His teeth flashed in a sudden feral smile. "We can find her, Wizard."

It is impossible to judge distance when the landscape never changes, and time loses meaning when the light remains a uniform grey. Only aching muscles and extremities growing numb from the cold gave them any indication of how far or how long. Magdelene's eyes were hooded, and she hummed as she walked. Zayd followed the cord, rejoicing that the pull grew stronger, and giving thanks that the way had, so far, not been blocked.

"It's the humming," Magdelene explained. "It keeps the lesser demons away."

"I'm not surprised," Zayd admitted. In any other circumstances he'd be well away from the tuneless drone himself.

Magdelene, who had a pretty good idea of what Zayd was thinking, only smiled and went on warning the demonkind of who walked their land.

They'd eaten twice of their supplies in Magdelene's satchel when four horseman appeared on the horizon. Magdelene and Zayd stood their ground as horses and riders thundered towards them. In less time than should have been possible, the dark rider was flinging herself off the pale horse and into Magdelene's arms.

The most powerful wizard in the world extracted herself from Death's embrace and caught the bloodless hands firmly in her own. "Calm down," she advised. "I'm glad to see you too, but I'm not trying to knock you over."

Death grinned and backed up a step. "You're looking well," she said in such a disappointed tone that both women broke down and roared with laughter.

Zayd found himself meeting the gaze of the rider on the black horse who rolled his eyes in cadaverous sockets and shrugged bony shoulders.

Finally, the laughter faded to giggles. One arm wrapped companionably about Magdelene's waist, Death wiped her streaming eyes and noticed Zayd. "Ooo nice," she crooned, jostling Magdelene with her hip. "Aren't you going to introduce me to your friend?"

"Not on your life," Magdelene crooned back.

That set them off again.

Pestilence buried his head in his hands and groaned, but Famine was made of sterner stuff. Bony fingers beat against equally skeletal thigh. "Put a sock in it, ladies," he boomed. "We have work to do."

"Okaay, okay." Death flipped a hand at her companions and fought to get her mirth under control.

Magdelene steadied herself against Death's shoulder and enquired innocently, "So, where are you headed?"

"Well, we..."

"Don't tell her!" War used the flat of her sword to pry the women apart and push Death towards her horse. "Remember what happened the last time!"

Famine and Pestilence shuddered at the memory, and Death shrugged. "Sorry."

"Never mind." Magdelene winked up at her. "Maybe next time."

Then the riders were gone.

Zayd emptied his lungs and tried to work the tension out of his shoulders. "You have weird friends, Wizard," he muttered.

"Have an oat-cake," was the wizard's reply.

ભ ભ ભ

The palace appeared to have sprung up between one heartbeat and the next. It was never on the horizon, never in the distance; it was just suddenly there. Made of the same dull grey stone as the rest of the Netherworld, it wasn't difficult to believe that the structure had sprouted from the ground like some particularly foul species of fungus.

Magdelene noted the seal etched over the door and sighed philosophically. "Well, it could have been worse."

She turned to Zayd, and for the first time, something in her eyes made the warrior believe she could indeed be what she was called.

"Your sister is the guest of Lord Rak'vol" — her tone made the name a curse — "one of the five demon princes." She waved a hand at the cold desolation around them. "Here, I can only contain his powers. You must defeat him."

"I do no magics," Zayd growled.

Magdelene's voice was grim. "Neither will he, but he'll still have his physical strength, and that fight is yours."

Zayd looked up at the prince's seal, leaned his spear against the wall, and began to strip off his clothes. He shook free the ends of his loincloth, tucked his dagger back under the fold, and stood as Magdelene had first seen him in the garden. "If I fight," he said, "I do it on my terms." Ignoring the cold, he began to murmur the warrior's chant.

A knocker of bone on the palace's door boomed a summons impossibly loud when dropped. The doorman was familiar; the red eyes, ivory horns, and features bore a startling resemblance to Kali's. A lower look, however, showed this demon to be very obviously male.

"You're here at last." He reached out a taloned finger to stroke the wizard's cheek. "But you'll have to get by me to get in." His chuckle was obscenely caressing. "The prince awaits, and you have no power to spare. What will you do to Muk to pass my door?" Gestures made the demon's preference plain.

Magdelene's eyes narrowed to slits. "Zayd," she said, and stepped aside.

A demon's knees are no more protected than a man's, and beneath the copper-bound butt of Zayd's spear, they crushed in much the same way.

Magdelene stepped over the writhing body and into the building. Zayd followed. Shrill shrieks of pain followed them both.

Torches that smoked and flickered lit the way, making even more unpleasant the inlay work of gold and gems that ran along the wall. They came to the end of the corridor, turned, came to a branching, turned, came to a dead end.

"If he thinks he can keep me out with this," Magdelene growled, glaring at the wall, "he can think again." She took Zayd's hand. "Close your eyes," she commanded. "Let me lead you."

"I'd rather see where I'm walking, Wizard."

"Suit yourself," Magdelene snapped and walked into the wall she faced.

Zayd closed his eyes as his hand and lower arm followed the wizard into the stone. Some moments later, when she released him, he opened them again.

The room they stood in was lovely; brilliant tapestries hung on the walls, thick carpets covered the floor, the light was soft and golden. On a pile of brightly colored cushions a young woman lay sleeping. Her skin was a rich, dark brown with warm velvety shadows and glowing highlights. Her body was an artist's dream and graceful even in repose. Just as the beauty that was to be hers as a woman had shown in the face of Joah the child, the innocence of the child showed in the face of the woman.

"Joah?"

"Joah." Magdelene confirmed.

Zayd took a step towards his sister who slept on unaware. "Has he — ?"

"No, he hasn't." Rak'vol answered for himself. "But he will."

The demon prince was taller than the warrior, but not by very much. Broader through the shoulders, but only barely. Curls like copper silk tumbled down his back. Golden brown skin stretched over sculptured muscle. His face was beautiful without being soft — straight nose, angles cheeks, generous mouth. Amber eyes were amused.

"The more human evil looks," said Magdelene softly to Zayd, "the more dangerous it is."

Rak'vol laughed and tossed his head. "You were a fool to come here, Wizard," he said, friendly, chiding.

"Once, there were six demon princes," the wizard replied. "Now, there are five."

The perfect smile broadened. "Kan'Kon was an idiot. He challenged where you were strongest. This is my domain, and I am stronger here." His eyes began to darken, and he turned to Zayd. "I assume you have come to fight for the fair maiden?"

"Don't look in his eyes!" Magdelene cried, jolting Zayd from what was intended to be a fatal hesitation.

The battle joined.

Zayd needed every advantage his spear provided. In spite of his human appearance, Rak'vol moved with in-human speed, using hands and feet as deadly weapons. Zayd took a kick to the thigh that would have broken the bone had it not been partially blocked. As it was, the muscles knotted in pain. He let the leg collapse and, as he twisted, dragged the blade of his spear along the demon's ribs.

The blood on the steel sizzled, and the metal began to melt and run. Zayd froze in horror as his spear became a wooden staff.

Rak'vol chuckled as his wound closed. "The wizard may hold my power" — he waved a magnanimous hand at Magdelene who stood eyes closed, hand clenched, ignoring them as she ignored the crimson drops that fell from her ears — "but she cannot change what is bred in bone and blood. What has never lived cannot harm the demonkind. You are welcome to do what you can with that stick of course."

The battle began again.

Zayd felt ribs break a moment later, but he got in blows of his own, and the demon was not as unhurt as he pretended. His spear shaft shattered against a golden elbow, and he tossed it away as Rak'vol twisted to protect his numbed arm. They closed, brown hands around golden throat, golden hands around brown. Zayd peered over the demon's shoulder, through the red mist that was rising behind his eyes, and screamed, "Magdelene!"

Too late, as Muk, who had crawled on his belly all the long way from the door, threw himself at the wizard's back. Magdelene went down.

Golden talons grew suddenly on fingertips and dug furrows of pain through the muscles on Zayd's back. He felt blood run down his legs, felt his hands loose their grip, and heard the demon call his name.

He had no choice. He looked into the ovals of onyx that had become the demon's eyes. The sound ripped from his throat was more than a scream. And he couldn't stop making it.

On the cushions, Joah stirred. She raised one hand as if to bat away the rising cadences of sound, frowned, opened her eyes.

"NO!"

The lightning bolt caught Rak'vol in the centre of his back. His cry of agony added to the din, and he dropped Zayd as he turned to face this new menace.

Zayd's whole awareness was centered on pain, but he dimly knew that he couldn't quit yet. He saw his sister facing the demon, her lips drawn back in a snarl, then he saw her fall, wrapped in blue light and shrieking. With both hands he drew his dagger, and with the last of his strength drove in, up, and under the demon's ribs.

The sudden silence was overwhelming.

Copper brows rose as Rak'vol sank to his knees. "Who," he demanded querulously, "carries an ivory dagger?"

"The sons of Tamalair," Zayd told him, and they collapsed together.

Joah was at her brother's side in an instant, but Magdelene was there first.

"Help me lift him," Magdelene commanded. "We've got to get out of here."

"But he's hurt," Joah protested. "And you're hurt. Can't we wait? The demon's dead."

Magdelene rolled Rak'vol's body out of the way with her foot. "Demons turn to ash when they die," she said shortly. "This one will be back."

"Then kill him!" Joah shrieked, cringing from half-memories of her time in the Netherworlds. "Kill him!"

Magdelene shook her head; her eyes were sunk deep in purple shadows, her skin was grey and clammy, and her ears were still bleeding freely. "I can't."

The two women half-carried, half-dragged Zayd from the room, disturbing a pile of ash and two ivory horns. Muk had clearly marked the route through the maze with his broken and bleeding knees.

Outside, the freezing wind dragged Zayd up from unconsciousness. He groaned and tried to stand.

Magdelene twisted around, searching the immediate area desperately, but there was nothing to find. She draped Zayd in Joah's arms, spread her own, and called, "Door!"

Still nothing.

She straightened and reached. Power crackled around her, and this time she didn't call, she commanded, "DOOR!"

"Onyx eyes," Zayd muttered as darkness claimed him again.

With a pop of misplaced air, the great brass-bound door appeared inches from Magdelene's nose. She flung it open, helped Joah get Zayd inside, then slammed it shut.

"Never forget," the most powerful wizard in the world snarled at the demon embedded above the door, "who put you there."

His terrified gibbering followed them up the stairs.

CR CR CR

"But how did you summon the door," Joah wanted to know, "if you had no power left."

"I tapped into the power of the Netherworld."

Joah's eyes went very wide, and she bounced on the end of Zayd's bed. "Wow! Can you do that?"

"I did it." Magdelene's eyes were still shadowed. Although she had healed Zayd, certain wounds of her own only time could take care of.

"Oh boy! When will you teach me?"

Magdelene's "Never!" and Zayd's "Are you crazy?" rang out at the same time. They looked at each other and laughed, but Joah only looked sulky.

"It's not like I'd do anything stupid," she protested. "I've learned my lesson." She stood and turned before them, a young woman in her mid-twenties who had lived only thirteen years. "I've lost ten years of my life."

"Balderdash," snorted Magdelene, sounding more like her old self. "You haven't lost anything. You are who you always were, not even the demon princes can change that. So, who are you?"

Joah glanced down at herself and shrugged. "I am Joah," she said at last.

"And who is Joah?"

"Me."

"Well?"

"Well, what?" Joah wanted to know. Then she looked down at her hands. Old hands. Young hands. Joah grinned.

"That's very good." Magdelene took a five-year-old by the shoulders and pushed an old woman out the door. "Go show Kali," she told a young matron. "Your brother has had a rough time, and he needs his rest." She closed the door on a giggling thirteen-year-old and leaned against it with a sigh.

Zayd looked up at her through his lashes. "Uh, actually, Magdelene," he murmured, "I'm not that tired."

Magdelene's smile said many things as she twitched back the covers, but all she said aloud was "Good."

Nothing Up Her Sleeve

Leather soles slapped down against sand and rock, and something in the sound convinced the small grey-brown lizard that it might be safer to move off the path. Claws scrabbling for purchase, it launched itself forward just as a booted foot came down smack on its patch of warm ground. Jewel bright eyes peered out from the safety of a pile of loose rubble and, if looks could kill, the wearer of the boots would have reached the end of the road.

As it was, the boots went only another seven paces forward then stopped at a low coral wall. The air crackled and the lizard dove deeper under cover. Over countless generations, lizards living on the headland had learned that magic meant trouble and this particular lizard had no intention of getting involved.

Edges wavering under brilliant sunlight, a gate appeared in the coral wall. Less than a heartbeat later, the wall was whole again. For some moments, the gate appeared, disappeared, appeared, disappeared — in the end, the wall remained whole. Not even a well placed kick had any effect although certain vehemently expressed profanities adding heat to the already tropical temperatures suggested that the wall had won that round as well.

At four foot high, it should have been easy enough to go over. It wasn't. Finally, the boots stomped back down the path, turned, and pounded towards the wall at full speed.

ભ ભ ભ

"He's going to hurt himself, Mistress."

"You're probably right, Kali," Magdelene admitted around a piece of papaya. She leaned one elbow on the wide stone sill of the kitchen window and sighed. Watching the intruder had been an amusing way to pass an afternoon too hot for physical activity but his repeated failures were becoming embarrassing — like laughing at a disability. "Well, I suppose as he wants to come in so badly, I'd better go out and talk to him." Popping the last bit of fruit into her mouth, she straightened.

"Shall I serve chilled juices in the garden?"

Magdelene shook her head. "Better make it something stronger," she advised. "He looks like he could use a drink."

CR CR CR

The coral wall loomed closer, closer.... Micholai put out one hand, stiff-armed himself into the air, and landed on his side with enough force to knock the breath from his lungs — a gate having just appeared under the point he was attempting to vault.

Gasping, he rolled over onto his back and squinted up at a pair of tanned legs exposed to an immodest height. Above the legs, a turquoise shift covered full curves, and above that pale grey eyes peered down at him from under a thick mass of chestnut hair. When he recognized the expression, he scrambled indignantly to his feet.

"My name," he said, attempting to dislodge a fine coating of sand from the surface of his black wool robe, "is Lord Wizard Micholai and I wish to speak with Magdelene, the one they call the most powerful wizard in the world." His tone clearly indicated that whoever *they* were, he didn't believe them. "You may take me to her."

Thick lashes lowered against the sun, the woman looked him up and down and smiled. "You're already talking to her," she told him.

He managed a strangled, "You?"

Her smile broadened. The alleged most powerful wizard in the world had a bit of fruit caught between two teeth.

CR CR CR

"You know, Micholai, you'd be a lot more comfortable if you took off that robe."

Micholai clutched the robe more tightly around him as he sat — with some difficulty — on the low, deep seat of a cane chair. He wasn't entirely certain why he'd agreed to join her for drinks in the garden or even if he actually had. "This robe," he declared, indignantly, "identifies me as a wizard."

"True enough," Magdelene acknowledged sitting down across from him and picking up a large palm-frond fan. "But as I know you're a wizard and you know you're a wizard don't you think it's rather unnecessary?"

"No!"

"Suit yourself." She leaned back and flapped the fan.

Micholai blinked sweat out of his eyes and tried not to lean towards the cool breeze the fan created.

An avid observer of young men, Magdelene placed Micholai's age somewhere between twenty and thirty. At the moment, he wasn't looking his best. His brown hair lay limp and matted with sweat, his nose was peeling, and his slightly blood-shot brown eyes darted back and forth between gritty lashes — searching, Magdelene deduced with some amusement, for an escape route. As she couldn't get him out of it, she had to assume the robe covered all the usual bits in the correct proportion.

She wondered if the self-important, stiff-necked attitude that made him refuse to relax was a result of his mission, his age, or an innate part of his character. Reaching across the tiny patio, she pushed at his knee with one bare foot. "Calm down. I don't bite."

"That, Mistress, is not entirely accurate." Kali set a tray holding two frosted glasses and a pitcher of liquid down on a three legged table.

Micholai paled as the green-skinned, ivory-horned demon stretched out a taloned hand and offered him a drink. "It's true," he gulped. "You ... you're served by demons!"

"Who is currently trying to serve you," Magdelene pointed out. "Take the glass and say thank-you."

Fingers shaking only slightly less than his voice, he did as he was told.

"You're welcome," Kali told him. She handed Magdelene the second glass. "Will we be having him for supper?" she asked, her expression unreadable.

Micholai choked.

Magdelene sighed. "If you mean will he be staying for supper, I think so. You'll have to excuse my housekeeper," she continued as Kali returned to the kitchen. "Her command of human language is a tad idiosyncratic. Now then," she took a long swallow and sat back contentedly, "you've told me your name but not why you're here."

Suddenly recalled to his duties, Micholai wiped his chin and squared his shoulders. "I," he declared, "represent THE COUNCIL OF WIZARDS."

"The what?"

"THE COUNCIL OF WIZARDS."

Magdelene scratched at the back of her right calf with the toes of her left foot and frowned. "Never heard of them," she said at last.

"But..."

"Look, Micholai, why don't you just relax, take off your robe..."

"I am not taking off my robe!"

"All right, all right, keep it on." She lazily pushed her hair back off her face. "But start at the beginning. Who or what are the Council of Wizards?"

Micholai took a deep breath and a long drink, only barely managing to keep them separate. This was not how he'd imagined this confrontation but the debacle at the gate had shaken his confidence and the wizard he'd come to confront was not like any wizard he'd ever imagined. Take control from the beginning, the council had said. Sure easy for them to say. They weren't being watched as though they were some new and not very interesting form of entertainment. "THE COUNCIL OF WIZARDS..." He felt blood rising up under the sunburn on his cheeks and began again. "The, uh, Council of Wizards are made up of the five most powerful wizards in the world..."

Magdelene's brows nearly touched her hairline.

"...and, well, they run things."

"What sort of things?"

"Wizard things."

"Ah. And why haven't I ever heard of them?"

"They tried to contact you." His voice picked up a decidedly defensive tone. "But they couldn't raise your crystal..."

"Don't have one."

Micholai's eyes widened and one hand rose to cup his own crystal protectively. It had been the greatest day of his life when after years of apprenticeship he'd been presented by the council with the badge of his accomplishment. "But all wizards wear a crystal."

She stretched, sweat-damp skin pressing against the thin cotton shift and sticking. "I don't."

As it was very obvious that she didn't, Micholai wet his lips and continued. "They tried to break into your scrying but you flung their power back at them with so much force that it knocked the Lady Wizard Gillian off her stool."

"Not that I noticed but it serves her right. Was she hurt?"

"She was very embarrassed." Micholai's lips twitched into an involuntary smile as he remembered how Lady Wizard Gillian had bounced back onto the floor, robe flapping, crystal swinging, perpetually sour expression overlaid with indignant disbelief. When he saw Magdelene sharing the smile, he forced himself to frown. "A wizard's dignity is not to be trifled with."

Magdelene's smile broadened. "That sounds like a quote."

His traitorous lips began to curve again. "Yes, well. Anyway, as conventional methods appeared to be of no use, the council sent me to contact you."

"And are you a member of the council?"

"No. That is, not yet."

Magdelene let that lie.

"A number of wizards work with the council. And they have a large training centre."

"I see. And what does The Council of Wizards want?"

"You're to appear before them for a disciplinary hearing."

She blinked. "For a what?"

"A disciplinary hearing." He pulled at the collar of his robe. "I was instructed to tell you that if you don't come with me, action would be taken."

"Action? Never mind." A lazy wave cut off his explanation. "So, where do they want you to take me?"

"They have a stronghold high in the Kurel Mountains."

"The Kurel Mountains..." Place names had changed more than once since Magdelene had settled in the south. "Isn't it late spring there now? With soft breezes and new grass and wild flowers?" She sighed and rubbed absently at a puddle of sweat caught in the crock of her elbow. "I think I'd like to see spring again. We'll leave tomorrow."

It had gone much better than Micholai had thought it would during his assault on the gate. "Fine. Tomorrow." He stood, ignoring protests from various parts of his body.

Magdelene stood as well. "And for now, I'll have Kali run you a nice cool bath. While you're in it, she can clean your clothes — including that robe you're so attached to. Then we'll sit down to a heaping platter of shrimp with a nice salad on the side.... What's the matter?" His shoulder was rigid under her hand.

"I can't..."

"Nonsense. You can so. Unless you'd rather sleep outside the gate in case I attempt to escape?"

He'd intended on doing exactly that. Somehow it seemed a little silly.

"Wouldn't you rather be comfortable and well fed? Of course you would." She steered him, unsure but unprotesting towards the house.

For the first time in his life, Micholai wondered if the Council of Wizards knew just what they were getting into.

CR CR CR

"A Council of Wizards, Kali. Can you believe it? What's next?"

"Breakfast." The demon set a plate of fresh bran muffins on the table.

Magdelene shook her head as she spread the butter. "All tucked neatly into one place..."

"Perhaps they are not aware of the danger."

"Well, they're going to be."

ભ ભ ભ

Some time later, Magdelene stared at the younger wizard in irritation. Bathed, fed, and rested, he was actually quite attractive. Unfortunately, his appearance had nothing to do with her mood. "What do you mean you can't just transport us? You've been there, Don't you know the spell?"

"Yes, but..."

"If you need more power, I can supply it."

"No, it's just..."

"Don't try to tell me I've got to spend an uncomfortable amount of time travelling because I won't do it."

"It's more complicated than that..."

"If I'm putting myself out to do something for somebody," Magdelene muttered — at the sink behind her, Kali rolled her eyes — "I don't like being inconvenienced."

"It's nothing personal!" Micholai protested, once again on the defensive. "No one can transport directly to the stronghold. The council has wrapped the area in spells so strong that the closest anyone can arrive is five days out."

"Why?"

"Demons." Shooting a nervous look at Kali's back, he leaned forward and lowered his voice. "The spell leaves too obvious a signature. The council is afraid demons will track it and mass for an attack, wiping out the cream of wizardry in one battle."

Magdelene snorted. "Leaving aside, for the moment, your rather loose definition of the cream of wizardry, hasn't it occurred to your council that the stronghold itself is probably leaving enough of a signature to attract some attention?"

"They've taken care of that."

"How? With more spells?" She shifted her small travelling bag from her right hand to her left and sighed. "Well, I'm packed, I'm dressed, I suppose I can find some way to survive five days on the road. Where can you transport us to?"

"Sherilac. It's a trading city where the Lea joins the Kan."

The names of what were probably rivers meant nothing to her. "It's been a long time since I was in a city of any size," Magdelene mused thoughtfully.

Kali made choking noises which Magdelene chose to ignore.

"Do you prefer to begin your transport spell outside or in?" she asked.

"Uh, outside."

When Micholai moved to follow her out the kitchen door the demon's voice brought him up short.

"Lord Wizard."

Preening a little at the honorific, he turned.

"A word of advice, Lord Wizard." Kali jerked her horns in the direction her mistress had taken. "When you get to the city, keep her moving."

Micholai frowned. "Keep her moving?"

The demon nodded. "It's safer," she said.

ର ର ର

"'Tis a wizard!"

The town had appeared nearly deserted until on a street by the harbour an old man had recognized Micholai and sent up the call.

Micholai inclined his head graciously as people began to gather. "It's the robe," he told Magdelene smugly, raised a near regal hand in salute, and added, "If you wore a robe, I'm sure they'd be this excited to see you."

Magdelene, who had forgotten that spring could mean grey and glowering skies, cold winds, and drizzle just as easily as gentle breezes and flowers, growled inarticulately. The growl became a pained grunt as a stout shopkeeper, his fine clothes soaked with dirty water, drove a beefy elbow into her side while attempting to shove her out of his way. Said shopkeeper found himself suddenly some distance outside the city gates wearing only his boots. Magdelene hated being cold, she really hated being cold and wet, and considering how she felt about being cold, wet, and bruised, she figured he could consider himself lucky she'd left him the boots.

She frowned as word continued to spread and more and more people scurried up from the waterfront. Although Micholai apparently accepted the crowd as his wizardly due, growing increasingly full of himself with every cheer, Magdelene rather suspected there was more to it. When the mass of townsfolk up ahead parted to allow an official delegation through, she jabbed her companion sharply in the ribs. "Looks like they're about to hand you the key to the city."

"Wizards," Micholai informed her down the length of his nose, "are highly thought of around here."

"So are ratcatchers," Magdelene pointed out tartly. "But there's a reason for that."

"Lord Wizard, thank Kelptro you've come in time." The mayor, his chain of office thrown on over a mud-stained jerkin, grabbed Micholai by the shoulder and dragged him forward. "We've got to hurry. The water's almost here!"

"I should think you've got quite enough of that already," Magdelene muttered pushing damp hair back off her face.

The mayor ignored her, propelling Micholai over rain-slicked cobblestones toward the harbor. "It's been weeks since we sent the messenger up the mountain. We were afraid no one was going to come."

"But," Micholai protested, trying unsuccessfully to free his robe from the larger man's grip.

The mayor ignored him too. "The sandbags are only just containing the flooding. If you hadn't come we'd have lost half the town."

"But..."

"We've done what we can, Lord Wizard. Now it's up to you."

"But..."

"Fall back! Fall back! Give the Lord Wizard room to work!"

"Now you say 'but' again," Magdelene prompted as Micholai stared in silent horror down the length of the harbor breakwater. Wet and exhausted townspeople scrambled past them to the relative safety of the shore and stood waiting expectantly.

Micholai shot her a panicked glance and cleared his throat. "Just, uh, what exactly is the problem?"

"The Lea's flooded," the mayor explained. "Mudslide upriver held most of the spring runoff. Kelptro-cursed thing cleared this morning. When it gets here..." Both hands graphically illustrated what the town could expect. "...we go with."

"And you want me to ... uh..."

Magdelene rolled her eyes. "Stop it," she suggested.

"That's right." The mayor looked at her for the first time. "Who are you?"

She gave him her second best smile. "I'm with the wizard."

A moment later, they were picking their way carefully along the top of the breakwater. The river water swirled brown and angry against the sandbags, surging over them in a number of places, forcing its way through in others.

"I can't do this," Micholai protested, unable to stop moving because of the firm pressure of Magdelene's hand between his shoulder blades. "Anything of this magnitude has to be cleared with the Council of Wizards."

"Sounds like they tried that."

"There are rules!"

"Break them."

"Wizards are not permitted to use their power to interfere in the lives of those who have no power."

"That's a stupid rule."

"We can't always be taking care of them. They've got to take care of themselves."

"They tried. They can't do anything about this."

He pulled away from her hand and turned to face her. "So then..."

"They die."

"No."

"That's what your rules say."

Micholai squinted past her to the townspeople grouped expectantly on the shore. He groped for his crystal. "Power without structure is chaos."

Magdelene grabbed him by the front of his robe and shoved him around to face upstream. "Structure without flexibility is bullshit," she yelled as the muted snarl of the river grew suddenly louder. "And you've just run out of time."

Sweeping up everything it passed, a seething wall of water roared towards them. Then it was closer to them than they were to shore.

"Raise your arm!"

"What?"

She grabbed his wrist and threw his arm into the air. The wall of water leapt up with it, curving over the harbor, over the docks, over the heads of the crowd. Huge trees, boulders torn from the mountain, the shattered remains of buildings ripped off their foundations twisted and spun in the muddy arch. The noise was nearly deafening. Magdelene stuck her fingers in her ears.

Micholai stood frozen, knowing full well he'd had nothing to do with this but afraid to lower his arm. Only when it was finally over, when the danger had been diverted past the town, did he let it drop to his side, pins and needles wrapped around it from elbow to fingertip. "Why?" he demanded.

Magdelene stepped back as the first of the hysterically grateful townspeople threw themselves down the length of the retaining wall. "I try to keep a low profile," she explained, not entirely truthfully. A dozen clutching hands all tried to get a piece of the wizard who'd saved the town. "Besides, you're the one in the robe."

ଓ ଓ ଓ

"It's a beautiful spring day out there, Micholai. Too bad you can't leave the room without being swarmed." Magdelene ignored the scowl he shot her and dropped her travelling bag on the floor by the wide balcony doors. "Wait until you see what I bought. It's exactly what we need for travelling up into the mountains. You know, this really is a very nice place." Her fingers stroked the soft nap of a brilliantly patterned multicolored shawl. "The weavers here do the most amazing things with sheep. Pity you couldn't have come with me."

"Magdelene..."

"Of course, that robe of yours does make you stick out like a tall, dark, sore thumb."

"Magdelene..."

"Still, everyone knows you're a wizard and that is what's important, people throwing themselves at your feet, kissing your hem, even if it does keep you cooped up on such a..."

"Magdelene!" He crossed the room and grabbed her shoulders. "I got the point the first time. I am not stupid!"

The corners of her mouth quirked up. "Of course you're not," she told him kindly, grey eyes sparkling. "You're a wizard."

It was probably fortunate that a sudden knocking at the door cut off his reply.

"Hey, Magdelene! Where do you want the carpet."

"Over there by the window, Bruno."

The burly man followed her pointing finger, the huge roll of carpet resting lightly on one broad shoulder. "You had to be on the top floor," he grumbled good naturedly. "Couldn't be down at street level. Oh no. Had to be up three flights of stairs."

"I did it on purpose." Magdelene watched appreciatively as he crossed the room. "I wanted to see those rippling muscles covered in a fine sheen of sweat."

He laughed and let the carpet fall. "Well, as long as you had a good reason." He turned... "Maybe we should try it out, you and I." ...saw Micholai and blushed a deep crimson. "Lord Wizard. Your pardon. I didn't see!" The speed of his exit invalidated the common belief that big men were slow men.

Micholai spread his hands helplessly at Magdelene's glower. "I didn't do it on purpose!"

"I know you didn't." Her expression softened as she realized how much the porter's reaction really had upset him and she decided that lessons were over for the moment. After all, she still had five days on the trail to make him into a human being. "Don't worry about it. Come and see what I bought."

"I thought you'd never been to Sherilac before?"

"I haven't." Tongue between her teeth, she worked at the cords holding the carpet rolled.

"But he spoke like he knew you..."

"Who? Bruno? I met him this morning."

Micholai shook his head and couldn't help a note of censure creeping into his voice. "You shouldn't tease strangers like that."

"I shouldn't or wizards shouldn't?"

"Uh..."

She laughed, much as Bruno had, and leapt up off her knees. "Then you'll be happy to know, I wasn't, in the strictest sense of the word, teasing."

He shook his head. "You couldn't have meant to... I mean, wizards don't!"

"Of course they do. Where do you think little wizards come from?"

"He was a porter!"

"He was a hunk," Magdelene corrected. "And a nice man. And your attitude is beginning to irritate me. Fortunately, I refuse to allow you to ruin my good mood." With a wave of her hand, the carpet unrolled. "What do you think?"

Greens and blues and oranges and yellows, in every possible variation of non-complementary shades, chased each other around and around and around the border. The central design was... Micholai squinted but it didn't help; he had no idea what the central design was. Was, in fact, willing to believe that it hadn't been designed at all. That it had just happened. It wasn't the sort of carpet any wizard would be caught dead on. He opened his mouth to tell her so, had a sudden memory of thousands of tons of moving water rising into the air, wondered just how irritated an honest response would get her, and said, "I bet you got a good deal on it."

"You wouldn't believe it." She set her travelling bag over a particularly virulent bit of pattern and dropped down beside it. "Well, come on."

Micholai took a step backwards. "Where?"

"To see the Council of Wizards. Remember?"

"On that?"

"Why not?"

He took a deep breath and let it out slowly, completely in control for the first time since his failure at the coral wall. Her stunt with the river had almost had him believing that most-powerful-wizard-in-the-world stuff. "Magdelene, flying carpets are a myth. Extensive research has proven that not only did the spell to energize them never exist but that carpets are basically so non-aerodynamic that they wouldn't ... wouldn't... uh..."

The carpet hovered two feet off the floor, fringes quivering as though it were anxious to be off.

Magdelene gave him her second best smile. "You coming or just breathing hard?"

"Magdelene!"

"Oh calm down and sit." She patted a luminously awful bit of weave beside her.

Fingers folded tightly around his crystal, Micholai shook his head.

"Either get on or I'm leaving without you."

A sudden vision of how the Council would react to Magdelene arriving unescorted moved him carefully onto the carpet. They deserved a warning at least. "Are you sure you know what you're doing?"

She shrugged as they flew out the window and began to climb. "How hard can it be? There's nothing up here to hit. Besides..." Lounging back against her travelling case, she waved at an astonished gull. "...if you think I'm spending five long, tiring days slogging up a mountain, you're out of your mind."

As the phrase *I'm out of my mind* had just been in the forefront of Micholai's thoughts, he closed his eyes, tried not to think about how far it was to the ground, and decided not to argue.

CR CR CR

The five days of travel differed only in that Micholai finally relaxed enough to open his eyes and look down. Once. Then he wished he hadn't as Magdelene, encouraged by his interest, put the carpet through two loops and a barrel roll.

But the nights...

ᚱ ᚱ ᚱ

The first night, Magdelene pulled a red and white striped tent, two folding beds, a four course meal, a pair of crystal goblets, and a bottle of very good wine out of a travelling bag six inches wide by a little over twice that high.

"H... h... how?" Micholai's fingers were white around the edges of the full plate he'd just been handed.

Magdelene looking confused. "Micholai, you're a wizard. How do you think?"

Micholai blushed. "Oh. Right."

ᚱ ᚱ ᚱ

On the second night, prompted by the screech of an owl in the darkness, Magdelene told of her encounter with the last of the great dragons and the half dozen knights who were determined to kill it. With her legs tucked up under her and the fire dancing flame colored highlights through her hair, she barely looked old enough to be dragon bait let alone dragon saviour.

Micholai listened, eyes wide. Had he heard the story from anyone else, about anyone else, he would have reacted with awe. It was, however, impossible to be in awe of Magdelene, no matter what she did — although an incident involving two of the knights had him as close to awe as he was likely to get.

ᚱ ᚱ ᚱ

The third night, after supper, she asked him what it was he liked about being a wizard. Something in her tone convinced him that she really wanted to hear the answer.

Although his list began in council approved places, under the power of her listening, he discovered joys he'd forgotten during the long years of training.

"...but, I guess what I really like is that, well, terrific feeling that comes from doing something so absolutely wondrous and impossible..."

Later, after the fire had died to white-red embers, he heard her say, so softly he wasn't sure she was talking to him, "You didn't mention the robe."

ↄ ↄ ↄ

On the fourth night, one of the crystal glasses shattered and without thinking, Micholai fused the pieces back into a seamless whole.

Magdelene gave him her second best smile but said only, "Thank you."

ↄ ↄ ↄ

On the fifth night, Magdelene discovered that Micholai possessed a fine tenor voice. She kept him singing until he pleaded for sleep.

"You couldn't have decided to sing four nights ago," she sighed as they made their way to their separate beds. "You just had to wait until the last night..."

ↄ ↄ ↄ

The stronghold of the Council of Wizards looked pretty much exactly the way tradition suggested it should. Thick stone walls surrounded a cluster of buildings dominated by the brooding bulk of a tower. The original builders had used the local granite and in the early morning sun the whole place gleamed a soft off-white.

"Almost pretty," Magdelene observed as they swooped over the last mile.

"Land outside the wall," Micholai told her, cracking one eye open just enough to see where they were.

"Don't be silly. Tell me where it is and I'll land right in the Council Chamber."

"Magdelene, there's a ring of defensive spells..."

The carpet passed over the outer battlements. Micholai made choking noises.

Magdelene reached over and patted him on one robe covered knee. "Look, I really don't want to get you in trouble so I'll set her down here in the courtyard. Okay?"

"Just land. Please."

The inhabitants of the stronghold froze at their tasks and watched in astonishment as the world's ugliest carpet drifted gently to the ground. They stared from windows and doorways as a chestnut-haired woman wearing turquoise trousers and a salmon pink tunic stood, stretched and declared in ringing tones, "There now, that wasn't so bad, was it?"

Expressions changed as they recognized her companion.

"Micholai! What do you think you are doing?"

Micholai scrambled to his feet and tried, unsuccessfully, to smooth the creases from his robe. "Lady Wizard Gillian! I, uh... That is, we... Uh, I mean... This is Magdelene?"

"So I assumed." Gillian shot a venomous glare over Micholai's shoulder. "I don't know what you're trying to prove, missy, but research has determined that flying carpets are not possible."

Magdelene blinked.

"And what's more, those defensive spells on the wall were put there for a reason. You had no business going through them in such a way."

"How should I have gone through them?"

"How should you have gone through them?" Gillian snorted. "And you call yourself the most powerful wizard in the world. Ha."

"Uh, Lady Wizard Gillian..."

"Be quiet, Micholai." Gillian turned, sketched two arcane symbols in the air and declaimed two lines in a language that seemed mostly made up of consonants. An unseen bell in the tower began to toll. "The COUNCIL OF WIZARDS will meet immediately," she declared, spun on one heel and strode away. "As you have brought her this far, Micholai, you can escort her to the council chamber."

"Did she have an unhappy childhood or something?" Magdelene asked as Micholai indicated they should follow the senior wizard.

His brows drew down and his right hand rose to wrap around his crystal. "Magdelene, you've got to start taking this seriously."

"Oh, I am," she told him, motioning for her travelling bag to go on ahead.

Somehow, he wasn't reassured.

ᘓ ᘓ ᘓ

"Magdelene, you stand accused before this COUNCIL OF WIZARDS of actions endangering all wizards." The Lord Wizard Wang Fu leaned forward, palms flat on the high oak bench the council used when it sat in session. "To wit, the stirring up the rancor of the demonkind by willfully destroying one of their princes."

"Is that what all this is about?"

"Isn't it enough!" Lady Wizard Fatima exclaimed, tapping one polished fingernail against the wood. "The completely unnecessary destruction of the sixth demon prince has upset the balance of power and put us all in a great deal of danger."

Magdelene stopped trying to find a comfortable position in the intricately carved marble chair, suspecting she'd found the reason why the council seemed so generally cranky. "You seem to be forgetting that I upset the balance of power in our favour," she pointed out.

Lady Wizard Tatianya shook her head, grey curls whipping back and forth. "No, no, no. Balance is the important factor when dealing with the Netherhells. Our favour, their favour — all that is completely unimportant."

"It was important to me at the time," Magdelene said dryly. "What does the council suggest I should have done when Kan'Kon challenged me?"

"You should not have accepted the challenge." Wang Fu was adamant. The rest of the council nodded agreement.

"Trust me on this one. Demons don't work that way."

"We know how demons operate." Lord Wizard Manuel sniffed. "We have devoted years to the study of the Netherhells."

Lord Wizard Manuel had lovely dark eyes and long sultry eyelashes. Magdelene decided she didn't like him anyway. "Ever been there?"

"Don't be impertinent. It is a well known fact that wizards can not survive in the Netherhells."

Magdelene rolled her eyes. "Suit yourself," she muttered. "You will anyway."

Lady Wizard Gillian, a white and purple crystal of truly immense proportions cupped in both hands, cleared her throat, the sound pulling the other members of the council around to face her. "Your willful and unnecessary action," she declared, "has stirred up the Netherhells. We are therefore decided to take action before we are all swept away on a crimson tide of revenge."

"Oh, puh-lease..."

"This council can no longer allow you to continue blithely doing whatever you wish." Gillian's lips thinned. "We were, in the past, prepared to be lenient..."

"About what?" Magdelene interjected.

"The demon you keep in your household for starters," Fatima declared.

"I saved her life. By demonic rules that makes her life mine."

Gillian waved that away. "We know you consorted with a bard."

Magdelene leaned forward. "Consorted?" she repeated.

"You bore him a son!" Fatima said scornfully. "Don't deny it!"

"Oh, I wasn't denying it," Magdelene explained. "I just thought you needed a stronger verb."

"As I said," Gillian snapped, "we were prepared to be lenient in spite of your refusal to act as befits your power. You have been, for all the centuries of this Council, a disgrace, a disgrace do you hear me, to the title Lady Wizard. You ignore our traditions, you scoff at our authority..."

"I didn't even know you existed until Micholai landed in my backyard."

"My point exactly. We are THE COUNCIL OF WIZ-ARDS. What are you? You have no crystal! You have no robe!"

"I wondered when we were going to get to that," Magdelene murmured.

Gillian surged to her feet, eyes blazing. "And yet you dare to place us in danger! Power confers a responsibility you have chosen to ignore. You have given us no choice. We are forced to remove your power!"

The silence that fell was terrible and profound. The Council stared at Magdelene, their expression ranging from gentle superiority to barely concealed glee. Magdelene stared back at the council, her expression nearly making it to polite interest.

"You think," Gillian continued, crystal swinging back against her chest with a meaty thud, that we can't do this. We have heard you call yourself the most powerful wizard in the world." Her eyes narrowed. "But there are five of us and only one of you. I think you'll find that our combined power is not to be scoffed at."

"Was I scoffing?"

"Research has proven," Manuel said smoothly, "That you can not win if you choose to fight."

"Fight?" Magdelene rested one hand against her breast. "Me? I readily admit to being lazier than any other five wizards of my acquaintance. You'll get no fight from me."

Gillian lowered herself slowly back into her chair. "I'm glad to see you're being so reasonable about the inevitable. You'll find we can be reasonable as well; have you any words to speak in your defense?"

"No." Magdelene stood and brushed her hair back out of her eyes. "But I have a couple to say about yours. One." She ticked the points on her fingers. "You might just as well transport in and out of this place, there's enough power gathered here that every map in the Netherhells has this place marked with a big red X. I may have stirred up the demonkind but if they attack here it's not my fault. Large concentrations of wizards never last long."

"We have lasted over two and a half centuries," Wang Fu sneered.

Magdelene sighed. "I have hickies older than that. Two, rules and regulations won't work against the demonkind. They don't follow your rules, they follow their own and those change without notice. Three," she spread her hands, "you'd be a lot more comfortable out of those robes."

"Enough of this mockery!" Gillian bellowed, slamming her fist down on the table. "We will deal with you now! Draw the circles. Light the incense."

Magdelene obliged.

"Not you!" Gillian shrieked.

With varying degrees of annoyance, the council moved to enclose Magdelene in their midst.

"Should I sit, stand, what?" she asked.

"It doesn't matter," Tatianya spat, taking her position. "You'll soon be put in your place."

On Gillian's signal, the council began to chant. With right hands cupped around crystals, they extended the left so that a quintet of palms faced inward. It didn't take long. The five crystals flared briefly then dimmed. The five members of the council looked pleased with themselves.

Magdelene scratched her nose. "So, I assume if I throw myself on the mercy of the council I can get a lift home?"

ରେ ରେ ରେ

Kali turned from the sink at the crack of displaced air. "Back already, Mistress?"

Magdelene shrugged and set her travelling bag down on the kitchen floor. "They've been warned."

"How did they take it?"

"They took away my powers."

"They took away your powers," Kali repeated, crossing her arms across her chest.

"Uh huh."

The demon looked disgusted. "Is that all?"

"Not quite." Magdelene frowned at the sudden realization. "Those pompous sons-of-bitches kept my carpet!"

ෆ ෆ ෆ

"Mistress, do you sense it?"

"Pretty hard to miss, isn't it?" Magdelene yawned, stretched and stood. It had been a wonderful six weeks — lying in the sun, swimming, eating, attempting get in and out of her hammock using no magic — but as parts of her house had got completely out of hand without supervision she supposed it was time to call an end. "Don't wait up, Kali."

Kali sniffed. "I never do, Mistress."

A heartbeat later, Magdelene stood just inside the gates of the council's stronghold.

"Magdelene!"

"Good grief, Micholai, you look awful!"

He staggered forward, swayed, and nearly fell. Grey-blue shadows ringed his eyes. One sleeve of his robe appeared to have been chewed off. "Demons ... From out of nowhere. We barely got the gate closed after the council..."

"The council opened the gate?"

"They went out to talk."

"To demons?" Inflated egos were one thing but blatant stupidity was something else again. "What happened?"

He shook his head. "What do you think?"

She shook her head in turn. "What a pity. With the council gone, who's going to give me back my power."

Micholai sighed and sagged down on a pile of rubble. "Don't be more difficult than necessary, Magdelene. After I thought about it for a little while, I realized that the council could no more take away your power than it could..." one corner of his mouth quirked up, "...force you to put on one of these stupid robes."

Leaning forward, she gently brushed a bit of slightly charred hair back off his face. "Could you use some help?"

"I'd be thrilled."

"Later," Magdelene muttered and turned to face the gates. They were no longer in the best of condition. As she watched, they took a direct hit, trembled and crumbled into a line of smoking ash.

A screaming horde of demons advanced through the opening and came to a complete halt.

"Oh shit," said one.

A less articulate demon stomped taloned feet, gouging great chunks out of the flagstones, and flung a serrated battle-ax in Magdelene's direction. Whistling obscenely, the axe made a complete three hundred and sixty degree turn and would have bisected the thrower had its shape allowed for two equal halves. As it was, the larger of the two pieces took out one of its smaller brethren as it fell.

Those at the front of the horde suddenly decided they'd rather be at the rear.

When the carnage died down and self-inflicted wounds were being licked, a green-scaled, ivory-horned demon, enough like Kali to be her twin, called out. "We heard you lost your power!"

"You heard wrong."

"But we have been observing you! You have used no power since you came from here!"

"So?"

"So, you..." Ruby red eyes widened and the demons tone grew peeved. "It's a trap!"

Magdelene smiled. "Of course it is. You know how I hate to exert myself."

"That's not fair!"

"Oh for pity's sake you're a demon, what do you know about fair?"

"Good point," the demon acknowledged.

The ground erupted under Magdelene's feet. Half a dozen tentacles with claw-edged suckers whipped around legs and arms and body, tightened, turned white, and flaked apart as Magdelene stepped out of their hold. The battle that followed didn't last long. When over half the horde had been destroyed, lowering the odds to barely fifty to one, the remaining demons, voluntarily disappeared.

"Demons," Magdelene explained, to the silent semi-circle of black-robed wizards she found watching her when she turned, "may enjoy nothing more than wholesale slaughter but they aren't actually stupid. Self-preservation almost always wins out over bloodlust."

"But why a trap?" Micholai asked.

"A demon exists only to gain power and status. While destruction of a wizard raises both, it comes with a risk. Demons don't like risk. In order to get his troops to assault me, Kan'Kon had to lead them himself. You know what happened. This place has probably been under discussion of assault for some time..."

"But why the trap," Micholai insisted.

"I'm getting to that." She wiped a bit of ichor off a block of stone that had been blasted out of the wall and sat down, ignoring the decomposing demon feet sticking out from underneath. "The council wouldn't listen when I explained they were in danger. If things continued the way they were, sooner or later, one of the Demon-princes would've decided that the potential gain from so many wizards in one place outweighed the risk. As he wouldn't want me to get involved, he'd probably goad one of his brothers into keeping me busy long enough to destroy this place and gain its power. Which," she looked around and shook her head, "wouldn't have taken long as the odds changed rather drastically in demonic favour when the council served themselves up on a platter."

"So you let them think you'd been removed already," Micholai began to pace. "Essentially, you made them attack on your terms."

"Essentially," Magdelene agreed. "And if the council had just stayed inside the walls it would have been a perfect plan and no one would've gotten hurt." She scratched at a sucker mark on the back of one calf and sighed. "Boy, am I hungry. I could really go for a plate of Kali's calamari about now."

"Look! Look what I found!" An apprentice, no more than twelve, came running through the ruins of the gate holding Gillian's massive crystal in both hands.

The assembled wizards stared at the huge stone. All but two lifted right hands to clutch the smaller crystals hanging around their own throats. No one spoke.

"Give it to me," Magdelene said at last.

As no one protested, the apprentice solemnly stepped forward and laid the crystal — worn for two hundred and fifty years by the head of the Council of Wizards — on Magdelene's outstretched hand.

Magdelene tightened her fingers.

The crystal shattered into purple dust.

Eyes dancing, Magdelene blew the dust off her palm. For a moment the breezes were purple and then the dust began to settle.

A pair of purple pigeons looked significantly unimpressed but the small flock of ravens, violet highlights gleaming in the sun, continued to feed uncaring on scattered piles of lavender entrails.

Micholai rolled his eyes. "Magdelene..."

"With great power," Magdelene interrupted, "comes great responsibility." She stuck out a purple tongue. "But no one ever said that we weren't allowed to have a good time." Then she disappeared.

Only to reappear a moment later, swooping out of the ruins of the tower and down into the courtyard.

"Well?" the most powerful wizard in the world asked, hovering a foot or so above the ground and offering Micholai her best smile. "You coming?"

Micholai started to protest, shrugged, grinned, and climbed cautiously aboard.

The carpet rose straight up and the last anyone heard, as a black wool robe drifted slowly down from the clouds, was a strangled, "Magdelene! We're going to fall off!"

We Two May Meet

Magdelene was beside herself when she woke that first morning home from Venitcia — which wasn't really surprising as she'd never been much of a morning person. If truth be told, she was more of a mid-afternoon, heading into cocktail hour kind of a person.

What was surprising was that the self she was beside, appeared to be snoring.

ᘓ ᘓ ᘓ

"Mistress?" Kali's red eyes widened as two wizards walked into the kitchen — identical but for the fact that one had her thick chestnut hair pulled back into a tight bun and seemed to be wearing an outfit in which all the items not only complemented each other but covered her from neck to knees. The demon housekeeper turned to the other wizard, whose hair fell in the usual messy cascade and who was wearing a vest and skirt in virulently opposing shades of green. "Mistress, there are two of you."

"No." Magdelene crossed the kitchen and pulled a mug embossed with the words, the most powerful wizard in the world off the shelf. "There's still only one of me. I just seem to have gone to pieces."

Kali sighed, but said, as was expected, "Well, pull yourself together."

"Not without a cup of coffee."

"Very funny," the second Magdelene snorted. "But neither misplaced humor nor your unseemly addiction to that beverage is getting us any closer to solving our problem!"

"We've managed to determine that she's my unfun bits," the first Magdelene informed the demon, sinking into a chair and reaching for a muffin.

"I hope you're not having butter on that!"

"Also my nagging, uptight bits."

"Mistress, how did this happen?"

The first Magdelene shrugged, spreading butter liberally on the muffin. "Beats the heck out of me. She was there when I woke up; large as life and twice as tidy."

"And I can't seem to get her to care," growled the second through clenched teeth. "We must find out who did this to us and why."

"It's too hot to care." The first stuck her foot out into a patch of sunlight and grinned down at the shadow of her bare toes on the tile floor.

"Mistress, if there is a wizard powerful enough to do this..."

"What difference does it make? I mean, really? It's been done."

"You see? You see what I've had to put up with?" The second glared down at her double. "Well, fine. I don't need you — I was only including you in the process to be thorough. I can get the answers on my own." Pivoting on one well-shod heel, she stomped out of the room, the door slamming behind her.

"What a bitch," the first snorted.

Mistress, if she is a part of you..."

"Then I'm well rid of her."

The door swung open hard enough to crash against the wall. "What have you done to my house!"

Magdelene-one sighed, reaching for another muffin. "What do you mean, your house? Try, my house."

"The tower is missing!"

"Is not."

Shaking her head, Kali went out into the hall. Not only was the tower missing but two of the hall's four doors opened into the garden and the door that should have returned her to the kitchen lead sequentially to the sitting room, the bathing room, Joah's old room, and a room the demon didn't recognize although from the piles of debris it appeared to be a storeroom of sorts. A half-grown calico cat meowed indignantly down at her from a stack of crates.

"I have no idea," she said, closing the door again. If the house was causing the cats problems, things were even more serious than they appeared.

A fifth attempt finally took her back to the kitchen. Magdelene-one was licking the jam spoon while Magdelene-two made notes on Kali's recipe slate.

"The house," she announced, "is out of control."

"That's just so unlikely," Magdelene-one scoffed stickily.

"Never-the-less, Mistress, it is the case."

Sighing heavily, Magdelene-one heaved herself up out of the chair and sauntered over to the door, Magdelene-two following close behind, arms folded and lips pressed into a thin line. They walked out of the kitchen and stood in a square hall, warmly lit by the large skylight overhead.

"Sitting-room, bathroom, stairs to the Netherhells..." The doors opened and closed showing the rooms behind them as they were named. "...stairs to the tower." Magdelene-one rolled her eyes and headed back to the kitchen. "You guys make such a fuss over nothing."

As the door closed behind her, the house shifted and the green and gold lizard who had moments before been sunning himself in the garden stared up at Magdelene-two in shock.

"You're right," she told it. "The situation is completely unacceptable. Fortunately, a reasoned analysis finds a simple solution." Opening a door, she reached into the kitchen, grabbed her other self by the back of the vest and hauled her into the hall. The lizard disappeared, the doors returned. "Clearly, we must stay together in order to maintain the house."

"Clearly," Magdelene-one mocked. "Why?"

"Let me think..."

"Oh, you're thinking. I can smell the smoke."

Magdelene-two ignored her. "As you observed previously, there is still only one of us, we have merely been separated into pieces. It's therefore logical to assume that our power has been equally divided between us. Together, we remain the most powerful wizard in the world. Separate, we are merely powerful — and not powerful enough to mindlessly support old magics."

"That sort of sucks."

"Indeed. We need answers." Clutching her other self's elbow, Magdelene-two threw open a door and marched them both up the steps to the cupola on the top of the tower.

"Stairs; what was I thinking?"

From the outside, the turquoise house on the headland seemed to be only one story tall. From the copula, the two wizards had an uninterrupted view of the surrounding countryside from fifty feet in the air.

Magdelene-one gazed down at the cove and the fishing village that hugged the shore. "Nothing much happening there. Wait a minute, that's Miguel working on his boat. Would you look at the shoulders on the man. And the ass — you could bounce clams off that ass." Leaning forward, she whispered something in Miguel's ear. The fisherman turned and waved. Even at such a distance, they could see his broad smile.

"What did you say to him?" Magdelene-two demanded suspiciously.

One giggled. "I told him that if the kaylie weren't running I knew something else he could spend the morning spearing."

"Have you no concern for your dignity? And if not," she continued before her double could reply, "have you no concern for mine? We are the most powerful wizard in the world and we have a position to maintain!"

"Prude."

"Slut."

Magdelene-one stuck out her tongue, flickered once, and glared across the room. "You stopped me! How dare you stop me!"

Hands on her hips, Two returned the glare. "Have you forgotten why we came up here?" A half turn and a sharp wave toward the large oval mirror in the rosewood stand. "We must discover who did this to us!"

"Why?"

"So that we can undo it."

"Why?" One asked again, dropping down onto the huge pile of multicolored cushions that filled most of the floor space. "Personally, I think I'm better off without you dragging me down."

"Me dragging you down?" the other Magdelene snorted turning to the mirror. "Oh, that's a laugh."

The mirror — an expensive replacement after a wizard wannabe had broken her original trying to use the demon trapped inside — showed nothing but a reflection of both Magdelenes.

"You've broken it!"

"I haven't done anything."

"Oh, you never do do anything do you?"

"At least I know how to enjoy myself," Magdelene-one pointed out. She flashed her double a sunny smile and vanished.

"At least I won't end up with sand in unmentionable places," Two sneered to an empty room.

ᘓ ᘓ ᘓ

"Where...?"

"The village," Magdelene-two snorted as she crossed the kitchen. "She is such an embarrassment, Kali." Lowering herself into a chair, legs crossed at the ankles, she quivered with indignation. "I shudder just thinking of how she's perceived."

"The villagers have always treated her — you — with respect, Mistress."

"But she's so..." Manicured nails beat out a staccato beat against the polished wood of the table as she searched for a description that managed to be both accurate and polite and managed only: "...enthusiastically athletic."

"From what I have heard, they respect that as well and I have received the impression on a number of occasions that some are rather in awe." Kali set a lightly steaming cup of tea on the table by the wizard. "Did you discover who is responsible for this division?"

Magdelene-two took a ladylike sip of tea and sighed. "I'm afraid not. The mirror is non-functional and showed only our reflections. Whoever divided us in two must have disabled it in order to cover their tracks."

The demon nodded thoughtfully.

ര ര ര

"What's this?" Magdelene-one blinked down at the lightly steamed vegetables and the poached fish on her plate.

Kali placed a pitcher of water and a glass on the table. "Lunch, Mistress. High in fibre, low in fat. Your double ordered it."

"Then why isn't my double here eating it?"

"She remains in the workshop, delving in eldritch realms to discover the cause of your affliction."

"Hey, it's nothing a little salve won't cure. Oh, our affliction. Right. Well, she's going to get us into trouble with that whole eldritch realms thing — it's likely to bring on an angry crowd of villagers with torches and pitchforks. And hang on, I don't have a workshop."

"She has added one on, Mistress."

"And you just let her?"

"I am her housekeeper as much as yours, Mistress. If you are unhappy with her decision, perhaps you should confront her yourself."

"Yeah, probably, but I don't really feel much like doing it now. Maybe later." A lazy flick of a knife point teased apart two translucent flakes of white flesh. "Any chance of getting some tarter sauce with this?"

ര ര ര

"What are you doing?"

"What does it look like I'm doing?" Magdelene-two demanded. She dropped a cushion onto the ground, dropped to her knees on the cushion and began inscribing runes in the fresh earth. "I'm laying out protective wards around the house."

"Didn't there used to be cat mint there?"

"Do you want what happened last night to happen again?" Magdelene-two sniffed ignoring the actual question.

Magdelene-one settled back down in the hammock and scratched at her bare stomach. "Don't see how it can. We're already in two pieces."

"And what would you say to four pieces?"

"Five card draw, monkey's wild, it'll cost you a caravan to open."

Magdelene-two sniffed again. "You're making absolutely no sense."

"With four," her double sighed, "we'd have enough for poker."

"You think you're very funny, don't you? You're just lucky you have me to take care of things."

A tanned hand waved languidly in the hot afternoon air. "Whatever makes you happy, sister."

"Don't call me that!" two protested, vehemently tucking an escaped strand of hair back behind her ear. "I'm not your sister, I'm you!"

"Then I really need a nap. I'm not usually this cranky."

CR CR CR

"Kali, what is this?"

"Supper, Mistress." Thankful that the kitchen was one of the more anchored rooms, Kali put down the plate of spiced prawns in garlic butter. "Your double ordered it." When faced with the inevitable, she felt she might as well just say the lines assigned.

Magdelene-two's lip curled. "Then why isn't my double here eating it?"

"There was a delivery from the village this afternoon."

"A delivery of what?"

"I do not know. He never reached the house."

"Why not?" Kali opened her mouth to answer but a raised hand and a scarlet flush on the wizard's cheeks cut her off. "Never mind. How can she take a chance like that? He might not be a mere delivery boy, he could easily be our enemy attempting to take us unawares. He could be the wizard who divided us, arriving to check on our weakened condition." Magdelene-two leapt to her feet. "He could have weapons designed to destroy us!"

The demon placed her hand on the wizard's shoulder and pushed her back down into the chair. "I believe he was searched quite thoroughly," she said.

CR CR CR

Magdelene-two looked up from placing her folded clothing neatly into a chest and clutched at her voluminous nightshirt. "What do you think you doing here?"

"This is my bedroom."

"Excuse me, I believe that it's my bedroom."

"Whatever." Magdelene-one shrugged. "It's a big bed." She began to work at the laces on her vest.

"I am not sharing this bed with you."

"You're not my first choice either but..." The vest hit the floor, quickly followed by the skirt. "...so what. It's late. I'm sleepy. And this is my bed."

"You can sleep in one of the spare rooms."

"I don't want to." She kicked her crumpled clothes into a corner. "Besides, I have dibs. I'm clearly the original."

"And how do you figure that?"

"I have all the dominant character traits."

"You're a lazy, lecherous, slob!"

"I rest my case." Triumphant, she dropped onto the bed. "And you're only angry because you know I'm ri.... HEY!"

Releasing her double's ankle, Magdelene-two stepped back and pointed toward the door. "Out. Now."

Magdelene-one scrambled up off the floor. "You shouldn't have done that."

"Really? What were you planning to d... AWK!" Pressed up against the back wall, she struggled to get an arm free.

"I plan to get some sleep if you'd just shu... OW!"

For every offense, an equal defense. For every spell, a counter spell. For every pillow slammed into a face or across the back of a head, there was a pillow slammed in return. The pillows were, by far, getting the worst of it.

CR CR CR

The villagers stared up at the lights and noises coming from the house of the most powerful wizard in the world and they wondered. Some wondered what fell enchantments were afoot. Most wondered why they hadn't been invited to the party.

One wondered why the ground seemed to be shaking slightly...

ଔ ଔ ଔ

The impact shook the house and knocked both Magdelenes to their knees, hands buried in each other's hair.

"Now what have you done," Magdelene-two demanded, eyes wild.

"Wasn't me," her double denied hurriedly. "It must have been you."

"Well, it wasn't. Unlike some people, I maintain perfect control at all times."

"So, if I didn't do it and you're maintaining perfect control," Magdelene-one mocked. "Who's doing all the bang...."

The second impact was more violent than the first.

The wizards' eyes widened simultaneously and together they raced for the hall.

Unencumbered by the tangled ruin of a nightshirt, Magdelene-one reached the door first and threw it open, peering down the long, long flight of stairs that lead to the Netherhells. Swinging free, the door began to tremble.

"DUCK!"

After impact the two wizards lifted their heads to peer wide-eyed at the object embedded in the wall. It was a large bone, almost five feet long and a handspan in diameter. Crude sigils had been carved around the curve of the visible end.

"That can't be good," Magdelene-one observed, standing.

Gaining her feet a moment later, Magdelene-two crossed to the bone. "It appears that one of the demon princes is attempting to breach the door. This sigil here is the sign of Ter'Poe, and this the sign of conquest, and this..." She tapped her finger lightly against another. "...this is what appears to be a corrupted version of my name with certain Midworld influences apparently creeping into the actual line and curves."

The other wizard gave an exaggerated yawn. "Even facing potential disaster you're boring."

"Potential disaster, Mistresses?"

They turned together to face the housekeeper.

"You don't think an invasion by the Netherhells where we all end up murdered in our beds and all manner of evils like sloth and gluttony..." Magdelene-two paused long enough to glare at her double. "...run loose in the world is a disaster?"

"I merely question your use of the word potential, Mistress. If their missile was able to reach the house, they are already through the door."

On cue: the distant sound of pounding footsteps rose from below.

Magdelene-one scratched thoughtfully. "At the risk of repeating myself, that can't be good."

"You idiot!" Magdelene-two charged across to the open door and lifted both hands to shoulder height, palms out, fingers spread. "And while the darkness from the deep doth into this world try to creep, I raise my powers from their sleep..."

"What are you doing?"

"Stopping an invasion by the Netherhells!"

"With bad poetry?" Accepting a dressing gown from Kali, Magdelene-one belted it then pointed down the stairs. "Go home."

"Ow!" The exclamation was distant but unmistakable. The footsteps paused.

And then they began again.

"That can't be..."

"Yes, we all know. That can't be good. Stop repeating yourself and start throwing things at them before we're horribly killed and responsible for the deaths of thousands."

"I don't think..."

"Fortunately for the world, I do."

"I can think of someone's death I'd like to be responsible for," Magdelene-one muttered.

ଔ ଔ ଔ

"That... was close," Magdelene-two gasped, sagging back against the now closed door.

"Too... close," Magdelene-one agreed from where she lay panting on the floor.

"As long as your power remains divided, I very much doubt you could stop a second assault," Kali pointed out. "And there will be a second assault, Mistresses. You may count on that as a certainty."

"She has... a point."

"Two. They're horns."

"She has a point about the two of us not being able to defeat the demon-kind a second time," Magdelene-two ground out through clenched teeth. "We have to do something before we're all destroyed. Before we're chopped into pieces and devoured. I'll return to the workshop and attempt to find the strongest spells we can perform with our reduced power."

"Good on you. I'll have a nap."

"No," Kali sighed. "You will both come with me to the tower."

"Kali, lest you forget I..."

"We," amended Magdelene-one.

"...are mistress here."

Kali ignored them both and started up the stairs. After a moment, they exchanged identical expressions of confusion, and followed.

"The mirror is not functioning properly," Magdelene-two reminded the demon.

"Yes, Mistress, it is. Ask it other than who divided you from yourself."

After a moment spent working out demonic syntax, and another moment spent jockeying for position, the wizards took turns asking questions they knew the answers to. The mirror performed flawlessly.

"Now," prodded the demon, "ask it who is responsible for this division."

Magdelene-one shrugged, leaned past her double and asked.

The mirror continued to show only the reflection of the two Magdelenes.

"See? It's busted."

"No." Kali shook her head. "It is not. Think, both of you, who is strong enough to do this to the most powerful wizard in the world? You did it to yourself," she confirmed as understanding began to dawn. "The mirror has been giving you the correct answer from the beginning."

"We did this to ourselves?"

"Bummer."

"How? When?"

"When? It happened in the night as you slept. How?" Scaled shoulders rose and fell. "I do not know. Only you know."

"I don't know." Magdelene-one flopped down on the pillows. "Do you know?"

Magdelene-two pushed back a straying strand of chestnut hair and shook her head. "I'm forced to admit that I have no memory of doing any such thing."

"But clearly, it was done. And it must be undone before the world is overrun with others of my kind who are less... nice." Kali folded her arms. "For reasons only you can know you have brought this division upon yourself. Only you are powerful enough to undo what you have done."

"Granted, but we don't know what we've done."

"It is in your heads, Mistresses. It must come out."

"Eww." One's lip curled. "Look, I have an idea, let's just stay like we are."

"I want you back as a part of me as little as you want me in you," Two snorted, "but we have a responsibility to everyone in the world. We must save them from the encroachment of the Netherhells."

"Why? We've been saving them from that encroachment for a very long time. I say let someone else take the responsibility so I can have some fun."

"You've been having fun!" Magdelene-two reminded her sharply, arms folded over the ruins of her nightshirt. "In fact, you've been having everyone who's come within twenty feet of this house and it's GOT. TO. STOP."

"Bitch."

"Tramp."

"Mistresses, enough. You must pull yourselves together before disaster overcomes us all! There is a man," Kali continued, shooting a warning glare toward Magdelene-one, "a Doctor Bineeni, in Harmon, a town three days travel inland. I have heard he attends to problems of the mind."

"Heard from who?"

"The baker's husband has a nephew whose friend had very good things to say about the man."

"The baker's husband's nephew's friend?" One shook her head in disbelief. "Oh, yeah, that's a valid recommendation."

"Do you have a better idea?" Two demanded.

"Sure. I leave and the demon princes do what they want to you."

"Fine. Two can play at that game."

"It is not a game and no one is playing." Kali's crimson eyes glittered. "If you have no consideration for the peoples of this world, then consider this: the demon princes have vowed vengeance for the death of their brother. They will not care how many pieces you are in when they begin but I guarantee you will both be in many more pieces when they finish. You may continue arguing and die or go to Harmon and live."

The only sound in the tower was the soft shunk, shunk, shunk of Magdelene-one stroking a silk tassel.

"Live?" she said at last, glancing up at her double.

"Live," Magdelene-two agreed.

ଊ ଊ ଊ

"We have to walk?"

Kali rolled her eyes, white showing all around the red. "You have never been to Harmon, Mistress. You can not go by magic to a place you have never seen."

"What about borrowing Frenin's donkey and cart?"

"You may not be seen in the village like this. It will cause them great distress."

Magdelene-two looked pointedly at her companion who was wearing wide-legged, purple trousers, an orange vest, and yellow sandals. "I can fully understand why."

"Ice-queen."

"Sleaze."

ભ ભ ભ

Kali stared up at the huge wrought iron gate over-filling the break in the coral wall and sighed. Deep and weary exhalations weren't something demons indulged in as a rule but over the last day she'd become quite accomplished. Had she ever stopped to anticipate their current situation, she might have expected two Magdelene's would be twice as much trouble as one. She would have been wrong. Twice as much trouble was a distinct underestimate.

"What the Netherhells have you got in that thing?" Magdelene-one drawled poking a finger at her companion's carpet bag.

"Clean handkerchiefs, water purification potion, bug repellent, extra sandal straps, desiccated dragon liver, a comb, one complete change of clothes, soap, a talisman for stomach problems... What?" Two demanded, the list having raised not one, but both eyebrows to the hairline of her listener.

"You do remember you're a wizard?"

"Your point?"

Magdelene-one held up a small belt pouch. "I have everything I need in here."

"And if we're unable to use our powers?" Two demanded.

"I still have everything I need."

"There's not enough room in there for a pair of clean underwear."

Rubbing at a rivulet of sweat, Magdelene-one grinned. "Good thing I don't wear them then. I still don't see why we can't take the carpet," she complained to Kali before her double could respond.

"With your powers divided it would take both of you working in concert to keep the carpet aloft," the demon explained again. "Should your attention wander, even for a moment, it could be fatal."

"Three days on the road with Ms. Knettles-in-her-britches here could be fatal too."

"No one ever died of boredom, Mistress. Or embarrassment," she added as the second Magdelene caught her eye. "And the sooner you begin, the sooner we can put all this behind us. Remember what is at stake." She all but pushed the wizards through the gate and onto the path. As they rounded the first turn, already squabbling, she sighed again and closed her eyes.

Which was how she missed the black shadows slinking around the corner behind them.

soon soon
at their weakest
away from home
away from help
soon soon

Harmon was a largish town, four, maybe five times, the size of the fishing village nestled under Magdelene's headland. It boasted a permanent market square, three competing inns, two town wells, a large mill, four temples, a dozen shrines, and one small theater that had just been torched by the local Duc who'd objected to having his name and likeness appear in a recent satirical production.

In its particular corner of the world, Harmon was about as cosmopolitan as it got.

Which could have been why no one gave the two identical wizards a second glance — although, it was more likely they passed unnoted because no one knew they were wizards and they weren't, after three days travel, particularly identical.

The shifting shadows of early evening hid the bits of darkness that entered the town on their heels.

soon

"Excuse me, we'd like a room."

'Two rooms," Magdelene-one corrected. "A dark, narrow uncomfortable room for her." She nodded toward her companion. "And a big, bright, comfortable room for me." Smiling her best smile, she leaned toward the barman. "With a big, bright, comfortable bed."

Totally oblivious to the beer pouring over his hand, the barman swallowed. Hard.

Magdelene-two gestured the tap closed. "One room," she repeated, her tone acting on him with much the same effect as a bucket of cold water. "The one at the end of the hall with the two beds will do and we will not..." A pointed look at her sulking double. "...be sharing it with any other travelers." As four coins of varying sizes hit the counter, she swept the common room with an expression icy enough to frost mugs and drop curious eyes down to the table tops. "First night's payment plus payment for use of the bathing room. I want the water hot and clean linens — clean, mind you, not just turned clean side out. And don't bother telling me you never do that," she cautioned, spearing the barman with a disdainful snort. "I know you do."

"How?"

"We're the most powerful wizard in the world," Magdelene-one told him brightly while being dragged toward the stairs. A shower of coin hit the bar. "I'll get the first rou... OW!"

Maintaining her grip, Magdelene-two leaned in close to what should have been a familiar ear. Except that one never sees ones own ear from that angle, she reflected, momentarily nonplused. "Don't you think we should be keeping a low profile?" she asked quietly, dropping her voice below the sudden noise of fourteen people charging toward the bar, tankards held out. "We shouldn't be letting the whole world know we're at half strength. That's just asking for trouble!"

"You worry too much." Rolling her eyes, Magdelene-one pulled her arm free. "Look, you have the first bath while I hang out here. I'll be fine." She sighed at the narrowed eyes and thin lips. "What? You don't trust yourself?"

"You are not the parts of myself that I trust!"

CR CR CR

"...so he said, Are you waiting to see the whites of his eyes? and I said, Not exactly!" Magdelene's gesture made it very clear just what, exactly, she'd been waiting to see. As the crowd roared its approval of the story, she upended her tankard and finished the last three inches of beer.

Before she could lower it, a hush fell over the room.

By the time she set the tankard on the table, the hush had become anticipation.

"Rumor has it, you're a wizard."

A quick inspection proved her tankard was definitely empty. Since no one seemed inclined to fill it, she sighed and turned. There were three of them. Big guys, bare arms; attitude. Since this particular tavern didn't cater to the "big guys with bare arms and attitude" crowd, they'd clearly dropped by to make trouble.

"You don't look like a wizard," the leader sneered. "You don't act like a wizard." He leaned forward, nostril's flaring over the dangling ends of a mustache adorned with blue beads. "You don't smell like a wizard."

His companions grunted agreement.

"We wanted to see a wizard and we get pissed right off when we don't get what we want." A booted foot kicked the end of a bench; two people toppled to the floor.

Magdelene knew how to deal with this sort. One way or another she'd been dealing with these kinds of idiots her entire life. Unfortunately, she couldn't remember what she usually did. And the bi-colored codpiece worn by the man on the right wasn't helping her concentration.

CR CR CR

The bath was helping. Deep, hot water to soak away the road and the indignities. How could she even consider becoming one again with that low minded, badly dressed hussy?

On the other hand, how could she consider allowing the Netherhells to visit death and destruction on the Midworld?

Vigorously exfoliating an elbow, Magdelene wondered how she'd gotten herself into a situation with no viable alternatives.

The sound of raised voices caught her attention. One of the voices sounded familiar, although the language left much to be desired and nothing at all to the imagination.

"Oh, for the love of..." The water sluiced off skin and hair as Magdelene climbed from the tub and by the time she reached her neat pile of clean clothes, she was completely dry. Dressing quickly as the noise level rose, she opened the bathing room door, stepped out into the hall, paused, and returned to hang the mat neatly over the side of the tub. Some things a wizard had to do to retain her self-respect.

She wasn't surprised to see herself as the center of attention in the common room. After pushing through the crowd, she was a bit surprised to see that the man who had her double by the vest was standing on chicken legs under the mult-colored arc of a rather magnificent tail. There were two others, also half-man half-chicken and a couple of dozen onlookers who seemed uncertain if they should be amused or appalled. Whatever her other half had done, it had only half worked.

In the midst of being shaken, Magdelene-one caught her double's eye and croaked, "Little help here?"

Two rolled her eyes. "Were you going up the scale, or down?" she asked pitching her voice under the roars of the chicken-man.

"D... d... down."

The three roosters, the largest marked with blue dots on the ends of its wattles, made a run for the door and the wizards found themselves alone in the center of the room. The noise building in the surrounding crowd began to sound like an angry sea.

In Magdelene's experience, crowds became mobs very quickly.

Familiar fingers interlocked, left hand to right.

One voice from two mouths murmured, "Forget."

ത ത ത

"Why roosters?" Two asked as they climbed the stairs.

One rubbed at a beer stain on her trousers. "Well, all three were acting like pricks and pricks are another word for co..."

"I get it. You have to be more careful. Just because it's on your body, doesn't mean I want some over-muscled idiot rearranging my face. The world can be a nasty, brutal place and you must be prepared for that at all times."

"I don't think I want to live in your world," One snorted, pushing open the door to their room and slouching inside.

Two glared down at the handprint on her double's right cheek. "I know I don't want to live in yours." Closing the door with more force than was necessary, she walked over to the window, and reached out for one of the shutters. Frowning, she stared down into the inn yard. "The shadows are roiling."

"Yeah, yeah whatever that means."

"They're excited about something."

Magdelene-one dropped onto the nearest bed and belched. "Probably not about the beer."

together
not now
not when together
when apart

"You Doctor Bineeni?"

The elderly man slumped over the scroll jerked erect so quickly his glasses slid down to the end of his nose. Half turning, he glared at the chestnut haired woman standing in the door to his inner sanctum. "Here now, you can't just barge in unannounced!"

A second woman joined the first. "That's what I said, but she never listens to me."

Magdelene-one jerked a finger toward her companion. "Thinks she's my better half. What a laugh, eh?"

Pushing his glasses back into position, Doctor Bineeni stared. "Twins? But at your age even identical twins would be less than identical as differing experiences would write differing histories on the face."

"At our age?" Two bristled.

"You look..." He frowned. "But you're not young."

One sighed. "You don't know the half of it sweet cheeks. We're the most powerful wizard in the world."

His eyes widened, strengthening his resemblance to a startled lizard. "You're Magdelene?"

Waving a bundle of dried herbs onto the top of the tottering pile across the room, One dropped into a chair. "He's heard of us."

"That should make this easier," Two agreed. She ran her finger along the edge of a shelf and clucked her tongue at the accumulated dust.

"But... you're a legend. You don't really exist."

"Oh, I exist. You can touch me if you like. Ow!" Shooting a steaming look at Two, she muttered. "I meant he could touch my hand."

"Sure you did."

Wide-eyed the doctor looked from one to the other. "You are the most powerful wizard in the world?"

"Yes."

"Both of you?"

"That's correct."

"There should only be one of you."

"Also correct." Two dusted off her hands, tucking them into the sleeves of her robe. "It appears that in the split, we both got half the power..."

"And she got the really shitty bits of the personality."

"...and we need you to put us back together before the Netherhells make another try for the stairs."

"The stairs?" Dr. Bineeni asked, looking from one to the other.

"Yes, the flight of stairs in my house that descends into the Netherhells."

He smiled and raised an inkstained finger, shaking it in their general direction. "Almost you had me, ladies. I can help with your delusion but you'll need to make an appointment."

"Under other circumstances, I'd be more than willing to follow protocol but we need to see you now."

"Ladies, I'm sorry...."

"Not as sorry as you will be if Ter'Poe gets up those stairs," One snorted. "We're not leaving until you help us."

The smile gone, Dr. Bineeni turned toward a back door. "Evan. Petre."

Two burly young men pushed their way into the room past the piles of books.

"Not bad." Magdelene-one fluffed out her hair and undid the top fastener on her vest. "One each."

Two stared at her in disbelief. "Is that all you ever think about?"

"No!" One's brows dipped in. "Well..."

"Slattern!"

"Anal-retentive!"

Evan, or possible Petre, reached for Magdelene-two's arm.

"Oh, go to sleep!" she snapped.

Both men fell to the ground.

"Horizontal. Very nice."

"Slut!"

"Ha! You're repeating yourself."

Two gestured. One countered. Power sizzled against power in the center of the room.

now

Darkness rose out of the shadows, divided an infinite number of times, took form and substance.

"Imps?" Two stared at the swarm of tiny figures scuttling toward her. "They dare to send imps against me?"

"Whatever." One didn't bother standing. She waved a languid hand and several imps imploded. The rest kept coming. Chestnut brows drew in. "That can't be good."

"Would you quit saying that!" Two shrieked as the first imps reached her.

They climbed into mouths and ears and noses. They tangled in hair. They tried to fit themselves into every bleeding wound they made. And for every dozen Magdelene destroyed, another dozen rose from the shadows.

Driven out of the chair, Magdelene-one staggered around the room, flailing power at her attackers. Stumbling over a muscular body, she began to fall and grabbed hold of the closest solid object: Magdelene-two's hand. As their finger tightened, the wizard looked herself in the eye and smiled.

An instant later, the only sign that a battle had been fought and nearly lost, was the tangled mess of Two's hair.

"I can't believe they'd send imps after us," she growled, her hair rearranging itself back into a tight bun.

"I can't believe the imps almost kicked ass," One added.

A whimper turned them to face Dr. Bineeni who was kneeling on the floor, staring up through the bars of his stool. "You're actually her!"

Yawning, One dropped back into the chair. "Yeah, we actually are."

"And we need your help. You saw what happens when we try to fight the darkness as two separate wizards."

"Yes. I saw." Drawing in a long, shuddering breath, the doctor seemed to come to a decision as he slowly stood. "Who did this to you?"

"Well, it's like, uh..."

"Are you blushing?" Two demanded taking a disbelieving step toward her double. "I wouldn't have thought you still knew how to blush!"

"Up yours."

"You know what your problem is? You're not willing to face reality." Straightening her robe, Two speared Dr. Bineeni with a irritated glare. "We did it to ourself. Ourselves."

"And you want me to...?"

"Put us back together."

Brushy gray brows rose above the rims of the glasses. "You want to be back together?"

"It doesn't matter what we want," Two explained over One's gagging noises. "We have a responsibility to the world to be back together before the Netherhells attack again."

"Not to mention a responsibility to not be personally sliced and diced."

"I see. You held hands to defeat the smaller darkness," he added thoughtfully.

"We can't keep doing that."

"Why not?"

"We can't stand each other."

"Again, why not?" He spread his hands. "Are you not both you? Do you dislike yourself so?"

"I like myself just fine," One broke in before Two could answer. "It's her can't stand. Bossy, up-tight, neat freak!"

"Lazy, lascivious — you don't care about anything but yourself!"

"Lady Wizards, please." Stepping over a sleeping body guard to stand between them, the doctor looked from one to the other and sighed. "What happened to make you dislike yourself so?"

CR CR CR

Dr. Bineeni's consultation room was as full of books and scrolls and candles and jars as his inner sanctum but it also held a wide chaise lounge. Magdelene-two created a second and the wizards — wearing identical apprehensive expressions — laid down.

"All right." Settling himself down into the room's only chair, the doctor picked up a slate and a piece of chalk. "Let's start with some stream of consciousness. I'll begin a phrase and you will finish it with the first thing that comes into your head. You..." A finger pointed toward Magdelene-one. "...will respond first and then you will alternate responses. Are you ready?"

"Sure. I guess."

"With great power comes great...?"

"Sex!"

Her chaise lounge collapsed.

"Hey! It was the first word that came into my head!"

"No surprise!"

"Lady Wizards! Please. Let's try something else. What is the last thing you remember before this happened."

"I went to bed."

"Alone?"

"Yes. I just gotten back from Venitcia and I was tired."

"Venitcia?"

"A city." Two frowned, trying to remember.

"And you were there because?"

"I don't know."

The doctor turned to One, who shrugged. "You got me, Doc."

"This is important." Dr. Bineeni pushed his glasses up his nose. "I will begin the thought, I want you to finish it. I went to Venitcia because...?"

"Someone asked for my help."

"Our help."

એ એ એ

Right hand gripping the rail with white knuckled fingers, Magdelene straightened and wiped her mouth on the back of her left. "Did I happen to mention how much I hate boats?"

"You did." Trying not to smile, Antonio handed her a water skin. "And then you called a wind to speed our passage, and then, if I'm not mistaken, you mentioned it again." He waited until she drank then reached out and gently caressed her cheek. "Did I happen to mention how grateful I am that you would not allow this hatred to keep you from helping my people?"

"You did." Leaning into his touch, Magdelene all but purred. Not even the constant churning of her stomach could dull her appreciation of a beautiful, dark-eyed man. She liked to think that she'd have agreed to help regardless of who the Venitcia town council had sent to petition her but she was just as glad that they'd hedged their bets by playing to her known weakness.

Until he'd climbed the path to the turquoise house on the hill, Antonio had thought he'd been sent on fool's errand — that the most powerful wizard in the world was a legend, as story told by wandering bards. Told enthusiastically by bards who'd wandered in the right direction. Magdelene had always been partial to men who made music.

And to those who actually made an effort to seek her out.

એ એ એ

"My village was built many, many years ago on the slopes of an ancient volcano, a volcano that has recently begun to stir. My people can not leave a place that has been home to them for generations."

"Can not?"

"Will not," Antonio had admitted smiling and Magdelene was lost.

෬ ෬ ෬

"We're close," he told her, tucking her safely in the curve of his arm as the boat rolled. "That is the smoke of the volcano. When we round this headland, we'll see Venitcia..."

When they rounded the headland, they saw steam rising off the water in a billowing cloud as a single lava stream continued to make it's way to the sea. There was no town. No terraced orchards. No temples. No wharves. No livestock. No people.

The captain took his vessel as close as he dared then Magdelene and Antonio took the small boat to shore. It took them a while to find a safe place to land and then a while longer to walk back to the town. Antonio said nothing the entire time.

Magdelene laid her palm on the warm ground, on the new ground, so much higher than it had been. "It happened just days after you left. Long before you found me. It was fast — ash began to fall and then the rim of the crater collapsed. The town was buried."

"How...?"

The lava told me." It had been bragging actually. She left that part out.

Antonio walked to the edge of the crust and stared down into the last river of molten rock. "Is everyone dead?"

"Yes."

He sighed, brushed a fall of dark hair back off his face, and half turned; just far enough to smile sadly at her. "It wasn't your fault," he said.

Before Magdelene could stop him, he fell gracefully forward and joined his people in death.

Until that moment, she hadn't even considered that it might be her fault.

෬ ෬ ෬

"I didn't take it seriously enough."

"I should have hurried."

"You called a wind to fill the sails of the boat," Dr. Bineeni reminded them gently.

"That was for my comfort," Two said bitterly. "Not for Venitcia."

Sitting with her back against the wall, legs tucked up against her chest, One wiped her cheeks on her knees. "I was too late."

The doctor shook his head. "It wasn't your fault. Antonio was right."

"Antonio is dead."

"Yes. But he made his choice. You have to let that go." Looking from one to the other, he spread his hands. "You can't raise the dead."

"Actually, I can."

Dr. Bineeni blinked. Then he remember to breathe. "You can?"

"If the flesh is still in a condition for the spirit to wear it," Two amended.

"Although I sort of promised Death I'd stop," One sighed. "It screws up her accounting."

"So, given the manner of his death, you couldn't bring Antonio back."

"No."

"Nor any of his people."

"No."

"But if I'd known," Two insisted, "I could have stopped it."

"So many things I could stop if I knew," One agreed.

"But I don't know. Because all I do is lie in the sun and have a good time."

The doctor's brows rose at Two's declaration. "All you do?"

"All I did." Two lips were pressed into a thin disapproving line as she nodded toward her double. "All she does. I recognize my responsibilities."

"But without her, you can't fulfill them." He rubbed his upper lip with a chalk stained finger as he studied his slate. "I have one final question."

One scooted forward to the edge of the lounge. "Then you can fix us?"

"No. Then you can fix yourself."

"If I'm going to fix myself," One muttered, "why'd I have to come see you."

Dr. Bineeni ignored her. "You have to learn to like yourself again."

"Myself, yes. Her..."

"...no." Two finished, lip curled.

"We'll see." He sat back, glanced from one to the other, and said quietly, "You have, in your house, a flight of stairs that descends to the Netherhells. Why?"

One snorted. "It's convenient."

"Convenient? To have demons emerge out of your basement?"

"Well, it's more of a sub-basement, but yes."

"Why?"

"So that I know where they are," Two interjected before One could answer. "The demon princes gain power by slaughter. You don't want them running around the world unopposed."

"No, I don't." As the silence lengthened, he added, "Legends say there were once six demon princes but the most powerful wizard in the world stood between the mighty Kan'Kon and the slaughter he craved and now there are five. Mourn for Antonio, mourn for his people, but do not define the rest of your life by his loss."

℞ ℞ ℞

Although she had the boiling oil ready at the top of the stairs, Kali stepped gratefully aside as a single pop of displaced air heralded the return of her mistress. The clothing suggested that only Magdelene-one had returned but then she noted the purposeful stride and the light of battle in the wizard's eyes and the demon-housekeeper gave a heavy sigh of relief.

Even given that the light of battle was more accurately a light of extreme annoyance.

"Mistress, they are very close."

"I can see that," Magdelene noted as the bone spearhead came through the door. Grasping the handle, she flung it open and smiled at the demon attempting to free his weapon. "Hi. I'm back."

It froze. Those members of the demonic horde pushing up the stairs behind it who were within the sound of her voice, froze as well.

From deep within the bowels of the earth, a fell voice snarled, "What's the hold up!"

"She's back."

Silence. One moment. Two. Then: "Oh, crap."

The demon at the top of the stairs curled a lipless mouth into what might have been a conciliatory smile.

"If it's any consolation," Magdelene told it, raising a hand, "you'll be at the top of the pile."

A moment later, the stairs were clear — although the bouncing continued for some time. Magdelene waited until the moaning and the swearing and the recriminations died down, then she leaned out over the threshold. "Don't make me come down there."

The lower door slammed emphatically shut, the vibration rocking her back on her heels.

"Temper, temper," she muttered, stepping back into the hall.

"I am pleased you are yourself again, Mistress." Lifting the vat of oil, Kali carried it into the kitchen. "I am happy the doctor was able to heal you."

"He got me moving forward again," Magdelene allowed, following her housekeeper. "Although I am the most powerful wizard in the world and I probably could have figured it out eventually on my own."

"We had time for neither probably or eventually, Mistress."

"True. I guess I needed someone to get into my head."

Kali stared at the wizard for a long moment then surrendered to temptation. "That's a change," she said.

Author's Afterword

This collection includes THIRD TIME LUCKY, the very first story I ever sold. I wrote it back in the early eighties while on vacation in Cuba, rewrote bits of it at the insistence of a couple of friends (primarily Bruce Schneier if I remember correctly, although Maia Cowan did move all the commas one word to the left), sent it off to Gardner Dozois at Asimov's who didn't want it (although he may have seen the pre-Bruce and Maia version), then sent it to George Scithers at Amazing who did. Given publishing schedules, the second story I sold (WHAT LITTLE GIRLS ARE MADE OF for Magic in Ithkar III) came out first but THIRD TIME LUCKY started the whole thing.

Sixteen novels and twenty-four short stories later, I still think it's a pretty good story.

Once I'd created the most powerful wizard in the world it was impossible to leave her alone; it was just too much fun to write about someone so cheerfully lecherous and unabashedly lazy who almost incidentally happens to be incredibly powerful. The fine people at Tesseract Books have set the Magdelene stories in as close to chronological order as is possible given the vague time markers within the stories but checking the dates on the copyright page will give you the order they were written in. The first is the order of Magdelene's life, the second of mine. I like to think the later stories show a matured writing ability. I like to think that, it may or may not be true.

If I could be any of my characters, I think I'd like to be Magdelene.

Terizan? Well, Terazin grew out of the punch line of SWAN'S BRAID which obviously needed a thief to pull it off. In many ways she is the antithesis of Magdelene — driven, competitive, emotions tightly under control. Terizan's stories are a little less lighthearted than Magdelene's; not being the most powerful wizard in the world, she's forced to be more involved in the world around her. But there's still room for a few laughs.

Will there be more Magdelene and/or Terazin stories? Probably.

There should always be room for a few laughs.

Author's addendum 2005

I wrote WE TWO MAY MEET, the new Magdelene story in this revised collection, for the DAW 30th anniversary anthology. Because the due date was September 30th, 2001, most of us were trying to write our stories in the weeks directly after 9/11. A number of people were having some trouble getting any work done and I mentioned on a couple of occasions that I was glad I was writing a Magdelene story since it was unlikely to be effected by the event. Then I discovered I was writing a story about survivor guilt.

Writing never happens in a vacuum.

Publication Credits

"The Last Lesson" by Tanya Huff © 1989
— first appeared in *Amazing Stories*, Volume 64, number 3;
September 1989
— reprinted in *On Spec*, Summer 1996

"Be It Ever So Humble" by Tanya Huff © 1991
— first appeared in *Marion Zimmer Bradley's Fantasy Magazine*,
Issue 11, winter 1991
— reprinted in The Best of *Marion Zimmer Bradley's Fantasy
Magazine*, Warner, October 1994

"Mirror, Mirror, On The Lam" by Tanya Huff © 1997
— first appeared in *Wizard Fantastic*, DAW, November 1997

"Third Time Lucky" by Tanya Huff © 1986
— first appeared in *Amazing Stories*, volume 61, number 4,
November 1986
— reprinted in *On Spec*, fall 1995

"And Who Is Joah?" by Tanya Huff © 1987
— first appeared in *Amazing Stories*, Volume 62, number 4,
November 1987
— reprinted in *On Spec*, Winter 1995

"Nothing Up Her Sleeve" by Tanya Huff © 1993
— first appeared in *Amazing Stories* volume 67, number 11,
February 1993

"We Two May Meet" by Tanya Huff © 2002
— first appeared in the DAW 30th anniversary anthology,
May 2002

Tanya Huff

Tanya Huff is best known for her Blood novels, about a modern vampire's crime-fighting alliance with a Toronto ex-cop: Blood Price, Blood Trail, Blood Lines, Blood Pact and Blood Debt. She has also written more than fourteen other novels, and her short stories have appeared in numerous fantasy magazines. She currently lives and writes in rural Ontario and is one of Canada's best selling and most beloved speculative fiction authors.

About Tanya Huff's Work

"Ms. Huff is a superlative talent who brings freshness and excellence to all of her work, also adding a depth of characterization that greatly enhances the appeal of her inventive fantasy novels."
                          - Rave Reviews re: *The Fires's Stone*

"This is fantasy at its finest, full of electrifying tension and wondrous events. Ms. Huff develops both plot and characters with sumptuous elegance, spinning a magical tale of high adventure and glorious triumph." - Rave Reviews re: *The Last Wizard*

"Contemporary urban fantasy at its best."
                 - Locus Magazine re: *Gate of Darkness, Circle of Light*

"The author's delightfully light touch lends a sense of timeliness to this effortlessly told fantasy mystery."
                          - Library Journal re: *Smoke and Shadows*

"Plot-driven, at a pace worthy of NASCAR, and the characters are well-drawn and compelling. Huff also takes aim with a freshly sharpened stake, skewering conventions with finesse and style. Huff's novel amply demonstrates that genre fiction doesn't have to be junk-food fiction." - The Globe and Mail re: *Smoke and Shadows*

"Ms. Huff is a marvelous talent whose vibrant characterizations and intelligent prose make each and every book a very special reading experience. Bring on the next verse!"
                          - Romantic Times re: *Sing the Four Quarters*

"Plenty of odd characters and touches of unexpected magic and humor to keep things moving, for a contemporary fantasy that's lots of fun." - Locus re: *Summon the Keeper*

Stealing Magic

A complete collection of short stories featuring Terazin, a top-notch thief and Magdelene, the world's most powerful (and laziest) wizard

by
Tanya Huff

EDGE SCIENCE FICTION AND FANTASY PUBLISHING

AN IMPRINT OF HADES PUBLICATIONS, INC.

CALGARY

Edge Science Fiction and Fantasy Publishing
An Imprint of Hades Publications Inc.
P.O. Box 1714, Calgary, Alberta, T2P 2L7, Canada

In house editing by Kimberly Gammon
Interior design by Brian Hades
Cover Illustrations by David Willicome
ISBN: 978-1-894063-34-0

EDGE Science Fiction and Fantasy Publishing and Hades Publications, Inc.
acknowledges the ongoing support of the Canada Council for the Arts and the
Alberta Foundation for the Arts for our publishing programme.

The Alberta Foundation for the Arts
COMMITTED TO THE DEVELOPMENT OF CULTURE AND THE ARTS

Alberta
COMMUNITY DEVELOPMENT

Canada Council   Conseil des Arts
for the Arts   du Canada

Library and Archives Canada Cataloguing in Publication

Huff, Tanya
Stealing magic / by Tanya Huff. -- Expanded ed.

ISBN-13: 978-1-894063-34-0
ISBN-10: 1-894063-34-1

1. Fantastic fiction, Canadian (English) I. Title.

PS8565.U328S73 2005   C813'.54   C2005-905375-5

FIRST EDITION
(k-20051016)
Printed in Canada
www.edgewebsite.com

Contents

Stealing Magic

Terazin

Swan's Braid

Horses. Terazin cocked her head to one side and sifted the sounds of the city. A lot of horses. And no one rode in Old Oreen although in the newer areas the laws had been changed. The sound of horses, therefore, could mean only one thing.

"Swan's back! The Wing has returned!"

Terazin grinned. Obviously, she wasn't the only one who realized what the sound meant.

Buzzing like a hive of excited bees, the crowd began to push back against the shops and stalls, treading both on merchandise too slowly snatched to safety and on each other. Terazin saw a number of small children being lifted to better viewpoints and decided the idea had merit.

Slipping sideways into a narrow alley, she leapt for a cistern pipe, touched toe to window-ledge, and awning pole, and swung up onto the sandal maker's flat roof. Settling down beside a large clay pot of hot peppers like she belonged there — few people stopped to question first impressions — Terazin lifted a hand to block the late afternoon sun just as Swan's Wing rode into view.

The crowd didn't so much cheer as scream its appreciation.

Helmless, her short hair glinting like a cap of mountain gold, Swan rode in front, flanked a half length back by her second, the man they called Slice, and her standard bearer, a girl no older than Terazin who bore a bloody bandage around one eye as proudly as she bore the banner. There were a lot of bloody bandages, Terazin noticed. It seemed that Hyrantaz's bandits had not been defeated without cost.

But, in spite of the popular belief that it couldn't be done, they had been defeated. Slice carried Hyrantaz's head on a pike, the jaw bobbing up and down to his horse's rhythm.

They'll be going to the Crescent, Terazin thought, eyes locked on Swan as she passed, the red gold of her life-braid lying like a narrow line of fire against the dusty grey of her backplate. Terizan's heart pounded harder and faster than usual. *If I hurry, I can be there first.*

☙ ☙ ☙

It seemed that half the city was already in the Crescent when Terazin arrived. She saw a number of people she knew, ignored most of them, and pushed her way in beside a friend in the front row. He turned languidly, and when he saw who it was his heavily kohled eyes widened in mock horror. "You're sweating."

Breathing a little heavily, Terazin wiped her forehead on her sleeve. "I beg your pardon, Poli. I forgot that you don't."

Poli smiled and patted her cheek. "Not without cash up front." His smile was his greatest asset; he had a way of using it that convinced the recipient that no other living being had ever been smiled at in such a way. Terazin wasn't at all surprised that he'd been able to make his way through the crowd to a place beside the Congress steps where he could not only see, but hear all.

The distant cheering grew louder and then spilled over into the surrounding crowd. Terazin wanted to leap up and down on the spot as others around them were doing, trying for their first look at the Wing, but she took her cue from Poli and somehow managed to stay calm.

"SWAN! SWAN! SWAN!" The chant became a roar as Swan reached the Congress steps and reined in her horse. The Wing spread out behind her.

Terazin counted, then counted again. There were only a dozen riders and two pack horses plus the standard bearer, Slice, and Swan herself. The twelve had seemed like a horde in the close confines of the old city, but here,

in a single line, they were frighteningly few. "That can't be all that survived."

"The rest are camped outside the city boundary," Poli said calmly, not so much to her as to the air. "Not in the same place they were camped when they made their kind offer to rid the trade road of Hyrantaz's pack of hyenas but close enough."

"How do you know?"

Poli raised an elegant brow. "Do you honestly think I wouldn't know where a great many mercenaries who have just returned from a dangerous campaign and will no doubt wish to celebrate their survival and are soon to have a great deal of money are camping?"

"Sorry." She wondered briefly how he'd managed the entire statement in one breath and then lost all further interest in Poli, the crowd, and the rest of the Wing as Swan raised a gauntleted hand.

"You're drooling," Poli murmured, his voice amused.

"Am not." But she wiped her mouth anyway. Just in case.

When the noise of the crowd finally faded in answer to Swan's command, the huge double doors of the Congress building swung open and the council that ran the city-state of Oreen stepped out. All seven were present and all in full robes of state; but then, they'd had plenty of warning, Terazin reflected, for the runner who brought the news of Hyrantaz's defeat had arrived at dawn, his shouted news jerking the city out of sleep.

"We have done what we were hired to do," Swan declared before any of the councillors could speak. Terazin shivered as the other woman's clear voice lifted the hair on the back of her neck. "We have come for payment."

Reluctantly dragging her gaze from Swan, Terazin could see how agitated some of the councillors were — constant small and jerky movements betrayed them. They didn't think she'd win; the idiots.

Councillor Saladaz, who'd recently been appointed to his sixth straight cycle as head of the Congress, stepped forward and cleared his throat. "There was the matter of proof," he said.

At a gesture from Swan the two pack horses were led forward and the bulky oilskin bundles heaved off to lie at the councillor's feet. "It was ... inconvenient to bring the bodies," the mercenary captain told him dryly as ropes were untied. "These will have to do instead."

Saladaz leapt backward as the battered heads rolled out onto the Congress steps and the crowd roared with laughter. Out of the corner of one eye, Terazin saw Poli raise a scented cloth to his nose even though the smell was no worse than a great many parts of the city in high summer.

"They will have to be identified," Saladaz declared at his most pompous, struggling to regain his dignity.

"I'm sure there are those about who would be happy to help." From all around the Crescent came cries of agreement. Caravans that surrendered without a fight, Hyrantaz had stripped bare of everything save lives — it amused him to see a line of naked, helpless people stagger off towards the city, not all of them surviving to reach safety. "I'll take a third of what we're owed now and the rest at the end of the week."

Councillor Aleezan, who most considered to be the best brain in the Congress, stepped forward, laid a slender hand on Saladaz's shoulder and murmured something in his ear. Too far away to hear what was said, Terazin saw Saladaz nod. He didn't look happy.

"It will take a moment to count the coin," he said, tucking his hands into the heavy embroidered cuffs of his robe and scowling up at Swan. "If we can have it sent to you later today..."

"By noon," Swan suggested, in no way making it sound like the ultimatum everyone knew it was. "Our headquarters are at The Lion."

"By noon," Saladaz agreed.

At a nod from his captain, Slice whipped his pike forward and with a moist thud, Hyrantaz's head joined the pile on the Congress steps.

Terazin felt her knees go weak as Swan smiled. "To complete the set," she said and pulled her horse's head around.

"SWAN! SWAN! SWAN!" The cheers that followed the Wing from the Crescent echoed off the Congress, battering the councillors from two directions.

"She's so..."

"Barbaric?" Poli offered. That at least one of Swan's immediate ancestors was a Kerber — from a loose confederacy of warring tribes that kept the west in constant turmoil — was obvious.

"Beautiful," Terazin snapped.

Poli laughed. "Well, you do know where she's staying. You could always wander in and..." He winked. "...introduce yourself." He laughed again as she paled. "Never mind, dear. I suppose you're still young enough for unrequited lust to have a certain masochistic fascination." Gathering up her hand, he tucked it in the crook of his arm. "I'm sure that with your skills you'll be able to get close enough to watch her without her ever suspecting you're there."

"I can't." Terazin pulled her hand free suddenly remembering what the Wing's return — *what Swan*, she corrected — had pushed out of her head. "I'm going to the Guild today."

Poli looked at her for a long moment. When he spoke his voice was softer and less affected than she'd ever heard it. "That fall really spooked you didn't it?"

She nodded, trying not to think about the carving crumbling under her foot, about the long drop, about the landing. "If I'd broken something..."

"But you didn't."

"I'm not fool enough to think it'll never happen again." She spread her hands. "The Guild takes care of you. You know that, Poli. The whores had one of the first Guilds in the city."

"Granted. But somehow I just can't see you meekly accepting a Guild's control over your life." His features fell into the nearest thing to a frown she'd ever seen him wear. "You don't even take advice well."

When she shrugged she could still feel the ache in bruised bone and the terror of lying in the darkness and wondering what would become of her if her strength and agility had been destroyed. "I've made up my mind, Poli."

He shook his head. "And you're not likely to change it, are you?" Sighing, he leaned forward and lightly kissed her cheek. "Be careful, sweetling." Then, just in case he should be accused of sentiment, added archly, "Friends who don't expect freebies are rare."

ભ ભ ભ

The Thieves' Guild believed that anyone who couldn't find them and gain access had no business applying for membership. The yellow stone building built into the inside curve of the old city wall showed no outward indication of what went on inside but Terazin had heard the stories about it most of her life.

"Getting into the house is just the beginning. You have to take a thieves' path to the Sanctum deep underground."

She didn't believe all the stories about the traps set along that path — wizards were too rare and far too expensive to use for such mundane purposes — but she believed enough to approach with caution. The roof would be guarded, likewise the windows that were even remotely accessible. Which left her with two choices; an inaccessible window, or the front door.

While there was a certain in-your-face kind of charm to walking in through the front door, Terazin decided not to risk it as that was very likely the kind of attitude the Guild could do without. Besides, for a good thief, no window was truly inaccessible.

ભ ભ ભ

A hair shorter and a half a hair wider, she mused, squatting silently under the tiny window tucked into the eaves, *and I wouldn't have made it*. As it was she'd very nearly had to dislocate a shoulder and slice the curve off both hips to get through. Strapping her pack to her chest — no point in carrying equipment if it couldn't be reached quickly — Terazin started looking for a path into the heart of the Guild house.

Some considerable time later, she sat down on the floor of a grey-tiled hall and thought seriously about going out the way she'd come in. She'd dealt with all the locks, all the traps, and a dog — who'd been incredibly surprised to have a live and very angry rat tossed at him — but was no closer to finding the Sanctum than she'd been. Her stomach growled and she sagged against the wall, about at the end of her resources, personal and otherwise. Her pack was almost empty and the tiny lantern, now closed and dark at her side, was nearly out of oil.

And then she heard the voices.

Someone was making loud, angry accusations. Someone else was making equally loud, angry denials. Terazin sank lower and lower until her ear pressed against the floor. She still couldn't make out the words but she didn't need to. Smiling in spite of her exhaustion, she traced the edge of the tile next to the one she was sitting on and felt a pair of hinges and a wire.

Movement of the wire would very likely ring bells or the equivalent to announce the imminent arrival of company. Resisting the urge to hum, she twisted it up so that the trap door no longer effected it and carefully applied pressure to the tile. Underneath was the traditional narrow chute. Bracing herself against the sides, she chimney-walked down, pausing only long enough to close the trap.

The voices were much louder.

"...pay for results!"

It was a man's voice but it made her think of Swan, dumping the heads in front of the councillors and demanding payment. Hardly surprising, as lately everything made her think of the mercenary captain. Earlier the tiny beam of light from her lantern had made her think of Swan's lifebraid gleaming against her armour. Sternly, she told herself to get her mind back on the business at hand.

"...received exactly what you paid for. If the end result was not what you desired that is not the fault of this Guild."

Her fingertips touched the bottom trap door. She could see the thin lines of light around three sides and knew this had to be the end of the line. The voices were directly below her.

"You haven't heard the end of this." The growled warning carried more force than all the shouting. A door slammed.

Muscles straining against the stone, Terazin turned herself around and gently pushed the trap door open a crack. She could see the edge of a scarred wooden table, piled high with junk.

"Although we fulfilled the terms of the agreement, he could cause trouble later," a new voice muttered.

A third voice sighed and admitted, "He could."

"Don't be ridiculous. He has no desire to have his association with us made public. Still, although I hate to do it, I suppose it wouldn't hurt to make some small attempt to mollify him." A woman's hand with long, narrow, ringless fingers, reached into Terizan's limited field of vision and picked up a parchment scroll. It took her a moment to realize she was seeing it through a lattice work of rope. A net. Obviously, she was intended to go flying into it whereupon half the supports would break away, leaving her dangling helplessly in mid air.

Her blood singing, she opened the door a little further, grabbed the edges and swung back with it. At the far end of the swing, she let go. Momentum carried her curled body past the edge of the net. She uncurled just before she hit the floor, landing heavier than she would've liked.

She could feel astonishment wash over her like a wave as she straightened.

A half a dozen lanterns banished all shadow from the small room. Two of the walls were covered, floor to ceiling in racks of scrolls, one in a detailed map of the city, the fourth held a pair of doors. Spread out over the floor was a costly, though stained, carpet. A man, a woman, and a person who could have been either or both, sat behind the table and stared at her, open-mouthed. No one knew their names but they called themselves the Thieves' Guild Tribunal.

Terazin bowed, conscious only of how exhausted she was. "I'd like to apply to the Guild," she said and stepped forward pulling out the last two items in her pack. "I took this dagger from the Captain of the City Guard, you may

have heard it was missing, and this is Hyrantaz's earring — I took it this afternoon."

"From his head?" The man leaned towards her, his bulk suggesting he no longer actively indulged in the Guild's business. "You took it from his head in the Crescent?"

Terazin shrugged. There'd been so many people crowding around it had been embarrassingly easy — but if they didn't know that, she wasn't going to mention it.

As the fat man started to laugh, the woman looked speculatively up at the trap door.

"You brought the rat in with you," the third person said all at once, as though they'd come to a sudden illuminating realization. "It distracted the dog long enough for you to get away and then convinced the dog's handler that he was only after the rat. That's brilliant! But what would you have done if there'd been two dogs?"

Terazin shrugged again. "Gone looking for another rat?"

The fat man was now laughing so hard tears were running down his cheeks. "Took it from his head," he kept repeating.

The woman sighed audibly and came around the table. "I think it's safe to assume the Guild is interested in admitting you. Your arrival here was very... impressive."

"I thought I was supposed to make my way to the sanctum."

The older woman nodded. "You were. But no one's ever done it before."

"No one?"

"We'd previously considered it a major accomplishment if someone got safely into the lower levels of the building." As Terazin glanced up at the trap door and the net, she added, "Of course, a good thief is prepared for every possibility."

Terazin heard the silent warning that she not get cocky about her accomplishment, and so merely said, "I agree..." and then had no idea of how to refer to any of the other three people in the room.

"You may call me Tribune One." The woman half turned, waving a hand at first the androgyne and then

the fat man. "These are Two and Three. You realize you must still complete an assignment of our choosing?" At Terizan's nod she turned her towards the door on the left, opened it, and pushed her gently through. "Balzador, get our candidate here some nourishment."

The thieves playing cards in the antechamber looked up in astonishment and Balzador leapt to his feet with such energy that a Queen of Destiny fell from his sleeve and fluttered to the table. "Candidate?" he squeaked.

The tribune smiled. "Yes. She's just dropped in and as we'd like to discuss her... test, I leave her in your capable hands."

As the door to the sanctum closed, Terazin heard Tribune One murmur, "You've got to admit, she's very clever." Then the latch clicked and the iron-bound oak planks cut off Three's reply.

The card players continued to stare. "Just dropped in?" Balzador said at last.

ᖇ ᖇ ᖇ

"All things considered," One murmured over her steepled fingers, "there's really no need for you to prove yourself to us. However, formalities must be observed."

Terizan, who'd been fed, fêted, and won six monkeys in a quick game of caravan, bowed slightly.

"We have, therefore," One continued, "decided to make your test showy but not especially difficult. You have five days to bring us Swan's braid."

It might have been only because of the blood roaring in her ears but the acoustics in the room suddenly changed. "Swan's what?" Terazin managed to stammer.

"Braid. In five days bring us Swan's lifebraid."

ᖇ ᖇ ᖇ

By thieves' standards, The Lion was not in what could be termed a profitable part of the city. Three storey sandstone tenements surrounded it, some with tiny shops on the first floor, the rest divided into small suites or single rooms. Almost all had external stairs, a few had roof gar-

dens. Terazin lived in nearly an identical neighbourhood — although closer to the centre of Old Oreen — and knew exactly what the area had that would be worth stealing. Nothing much.

Except that Swan was at The Lion.

"In five days bring us Swan's lifebraid."

She'd been too astounded to protest and had submitted without comment to being blindfolded and lead by Balzador up to a concealed door in an alley near the Guild house. "When you come back," he'd told her. "Come here. Someone will meet you and guide you down."

When she came back. With Swan's braid.

She couldn't do it. Couldn't offer that kind of an insult to the most beautiful, desirable woman she'd ever seen. *Face it, Terizan,* she sighed to herself as she watched The Lion from the shadows across the street, *if you got close enough to actually touch the braid, your heavy breathing would give you away.*

The large louvered panels in the inn's front wall had been folded back and the celebration in the common room had spilled out onto the small terrace. A number of the celebrants wore the red swan on their tunics but Swan herself remained inside.

Wondering just what exactly she thought she was doing, Terazin crossed the street and entered the inn. No one noticed her but then, not being noticed was one of the things she did best. With a mug of ale in her hand, she became just another of the townfolk who wanted to get close to the heros of the day.

Swan, holding court in the centre of the common room, had been drinking. Her eyes were bright — *like jewels,* Terazin thought — and her cheeks were flushed. In one hand she cradled an immense flagon and in the other a slender young woman who, as Terazin watched, leaned forward so that ebony curls fell over her face and whispered something in the mercenary captain's ear.

"You think so?" The flagon emptied, Swan stood, kicked her chair back out of her way, and tightened her grip around the young woman's waist. Red-gold brows waggled suggestively. "Prove it."

"Here?"

The Wing roared with laughter at the matter-of-fact tone and a couple began clearing bottles and tankards off the table.

Swan cuffed the nearest one on the back of the head and then turned the motion into a courtly gesture towards the stairs. "I think not," she declared. "This lot has a hard enough time keeping up to me without my setting yet another impossibly high standard."

As the two women made for the stairs, amidst renewed laughter and advice, Terazin slipped back into the shadows.

CR CR CR

The next night, she watched a nearly identical scene. Nearly identical in that while the young woman was again dark and slender, it was a different young woman. By the time Swan elbowed open the door to her room — both her hands being occupied — Terazin was on the tiny balcony of the building next door. By the time Swan began testing the strength of the bed, she was outside the window.

She'd spent the day thinking about the Guild. Without intending to, she'd found herself outside the building she'd fallen from, picking a bit of plaster off the ground. It couldn't have fallen when she had but it could easily have been from the same disintegrating carving. She'd turned it over and over and finally crushed it, wiping the grey powder off on the edge of someone else's tunic.

Dying didn't frighten her as much as an injury that would put her out on the street to starve.

The Guild took care of their own.

When they were finished, and the sweat-slicked bodies lay tangled and sleeping, Terazin measured the distance from the window to the bed, judged the risk, and decided it was twice as high as it needed to be. After all, Swan had a preference for slender, dark-haired women.

"...*a good thief is prepared for every possibility.*"

Including, it seemed, the possibility of stealing Swan's braid.

ଦ୍ଧ ଦ୍ଧ ଦ୍ଧ

"Poli, I need you to make me noticeable."

One delicately plucked brow rose as Poli turned from his mirror to face her. "I beg your pardon?"

"I've decided to take your advice."

"Which bit of advice, sweetling?"

Terazin felt her cheeks grow hot and wished he wouldn't look at her like he was looking inside her. "Your advice about Swan," she growled.

"Did I give you advice about Swan?" He absently stroked cosmetic into his neck. "I don't remember but then you've never taken my advice before so I admit I'm at a loss."

"You said that since I knew where she was staying I should wander in and... and..." Unable to finish as memories of Swan and the dark-haired young woman got in the way of her voice, she waved her hands and assumed Poli would understand.

His smile seemed to indicate he did. "How noticeable?"

ଦ୍ଧ ଦ୍ଧ ଦ୍ଧ

"Do I really look like this?" Staring into Poli's mirror, Terazin found it difficult to recognize the person staring back at her.

"No, dear, I created this out of whole cloth." When she went to brush a feathering of hair off her face, Poli gently caught her hand. "Don't touch. That's not for you to mess up." He twitched at the silk tunic he'd insisted she borrow and smiled proudly at her reflection. "I merely emphasized features you usually keep hidden," he told her, touching her temples lightly with scent. "And if we add my small contribution to your natural grace — try not to move quite so much like a cat on the hunt, sweetling — you should be impossible for our mercenary captain to resist."

Her heart beginning to race, Terazin managed a strangled, "Thank you."

ભ ભ ભ

She felt Swan's eyes on her when she walked into The Lion and only the thought of lying in that alley with broken bones kept her moving forward. Tossing her hair back out of her eyes — why Poli thought being half blind was attractive she had no idea — she hooked a stool out from under the end of a trestle table and sat down. When a server appeared she ordered a flagon of the house white, mostly because she'd heard the landlord watered it. While she had to drink, she couldn't risk slowing her reflexes.

After a couple of long swallows, she looked up, met Swan's eyes, and allowed her lips to curve into the barest beginning of a smile. Then she looked down again and tried to stop her hands from shaking.

"Move."

"Ah, come on, Captain..."

"Zaydor, how would you like to stand fourth watch all the way to the coast?"

Terazin heard the man beside her laugh, obviously not taking the threat at all seriously. "Wouldn't like it at all, Captain."

Swan sighed. "How would you like me to buy you another pitcher of beer?"

"Like that a lot, Captain."

"How would you like to drink it on the other side of the room?"

Zaydor laughed again and Terazin heard his stool scrape back. He murmured something as he stood but all Terazin could hear was the sudden roar of her pulse in her ears. When Swan sat beside her, knee brushing hers under the table, she had to remind herself to breathe.

Although even Poli had long since given up trying to teach her to flirt, Terazin found her inability was no handicap as the mercenary captain needed little encouragement. She listened, she nodded, and she let her completely besotted admiration show. That was more than enough.

"Shall we?"

It took a moment before she realized that Swan was standing and holding out her hand. *I don't have to decide about the braid now*, she thought, allowing the other woman to draw her to her feet. Desire weakened her knees but she made it to the stairs. *I can wait until after*.

လ လ လ

After.

Terazin stroked one finger down the narrow, red-gold braid lying across the pillow and tried to force herself to think. It wasn't easy as her brains appeared to have melted during the last couple of heated hours and dribbled out her ears.

Swan sighed in her sleep and shifted slightly, brushing damp curls against Terizan's hip.

If I'm going to do it, I should do it now. Do it and get it before she wakes. As she tensed to slip from the bed, she realized that she'd decided, at some point, to take the braid. It may have been when a particularly energetic bit of sex had pulled at joints still bruised from the fall; she didn't know and it didn't matter.

She dressed quickly, quietly, slipping her sandals under her borrowed sash — there'd be climbing when she left the inn. Picking up Swan's dagger, she bent over the bed and lifted the braid.

A hand slapped around her wrist like an iron shackle and she found herself flat on her back, Swan crouched on her chest, and Swan's dagger back in Swan's hand.

"And with my own dagger." Gone was the cheerful lechery of the common room, gone too the surprisingly considerate lover — this was the mercenary captain who'd delivered Hyrantaz's head to the council. "Were you planning on making it look like a suicide?"

Terazin swallowed and managed to squeak out, "Suicide?"

"Or perhaps," Swan continued, her thoughtful tones in direct and frightening contrast to her expression, "you'd planned on making it look like an accident. Was I to have

become entangled with my blade at the height of passion? I doubt you could make that sound believable but then, I'd be dead so I wouldn't have to be convinced."

"Dead?" Incredulity gave her voice some force. "I had no intention of killing you!"

"Which is why I caught you with a knife at my throat?"

"It wasn't at your throat," Terazin snapped, temper beginning to overcome fear. "If you must know, I was going to steal your braid!"

"My braid?" Frowning, Swan sat back. Her weight continued to pin Terazin to the bed but the dagger was no longer an immediate threat. One hand rose to stroke the narrow, red-gold plait hanging forward over a bare shoulder. "Why?"

"To prove that I could."

Swan stared down at her in confusion. "That's all?"

"Of course..."

"...*I suppose we should make an attempt to mollify him.*"

Her eyes widened as she suddenly realized who the Guild had decided to mollify. Councillor Saladaz had hired the Guild, had not been entirely satisfied, and Councillor Saladaz was a powerful man who could be a powerful enemy. If Swan's braid was stolen the mercenary captain would be humiliated and apparently that would make the councillor happy. The thief sighed as deeply as she was able considering that the larger woman still sat on her chest. The thought of Swan's humiliation didn't make her happy at all — although she supposed she should've thought of that before she tried to steal the braid.

Terazin stared up at the mercenary captain and weighed her loyalties. Adding the knowledge that she was at Swan's mercy to the scale — and ignoring the spreading heat that realization brought — she came to a decision. "I'm pretty sure the Thieves' Guild sent me to steal your braid in order to humiliate you."

"What?"

"They're sucking up to Councillor Saladaz. He wasn't entirely happy with something they had done for him."

Swan's eyes narrowed. "Why would Saladaz hire a thief?"

"To steal something?" Terazin bit her lip. *Oh great. Now on top of everything else she'll think I'm an idiot.*

To her surprise, Swan repeated, "To steal something," as though it were a brilliant observation. "Could a thief," she demanded, "be sent to steal through a mercenary troop and warn a bandit leader of an attack?"

"Someone warned Hyrantaz that the Wing was coming?"

"Someone, yes. One of my pickets said thought he saw a slender, dark-haired woman slip through our lines. Moved like a thief in the night, he said. We found no trace of her and we've had trouble with dryads before but Hyrantaz was warned and now you tell me that Councillor Saladaz..." The name came off her lips like a curse. "...has been dealing with the Thieves' Guild." She leaned forward and laid her blade back under Terizan's ear. "Could Saladaz have hired a thief to warn Hyrantaz?"

Terazin sifted through every commission that she'd ever heard the Guild was willing to perform. "Yes. It's possible."

"It wasn't you, was it?"

Her mouth gone completely dry, Terazin had never heard so deadly a threat spoken so quietly. Mutely, she shook her head.

Swan nodded. "Good." Then in a movement almost too fast to follow, she was off the bed and reaching for her clothes.

Terazin drew her legs up under her, ready to spring for the window but unable to leave. "You've been waiting for the dark-haired woman haven't you? That's why you've been..."

"Taking dark-haired women to bed?" Swan yanked the laces on her breeches tight. "I thought she might come back to finish the job so I made myself available."

She should've known that there'd be a reason and she should've known that the reason had nothing to do with her. She tried to keep from sounding wistful. "Why do you believe me when I say I'm not the woman you're looking for?"

Swan twisted around and, just for an instant, so quickly that Terazin couldn't be certain she actually saw it, her expression softened. "Maybe because I don't want you to be." Then she bent and scooped her swordbelt off the floor.

"Where are you going now?"

"To separate Saladaz's head from his shoulders."

"You're just going to march into the Congress and slaughter a councillor?"

"Not slaughter, execute" Her lips drew back off her teeth. "I lost a lot of good people out there and that asshole is going to pay."

"And then?"

Hands on her hips, Swan turned to face the bed. "And then what?"

"And then what happens?" Terazin slid her feet into her sandals and stood. "I'll tell you. You'll be arrested because you have no proof Saladaz did anything and then a lot more good people will get killed when the Wing tries to get you out of jail."

"So what do you suggest?"

Terazin ignored the sarcasm. "I suggest we get proof."

Both red-gold brows rose. "We?"

"Yeah, we. I, uh, I mean I owe you for not killing me when you had the chance."

One corner of Swan's generous mouth quirked up in the beginning of a smile. "Not to mention, for not turning you over to the city constables."

"Not to mention." She spread her hands. "The most obvious reason for Saladaz to want to warn Hyrantaz is that he wanted to keep him in business and he could only want to keep him in business if he was taking a percentage of the profits."

Swan nodded, slowly. "That makes sense."

"The councillor has a reputation for admiring beautiful things, so just suppose some of his payment was not in plain coin but in the best of the merchandise taken from the caravans."

"Suppose it was."

"Well, if someone should go into his townhouse, they could likely find that merchandise."

"And how would this person know what merchandise to look for?"

"Easy; every fence and constable in Oreen has a list."

Swan looked surprised. "They can read?"

"Well, no, but scholars are cheap."

"All right." The mercenary captain folded her arms across her chest. "What does this person do once she's found the merchandise in the councillor's house? It won't prove anything if you steal it."

"We could take it to one of the other councillors."

"We don't know that the other councillors weren't in on this deal as well."

Terazin smiled; if only for the moment Swan had referred to them as we. "Then we take it to the people."

ରେ ରେ ରେ

"Are you sure you're good enough for this?" Swan hissed, scowling at the iron spikes set into the top of the wall surrounding Councillor Saladaz's townhouse.

"If you hadn't been expecting a dark-haired woman to try something, I'd have had your braid."

"You think." She shook her head. "I don't like this. It's too dangerous. I don't like sending someone into a danger I won't face myself."

Terazin flexed fingers and toes, preparing for the climb. "First of all, you're too good a captain not to delegate when you have to and secondly, you're not sending me. It was my idea, I'm going on my own."

"Why?"

Because I'd cheerfully roll naked on a hill of fire ants for you. Something of the thought must have shown on her face because Swan reached out for her. Terazin stepped back. That kind of a distraction she didn't need right now. "We settled that already. Because I owe you for not killing me."

"So you're going to kill yourself?"

She wanted to say it was perfectly safe but she didn't think she could make it sound believable. "Just make sure there's a constable or two ready when I come back over the wall. Are your people in place?"

"Everyone's ready."

"Good."

Terazin had spent the early part of the day investigating the councillor's security arrangements while Swan readied her Wing for the evening's work. If it was to be done at all, it had to be done before full dark. The wall wasn't much of a problem. That it hid nearly everything behind it, was.

She'd heard dogs in the garden so she planned to avoid the garden entirely. Saladaz probably thought that the jump from the top of the wall to the twisted wrought iron of a second floor balcony was impossibly far. He was almost right. Two fingers on each hand hooked around the railing and Terazin just barely got her feet forward in time to stop her body from slamming into the house.

The tall louvered shutters were closed but not locked and before anyone could come to investigate the sound of her landing, she moving silently down an upper hall-way.

They won't be in the public rooms; they'll be some place private, but not locked away. He'll want to enjoy them, gloat over them, or there'd be no point in taking the risk of owning them.

She passed a door that gave access into a room over-looking the inner courtyard and all the hair on her body lifted. Unlike the Thieves' Guild, the councillor had obviously considered it worth the expense of having a wizard magically lock at least one of his doors.

Terazin smiled and kept moving. Might as well hang out a sign... She had no intention of trying to get around the spell and pick the lock. Thieves who held exaggerated ideas of their skills quickly became decorations on the spikes of the Crescent and a sensitivity to magic kept her safely away from things she couldn't handle.

At the next door, she sped though a bedchamber — in use but, given the hour, empty, — went out the window, and onto the inner wall. There were servants working in the courtyard but her long-sleeved tunic and trousers were close to the same shade as the brick, the short, corn-colored wig she wore was only a bit lighter, and, as good thieves learned early in their careers, people seldom looked up.

Fingers and toes splayed into nearly invisible cracks, Terazin inched across the wall. For one heart-stopping moment she thought there was a spell on the window as well but then realized she was reacting to the distant feel of the door lock. The window had no lock but then, why should it? The window looked over a private courtyard.

The room behind the window was a study. It held a massive table with a slanted writing surface, racks and racks of scrolls, a number of very expensive glass lamps — had she been on personal business the lamps alone would've brought a tidy profit — and a cushioned lounger with a small round table drawn up beside it. There were beautiful ornaments on display all over the room. The three she recognized immediately, Terazin slipped into her pack. A quick search of the scrolls discovered two sets of ebony handles chased with silver from the merchants' list of stolen goods. She took one and left the second. After all, something had to remain for the constables to discover. A malachite inkwell was far too heavy so she contented herself with removing the set of matching brushes.

Even without the inkwell, the extra weight made the trip back along the courtyard wall much more interesting than the initial journey had been. A handhold, barely half a fingerwidth, began to crumble. She shifted her weight and threw herself forward; stretching, stretching. Her toes clutched at safety and she started breathing again.

Down below, the servants continued doing whatever it was that servants did, oblivious of the drama being played out over their heads.

Bedchamber and halls were crossed without incident. Chewing the corner of her lip, Terazin measured the distance from the balcony back to the wall. Logic said it had to be the same distance going out as coming in but logic didn't have to contend with a row of iron spikes and a weighted pack. *If I jump a little short, I can catch myself on the base of the spikes and listen for Swan. Once I hear her, I can pull myself up to the top.* She flexed her knees and tried not to think about what would happen if she jumped a little too short.

Then her hands were wrapped around the spikes. She bit back a curse as one knee slammed into the bricks and held her breath listening for the dogs.

"I'm telling you, Constable, I saw someone climb over this wall."

They were directly opposite her. Gathering her strength, Terazin heaved herself up onto the top and began to run, bow-legged, for the far end, her heels touching down between every fourth spike.

"There! Up there! Stop thief!"

Heart in her throat, Terazin threw herself up into a young sycamore tree and down onto the roof of a long, two story building. She had to get to the centre of the city. At the end of the building, she danced along a narrow ledge, spun round a flag pole, bounced up an awning and onto the top of another wall. Behind her, the hue and cry grew as more and more people took up the chase.

"There he is! Don't let him get away!"

She touched ground, raced through a tangle of back streets — peripherally aware of the occasional large body that delayed pursuit — crossed the High Street with what seemed like half of Oreen after her, darted between two buildings and shrugged out of her pack. An ancient addition had crumbled leaving a dangerous stairway to the rooftops. Terazin skimmed up it, hanging the pack on a projection near the bottom, and threw herself flat behind the lip of the roof just as the chase reached the alley.

"Look! There's his pack!"

Wincing a little as the thieves' stair crumbled under purposefully heavy footsteps, Terazin stripped off her trousers and turned them inside out to expose the striped fabric they'd been lined with. The sleeves came off the tunic and were stuffed into her breast band, significantly changing her silhouette. The wig she added to a pigeons nest and couldn't see much difference between them.

With all the attention on the alley and her pack, it was an easy matter to flip over the far side of the building and into a window before anyone reached the roof by more conventional methods. It helped that two very large mercenaries were having a shoving match on the stairs.

By the time she reached the street, the mob had turned and was heading back to Councillor Saladaz's townhouse. Out in front were a pair of merchants who'd lost everything to Hyrantaz's bandits.

"Your left tit is lopsided."

Terazin slipped a hand inside her tunic and shoved at the crumpled sleeve. "Better?"

"Much." Swan grinned and stepped out of the shadow of the doorway. She linked her arm through the shorter woman's and they began to walk back to The Lion. "Everything worked out just like you said it would. When the constable pulled the drawstring on the pack everything in it fell out at his feet. He stared open-mouthed and a number of my louder officers stirred up the crowd, demanding to see each piece. When he held up the scroll ends, I thought the merchant they'd been taken from was going to spit fire. I've never seen anyone so angry. One of my people bellowed that the thief came out of Councillor Saladaz's house and that was all it took. The councillor is not a very popular man right now."

They could hear the roar of the crowd in the distance. If anything, it appeared to be growing both louder and angrier as it moved away from them.

"I left plenty for them to find," Terazin murmured. "And I expect when they're done with Saladaz it'll occur to someone that perhaps the other councillors ought to be checked out as well."

"You're quite the strategist."

Terizan's face flushed at the emphatic admiration in Swan's voice. She mumbled something non-committal and kept her eyes on her feet.

"Given that what you do is illegal and the odds have to catch up to you sooner or later — which would be an incredible waste — have you ever considered taking up another profession?"

"Like what?"

"Oh ... mercenary perhaps."

Terazin stopped dead and turned to stare up at the taller woman. Although her night sight was very good, the shifting shadows of dusk made it difficult to read Swan's expression. "Do you mean..."

"Thanks to that son of a leprous baboon..." She cocked her head as the background sounds of the crowd rose momentarily to a foreground scream of victory. "...who is even now being taken care of — I have a few openings."

"But I don't, I mean, I can't..." Terazin took a deep breath and tried again. "That is, I won't kill anyone."

Swan shrugged. "I can always get plenty of swords; brains are harder to come by. Besides," her voice softened and one hand rose to cup Terizan's face, "you're smart, you're beautiful, you're amazingly flexible; I think I'd like to get to know you better."

The thief felt her jaw drop and the evening suddenly grew much warmer.

"There's no need to decide right away," Swan continued, her grin suggesting she could feel the heat of Terizan's reaction. "I'm not taking the Wing anywhere until we're paid so we've got another two nights to see if we'll suit."

☾ ☾ ☾

"Swan! Swan! Swan!"

The people of Oreen screamed their approval as Swan and twelve members of the Wing rode into the Crescent. Although all seven members of council waited on the steps of the Congress, only four were actually standing. Councillor Saladaz and two others stared out at the crowd with sightless eyes, their heads having joined Hyrantaz and his bandits.

"So is it love?"

Eyes locked on Swan, Terazin shrugged. "I don't know."

Poli shook his head and sighed. "So are you going to accept her offer?"

"I don't know."

"Does she know that you're responsible for all this renewed adoration?"

"Don't be ridiculous."

"I am never ridiculous. But I do recall being asked to spread a rumor that Swan was behind the discovery of Saladaz and his little business arrangements." He smoothed down his tunic and smiled. "I guess he should have paid her right away and got her out of town."

Terazin grinned as Councillor Aleezan handed over the rest of the Wing's payment and the crowd went wild. Then the grin faded. "Poli, what should I do?"

He had to place his mouth almost on her ear to be heard over the noise. "What do you want to do?"

What did she want to do? Swan was exciting, exotic, exhausting, and not an easy person to live with. The Wing would accept her initially for Swan's sake and in time for her own but would she ever accept the Wing? They were as good at killing people as she was a stealing from them and she'd never really approved of slaughter for a living.

His manicured nails digging into her shoulders, Poli shook her. "Terizan, you have to make a decision. What do you want to do?"

"I want..." She didn't want to worry about injury or sickness or age. She didn't want to leave the city. And as much as she desired her, adored her, maybe even loved her, she didn't want to spend the rest of her life trying to keep up to Swan. Not to mention that she strongly suspected she'd hate sleeping in a tent. "I want to join the Thieves' Guild."

Poli released her and gracefully spread his hands, the gesture clearing asking, "So?"

"SWAN! SWAN! SWAN!"

Terazin watched the Wing, and Swan, ride out of the Crescent on a wave of adulation. She'd agreed to meet them at the Lion and give the mercenary captain her decision. Fortunately, she thought Swan would understand. Unfortunately, if she wanted to join the Thieves' Guild, she had a small problem.

"SWAN! SWAN! SWAN!"

The lifebraid gleamed like a line of fire down the back of Swan's armour. Terazin chewed on a corner of her lip and suddenly smiled.

Maybe not.

ය ය ය

"Uh, Tribunes...

His eyes wide, Balzador peered into the Sanctum. "Uh, Terazin is back."

One looked up from a detailed plan of the Congress and frowned at his expression. "Did you forget to use the blindfold again?"

"N-no. I used the blindfold but..."

"Good." Two cut him off. "Remember, she isn't a member of the Guild until she fulfills our commission. Although," he added in an undertone, "all things considered, we no longer really need to mollify our late client."

"Y-yes, I know but..."

Tribune Three sighed and turned from racking an armload of scrolls. "Well, if she's back, where is she?"

"Right here." Terazin pushed past the stammering Balzador and into the Sanctum.

One glanced up at the trap door in the ceiling, then smiled. "And did you bring us Swan's braid?"

"I did." Reaching behind her, she pushed the door the rest of the way open.

Swan swept off her blindfold, and bowed, eyes gleaming.

The tribunal stared, open mouthed, fully aware that if anything happened to their Captain, the Wing would tear the city apart.

"What is the meaning of this," One demanded at last.

Terazin echoed Swan's bow. "You never specified that I had to remove the braid from Swan."

"We, we," Two sputtered, then Three began to laugh.

"We never did," he chuckled, slapping meaty thighs. "We never did. We said bring us Swan's braid and she most assuredly has done that."

Two's narrow lips began to twitch.

Finally, One sighed and spread her hands in surrender. "Welcome to the Guild, Terizan." Almost in spite of herself, she smiled. "We'll remember to be more specific in the future."

CR CR CR

"I'm almost relieved you didn't take me up on my offer." When Terazin looked hurt, Swan cupped her chin with one hand. "You'd steal the company out from under me in a month."

"I don't think so," Terazin began but Swan cut her off.

"I do. I've seen you operate. Next time I'm back this way, you'll be running that Guild."

Terazin frowned. There were a number of things she'd like to change. Most of them ran out her ears as Swan bent and kissed her good-bye, but she was sure she'd think of them again. Just as soon as she could start thinking again. She swayed a little as Swan released her.

Swan swung up into the saddle and flicked her braid back over her shoulder. "You've stolen my heart, you know."

"Come back and visit it."

"I will."

Terazin raised a hand in farewell as Swan rode out of the stableyard then climbed to the top of the tallest building in the neighbourhood to watch the Wing ride out of Oreen.

"Next time I'm back this way, you'll be running that Guild."

She dropped onto a balcony railing and danced along it to a narrow ledge. The day was fading and she had a lot to do. Plans to make. She grinned and touched her hip. Safe in the bottom of a deep pocket, sewn into a tiny, silk pouch, was a long red-gold hair, rippled down its length from the weave of the braid.

In Mysterious Ways

"You want me to steal what?"

"The Eye of Keydi-azda."

Terazin stared at the Tribunal in disbelief. Her question had been rhetorical; she'd heard them the first time. "Keydi-azda is a god."

"One of the so-called small gods." Tribune One cocked her head and raised a slender brow. "Do you have a problem with that?"

"Actually, yes. People who steal from gods spend the rest of their very short lives in uncomfortable circumstances then they endure a painful eternity of having their livers eaten by cockroaches."

Tribune Three snickered.

One ignored him so pointedly his cheeks reddened. "You're saying you don't think you can do it?"

"No. I'm not saying that." Terazin spread her hands in what she hoped was a placating manner — the last thing she wanted was to irritate the Tribunal. Actually, the last thing she wanted was to steal the Eye of Keydi-azda but not irritating the Tribunal came a close second. They weren't particularly fond of her as it was. "I'd just rather not."

Tribune Two's pale eyes narrowed and thin lips opened to make a protest. A sharp gesture from One closed them again.

"Very well. As you don't seem to approve of this job..."

Terazin winced, realizing that the Tribune's choice of words had not been accidental and reflecting that she really had to learn to keep her opinions to herself.

"...you may go."

A little surprised it had been that easy, Terazin bowed gratefully. She had her fingers around the heavy iron latch that secured the door to the Sanctum when One added, "Send in Balzador, would you?"

"Balzador?" She whirled around and swept an incredulous glance over the three who ran the Thieves' Guild. "You're going to send Balzador to steal the Eye? There's no way he's up to something like that."

"Then who is?" One asked, steepling long, ringless fingers and examining Terazin over the apex. "If you are unwilling, who do you suggest we send to the Temple of Keydi-azda in your place?"

Who indeed. Mere days before she'd joined the guild, Terazin had found herself on a narrow ledge that led nowhere. To go back meant almost certain discovery and her head adorning a spike in the Crescent. To go on meant trusting her weight to an ancient frieze of fruiting vines carved into the side of the building. That feeling of having no choice but a bad one had been remarkably similar to what she felt now.

The only sound in the Sanctum was the quiet rustle of fabric as Three shifted his bulk into a more comfortable position. Even the lamps seemed to have stopped flickering while they waited for her reply.

Either she became responsible for the thief they sent, or they sent Balzador, who didn't stand a chance.

She lived again through the moment when the carving crumbled under her foot and she plummeted two storeys down, only luck keeping her from finishing the fall as a crippled beggar.

The guild took care of their own, but at a price.

"You've already accepted the contract?" she said at last.

"We have."

"To steal the Eye of Keydi-azda?"

"Yes."

"I'm going to need more information than that."

Three picked up a narrow scroll from among the junk piled high in front of him and began unrolling it. "We assumed as much."

"You assumed rather a lot," Terazin muttered sinking cross-legged down onto a stack of recently acquired carpets.

One smiled, her austere expression growing no warmer. "Yes," she said, "but then, we can."

ભ ભ ભ

Terazin walked slowly down the Street of Prayers, grinding her teeth. She hated being backed into a corner and she really hated the smug, self-satisfied way Tribune One had done it. When an orange-robed follower of Hezzna stepped into her path and attempted to hand her a drooping palm frond, she glared up at the veiled face and growled, "I wouldn't."

Behind the orange haze, the kohled edges of the acolyte's eyes widened. Holding the frond between them like a flaccid green sword, he stepped back out of her way.

Feeling a little better, Terazin quickened her pace. Traffic picked up in the late afternoon and she didn't want to waste the anonymity the crowds provided. At the top of the street, junior priests, robed in pale blue, stood on the four balconies of the Temple of the Light and sang out the call to the sunset service. At the bottom of the street, junior priests, wearing identical robes of dark grey, stood on the balconies of the Temple of the Night and did the same. Up and down the Street of Prayers, the people of Old Oreen hurried to complete the day's business. Very few of them were heading to either service. As far as Terazin could see, none of them were praying.

According to the Tribunal, Keydi-azda's Temple shared a wall on one side with the imposing bulk of the Temple of the Forge and on the other with the building where the Fermentation Brotherhood held their weekly meetings. Two storeys high but only one room wide, its fronting built of the same smoke-blackened yellow brick that made up most of the rest of the city, it was an easy temple to overlook. A weather worn eye carved into the keystone over the arched door gave the only indication of what waited inside.

The door led to a short hall and another door. Drawing in a deep breath and reminding herself that she was only scouting the job, Terazin stepped over the threshold.

It was quiet, dim, and smelled of sandalwood.

At one end of the rectangular room, shelves rose from tiled floor to painted ceiling. Petitioners could either leave an offering or remove an item they felt they needed. The shelves were half empty. At the other end of the room stood a small altar where a cone of incense burned in a copper dish.

Above the altar was a second carving of an eye. More ornately carved than the exterior eye, it also boasted an iris of lapis lazuli centered by an onyx pupil.

Keydi-azda was the god of comfort. After a meal, fat men would loosen their belts and sigh, "Bless Keydi-azda." Terazin had murmured the blessing herself on occasion when a good night allowed her to pay for more than bare necessities. Everyone knew the name of Keydi-azda.

Not many, it seemed, came to the temple.

Terazin sang The Drunken Baker quietly to herself. Twelve verses later, she was still alone.

"The priest is old," Tribune Two had said, "and sleeps soundly."

"Must be napping now," Terazin muttered, walking silently toward the altar, another hair rising off the back of her neck with every step. She'd just have a closer look and be gone before anyone noticed she was there.

The Eye sat loosely within its collar of stone.

If I slid a blade behind it, it'd just pop off into my...

"...hand."

Surprise, as much as the unexpected weight, nearly sent the disc crashing to the floor. Although barely larger than her palm, it curved out two fingers thick in the centre of the onyx and was heavier than it looked.

Heart beating so loudly an army could've marched through the temple without her hearing it, Terazin slipped the Eye under her clothes and sashed the flat side tight against her belly. Braced for contact with cold stone, she found it unexpectedly warm.

Then she turned and walked out.

No one tried to stop her. Feeling slightly separated from the world as she knew it, she made her way back to the Thieves' Guild and handed the Eye of Keydi-azda over to a grinning Tribune Three.

It was as simple as that.

Even Balzador could've done it.

ભ ભ ભ

A triple knock jerked Terazin up off her pallet, heart in her throat, and propelled her halfway out the narrow window before her brain began working.

Constables didn't knock.

"Get a grip," she told herself firmly, drawing her leg back over the sill and rubbing at the place where her knee had cracked against the edge of the sandstone block. "It's probably just Poli wondering if you want to go to the dumpling maker's with him." The sun suggested it was past noon, late enough for Poli to be up and thinking of his first meal of the day.

Tugging the worst creases out of her tunic, she limped to the door, drew the bolt, and swung it open.

One artificially arched brow arched even higher as Poli's critical gaze swept over her and around the tiny room. "You're sleeping late. Busy night?"

Terazin ignored the implication. "Bad dreams." She stepped aside to give him room to enter. "I must've woken up a hundred times."

"Guilty conscience." Removing a pile of clothing from the only chair, he sat and smiled beneficently. "Nothing a little food won't cure. Do try to wear something that won't embarrass me."

"Like there's a lot of choice," she muttered dragging her only clean pair of trousers down off a hook. Shoving one foot into a wide leg, she caught her toe in the thieves' pocket above the cuff, bounced sideways, tripped over the tangled blanket, and fell to the sound of ripping cloth, missing a landing on the pallet by inches.

As she swore and rubbed her elbow, Poli surveyed the split seam and shook his head. "You've got to start shop-

ping off a better quality of laundry line, sweetling. Wear the dirty ones before we starve to death."

"The worst of it is," Terazin sighed, doing as he suggested, "I didn't steal them. I bought them from old man Ezakedid and he told me they were only second hand." She shoved her feet into her sandals and bent to pull the straps tight. Without straightening she looked from the piece of broken strap in her left hand, to Poli. "This is not starting out to be a very good day."

૨૨ ૨૨ ૨૨

The dumpling maker had sold out of cheese dumplings so Terazin rolled her eyes, ordered lamb, and bit through her tongue while trying to chew a chunk of gristle soft enough to swallow. She spit out a mouthful of blood and picked up her cup.

"There's a dead fly in my water."

"Not so loud," Poli advised, wiping his fingers on the square of scented cloth he was never without, "or everyone will want one." Leaning forward, he lowered his voice. "Do you see the young lady in the yellow scarf? There by the awning pole? I think she's trying to catch your eye."

Terazin refused to look. "The way my luck's been going today, she's probably an off duty constable."

"I don't think so."

"Poli, I'm not interested." She shifted in place and slipped a hand up under her tunic to scratch at her stomach.

"You're never interested, sweetling."

"That's not true."

"No? If everyone in the city had your libido, I'd starve. You're not harboring a broken heart are you? I told you not to pursue a relationship with a mercenary."

"What are you talking about? You practically threw me into her bed."

"Nonsense." His lazy tone sharpened. "Can I trust that the itch you're chasing is not caused by some sort of insect infestation?"

"I have no idea but its driving me crazy." Fleas would be just what she needed.

"Let me look."

Figuring that the little Poli didn't know about skin could be inscribed on a grape with room left over for the entire Book of the Light, Terazin leaned away from the table and lifted her tunic a couple of inches.

"It's just a rash," he announced after a moment's examination. "Most likely caused by something you've leaned against — something circular from the look of it. I don't think it's dangerous, merely uncomfortable."

Something circular.

Through the sudden buzzing in her ears Terazin heard her voice tell the Tribunal, "People who steal from gods spend the rest of their short lives in uncomfortable circumstances." She hadn't meant uncomfortable literally but why not; Keydi-azda was the god of comfort after all. And it certainly explained the way her day had been going.

"All right, sweetling. What have you done?"

She shook herself and pulled down her tunic. A quick look around the dumpling maker's cantina showed no one sitting close enough to overhear. "I did a job for the guild..."

By the time she finished, Poli had paled beneath his cosmetics. "You stole the Eye of Keydi-azda?" he hissed. "Are you out of your mind?"

"I can't see as I had much choice."

"They gave you a chance to send someone else. Any other thief would've taken it."

She laid both hands flat on the scarred table top and leaned forward until their noses were almost touching. "I'm not any other thief."

Poli closed his eyes for a moment, then he sighed. "No, you're not, are you. Well, there's only one thing to do. You've got to put it back."

"I can't. I gave it to the Tribunal. I don't know who has it now."

"Can't you find out?"

"Sure, I mean the guild always insists on a written contract for blackmail purposes. All I'd have to do is break into the Sanctum and steal it."

Poli ignored the sarcasm. "Good."

Terazin opened her mouth to protest then closed it
again. People who steal from gods spend the rest of their
short lives in uncomfortable circumstances. A short, uncomfortable life. She'd planned on a long life. She had
too much to do to die young. "Oh bugger," she sighed.
Although she'd certainly intended to challenge the
Tribunal's authority, she'd expected to have a little more
time to strengthen her position in the guild. Fighting the
urge to scratch, she dipped her finger in her cup and
traced a circle within a circle on the table — driving a
splinter in under the skin far enough to draw blood. "All
right, you win. I'll find out who has it and I'll steal it
back."

"Your guild encourages free-lance work," Poli reminded her.

"I doubt this is what they had in mind," she muttered
around her injured finger.

He waved a dismissive hand. "Then they should have
been more specific."

"You're not helping, Poli. First problem, there's always
at least one member of the Tribunal in the Sanctum."

"Don't they trust you?"

"We're thieves, of course they don't trust us." Eyes
narrowed, she stared down at rapidly evaporating sketch.
"I think I can get rid of the Tribune, at least for a few
minutes…"

ଓଃ ଓଃ ଓଃ

The herbalist Terazin decided to use had a small shop
facing the cramped confines of Greenmarket Square. As
it wasn't an area she frequented, personally or profes-
sionally, she hoped she'd be neither recognized nor
remembered. Ignoring sales pitches as wilted as the vegetables, she made her way around the edges of the square
and, just outside her destination, stepped on something
soft that compacted under her sandal.

It turned out not to be a rotting bit of melon rind.

The dim interior of the shop smelled of orange peel
and bergamot. Bundles of dried herbs hung from hooks

in the ceiling and were packed into stacks of loosely woven baskets. Bottles and boxes crammed the shelves along one wall. In one corner, a large terra cotta jar sweated oil. Dust motes danced thickly in the single beam of light that managed to penetrate the clutter.

As Terazin entered, stained fingers parted the beaded curtain in the back wall and an ancient man shuffled through the opening. "How may I help you?" he wheezed. "Love potions? Women's problems? A soothing balm to ease the pain of inflamed eyes?"

"Cazcara zagrada powder."

"Ah, constipation." He squinted in Terizan's general direction. "I should have known from the smell."

"That's on my shoe!"

"Of course it is. Two doses, one monkey."

"I need four."

"Four?" Shaking his head, he lifted a stained basswood box onto the counter, opened it, and spooned the coarse brown powder onto a piece of fabric with an amazingly steady hand. "Be careful," he told her as he twisted the corners up and tied them off with a bit of string. "I don't care how backed up you are, just one dose of this will put you in the privy blessing Keydi-azda. And that's no laughing matter, young woman!"

"Trust me, I'm not laughing." Wiping the snarl off her face, Terazin handed over the two copper coins.

ଔ ଔ ଔ

The large antechamber outside the Sanctum smelled strongly of onions. Peppers would've been better but onions would have to do. Terazin traded jests with a group of thieves playing caravan then made her way across to the pair of kettles steaming over small charcoal fires, the four doses of cazcara zagrada palmed and ready. "Is it done yet?"

"Is it ever done before sunset?" Yazdamidor growled. He'd been a thief until a spelled lock cost him the use of one arm. Now, he cooked for the Guild.

"Look, Yaz, I'm in a hurry..."

"Got a job, does you?" He snorted, not waiting for her answer. "Course you do, smart one like you." Scooping a bowl of barley mush out of the first kettle, he thrust it at her. "There's always someone what can't wait. Go ahead, just don't blame me if it ain't cooked through."

She doctored the stew as she scooped it onto her mush, stirring in the powder with the ladle and hoping that she'd got as little of it as possible into her own food. Unfortunately, the way things had been going, she expected an uncomfortable evening. The meat was cooked through but, since the goat had probably died of old age, she couldn't see as it made much difference.

She finished before anyone else started. As the caravan players filled bowls and moved to join her, she clutched her stomach, muttered a curse, and hurriedly left the room. Racing up the stairs, only partially faking, she heard Yazdamidor laugh and shout, "Told you so!"

Now, it was all a matter of timing.

Most thefts were, patterns being easier to break into than locks.

In order to join the guild, thieves were expected to make their way through the guild house to the inner Sanctum. The rumors that reached the city of deadly traps and complicated protections were exaggerated but not by much. Terazin was the first thief to have ever made it all the way. Since no one had done it since, it was safe to say she was also the only thief to have made all the way.

As a member of the guild, her access to the House had improved since that afternoon and, this time, it wasn't necessary to enter through an attic window. Even avoiding the dogs, she only had to cover half the distance. Disconnecting the wire set to ring warning bells inside the Sanctum, she pried up a tile and laid an iron bar — removed from a trap she'd disabled a few moments earlier — across the opening. The rope tied to the middle of the bar she uncoiled as she chimney-walked down the narrow chute to the trap door at the bottom. Easing it open a fingerwidth, she listened.

Nothing.

The Sanctum was...

Then she heard the scraping of a horn spoon against the side of a wooden bowl and hurriedly rebraced her feet. Regrettably, since she'd already begun to move, the angle was bad and she wouldn't be able to hold her position for long. As the muscles in her lower back began to cramp, she wondered if the Tribune about to be so abruptly visited would believe she was just reliving past glories. Probably not.

It didn't help that her stomach felt as though fire ants were nesting just below the surface of her skin. She squirmed to ease the itch and her left shoulder slipped.

Oh crap...

As she fell, she grabbed the edge of the trap door and used it to swing out past the net waiting to scoop up those who entered without proper planning. A somersault in midair and she landed facing the Tribune's table.

The empty room echoed to the sound of footsteps pounding up the long flight of stairs used to bring clients unseen into the Sanctum. It was the only direct route into the heart of the guild house and the upper end was both trapped and guarded. It was also the most direct route to the privies.

Silently thanking whatever gods she hadn't pissed off, Terazin wiped sweaty palms on her thighs, vaulted the table, and jerked to a stop in front of the shelves of scrolls. There were a lot more than she'd noticed from the other side of the room.

Think, Terizan, think. They have to have a system or they'd never find anything themselves. There appeared to be three sections. One for each Tribune? Why not. She moved to left. Tribune One had given her the job. Okay. *This happened yesterday, it's got to be right on top.*

It wasn't.

Terazin couldn't read but she figured she'd recognize the hieroglyph for the Eye. Nothing looked familiar on any of the scrolls she opened.

I don't believe this...

"...eats anything. It's no wonder he's made himself sick." Tribune One's unsympathetic observation drifted down the stairs.

If the Tribunes caught her in the Sanctum, they wouldn't just throw her out of the guild, they'd throw her out in little bleeding pieces.

Heart pounding Terazin leapt up onto the table and jumped for the hook that supported the near end of the net. Something moved under her foot and she almost didn't make it. Glancing back, she saw she'd crushed the middle of a scroll as big around as her fist.

Bugger, bugger, bugger...

Blood roaring in her ears, she dropped back onto the table, scooped up the scroll, stuffed it down one trouser leg, and jumped again.

"Look at that, he's left the door open."

Her fingers closed around the end of the rope she'd left hanging and, knees tucked up against her chest to avoid the net, she transferred her weight. Her swing forward reopened the trap door. She scrambled into the ceiling, braced herself against the sides of the chute and flicked the rope up out of the way so the springs could close the door again.

"What was that?"

One snorted. "Probably rats."

"Four legged or two?"

High overhead, pulling herself out into the corridor, Terazin missed the answer.

ଔ ଔ ଔ

She couldn't take the scroll back to her room — if the information it contained was important enough the Tribunal would hire a wizard to search for it — so she took it to the only safe place she could think of.

Although there were three lamps lit, the temple of Keydi-azda was deserted — no petitioners, no priest. A linen cloth hung over the empty socket that should have held the Eye. Fully intending to leave the scroll on one of the shelves, Terazin leaned against the wall under a lamp and unrolled it. If it came to a confrontation with the Tribunal, any information she could glean might help to keep her head on her shoulders.

Within the outer sheathing, a number of parchment pages were attached to the upper handle. Nothing on the first page looked familiar.

"I've got to learn to read," she muttered. Centered in the top of the next page, the Eye of Keydi-azda stared out at her. "I'll be fried..." Remembering the near fall that had ensured she pick up this particular scroll, she glanced toward the altar and added a quiet, "Bless Keydi-azda." Just in case. She couldn't make out who'd paid for the job so she turned another page.

"The Staff of Hamtazia?"

And another page.

"Amalza's Stone?"

Altogether, since the last dark of the moon, seven icons had been stolen, all from small gods. Two days ago, Terazin wouldn't have much cared but she was beginning to realize it was the small things that made life worth living.

The hieroglyph on the bottom of the last page had to represent the people who'd hired the Guild for all seven thefts. Unfortunately, it was a incomprehensible squiggle as far as Terazin was concerned.

"May I help you, child?"

She hadn't heard the priest approach. His quiet question provoked a startled gasp and a few moments of coughing and choking on her own spit. When she finally got her breath back, she wiped streaming eyes with the palm of one hand and glared at him.

"Oh my, that didn't look to be very comfortable at all," he murmured sympathetically.

All things considered, Terazin bit off a rude reply and shoved the scroll under his nose. "Do you recognize this?"

"Oh yes. It was made by one of the priests of Cot'Dazur. See the three points and the dots below..."

"Who?"

The priest sighed and folded his hands over a comfortable curve of belly. "One of the new gods. There's a huge temple in the new town, all painted plaster and lattice work. Very stylish but not much substance, I'm afraid."

Scratching thoughtfully, Terazin frowned and wrestled these new pieces into place. "How does a god get substance?"

"Time." He smiled a little sadly. "Those who believe build it up, over time."

"Suppose you didn't want to wait?"

"You wouldn't have a choice, child. It isn't something you can suddenly acquire." Over their heads, the lamp sputtered and went out. "Oh my, I'd best get more oil." He patted her arm with one soft hand and waddled off toward the altar.

Uncertain of how to address him, Terazin took a step forward and called, "Your worship?"

"Yes, child?"

"I've heard that the Eye of Keydi-azda is missing."

Together they glanced over at the linen drapery.

"Yes, I'm afraid it is."

"You don't seem very upset."

"I have been assured it will be returned."

"Assured? By who?"

"Why by Keydi-azda, of course."

Terazin sighed. "Of course," she repeated, laid the scroll on one of the shelves beside a small clay cup, left the temple, and ran into half a dozen of the Fermentation Brotherhood just leaving a meeting. As they attempted to stagger out of her way, one of them puked on her foot.

ᘍ ᘍ ᘍ

Cot'Dazur turned out to be the god of nothing in particular although there seemed to be a divine finger stuck in a great many pies.

"Is your business not what it could be? Are you suffering from a broken heart? Do you want to impress an employer? A certain someone?" Colored flames from half a dozen flickering torches throwing bands of green and blue and gold across her face, the priest leaned forward and pointed an emphatic finger at a plump young man. "Would you like to have an application considered by the governing council?" She leaned back and spread her arms, her voice rising, her volume impressive. "Why run about to a half a dozen different temples when your problems can be dealt with under one roof." As music started up inside the

building, she stepped aside and gestured through the open door. "Come. Petition Cot'Dazur."

It was a catchy tune and Terizan, hidden in the crowd pouring up the steps, found herself moving in time to the beat — until she stubbed her toe and the pain distracted her.

Inside, lamps burning scented oil fought futilely against the smell of fresh paint mixed with half a hundred un-washed bodies. Had the ceiling not arced better than two full stories high with a row of open windows running below both sides of the peak, the combination would have quickly overpowered even the most ardent supplicant.

Painted into the plaster over the door was a represen-tation of Cot'Dazur with features so bland they seemed designed to appeal to just about everyone. From where Terazin stood, the paint looked wet. *When the priest of Keydi-azda said this was a new god, he wasn't kidding.*

Pushed up against a stucco wall, she scowled and brushed fresh plaster off her shoulder. A good thief avoided stucco — it not only crumbled easily, it also marked those who came in contact with it. Tonight it looked like she wasn't going to have a choice.

Most of the crowd had broken into smaller groups, each clustered around a red robed priest. Somehow, even though the music continued in the background, the noise never quite rose to unbearable levels.

"Would you like some sweet-dough?"

Terazin eyed the tray of deep fried dough and her lip curled. "No, thanks." Grease and stucco combined would be just what she needed.

"A cinnamon tea?"

"No. I'm, uh, fasting."

The acolyte smiled down at her. "This is your first time, isn't it?"

Since he didn't seem to expect an answer, Terazin didn't bother giving him one. Something about him set her teeth on edge. It wasn't his height, most people were taller than she was. It wasn't the blinding glory of his smile, or the cleft in his square jaw, or the breadth of his shoulders under his robe. It wasn't any single feature — it was the way they

combined that she disliked. While she might've responded better to a woman, she doubted it. Glancing around the temple, she saw that all the acolytes, men and women, shared a similar bland prettiness — they were young and cheerful and completely interchangeable. The priests, who had to be at least a little older, seemed much the same. In fact, they all looked rather remarkably like the painting of their god.

"How much does all this cost?" she asked as a trio of dancers began preforming on a small raised dais.

"Nothing at all to you," the acolyte assured her. "But donations are gratefully accepted."

Which explained the empty copper pot in the middle of the tray of sweet-dough. And the rosewood boxes carved with the hieroglyph of Cot'Dazur scattered strategically about.

"Gee, too bad I haven't got a monkey on me." She almost admired the way his smile never wavered as he disengaged and moved on. When his attention seemed fully occupied by a petitioner with a little more coin, she worked her way toward the front of the temple.

Compared to the quiet, contemplative temple of Keydiazda, all the rah, rah Cot'Dazur set her teeth on edge — although she had to admit as she paused a moment to listen to an impassioned prayer for the speedy recovery of a sick camel that involved some very realistic spitting, it was the more entertaining way to spend an evening.

The Guild of Thespians could take lessons from these guys...

There was the expected small door beside the altar. Terazin waited until a particularly athletic solicitation drew most eyes then slipped through it.

The sudden quiet made her ears ring.

It took time for a god to gain substance and first impressions suggested this lot wouldn't care to wait. If they planned to use the stolen icons as a shortcut to achieving divine power then all seven would have to be grouped together at a focal point somewhere in the temple. Inside the altar was the most obvious spot but not even the best thief in Oreen could get to them until after the crowd ate its fill of sweet-dough and went home.

A short flight of dark stairs led to narrow room lit by a single lamp. Street clothes hung neatly on hooks over polished wooden benches and a large wicker basket probably waited for dirty robes. Terazin squirmed into the darkness below a bench and settled down to wait.

Laughing voices woke her.

Feet flickered past her hiding place, shadowed shapes against the shadows by the floor. Most of the conversation seemed to centre on how full the collection boxes had been and on how much sweet-dough had been eaten. Since Terazin had always believed that priests were people just like any other people, she couldn't understand why it bothered her so much to be right. The smell of fresh varnish made her want to sneeze but that, at least, was a discomfort she was used to.

When the laughing voices left, she thought she could hear two, maybe three people moving quietly about the room.

"How much longer?"

"Patience, Habazan, patience."

Terazin recognized the voice of the priest who had drawn the crowd into the temple. She had an unmistakable way of pronouncing every word as if it came straight from her god.

"But we have the icons."

"Granted, but even small gods will be able to hold their power for a while."

"I thought if we took the symbol of their power we took their power."

"We did. The small gods and their icons have become one and the same in most people's minds. With the icon gone, the people assume that the god is gone and will stop believing. When enough of them stop, the gods will end, and their power — through the icons — will be ours."

"Will be Cot'Dazur's."

"Of course. That's what I meant."

"But how much longer?"

"Not very."

Not very, Terazin repeated to herself as the priest and her companion took the lamp and left the robing room. Not

very long before the small gods end. She lay where she was and scratched at the rash on her stomach. She didn't have to do this, didn't have to risk anything to return the Eye of Keydi-azda. If the priest of Cot'Dazur was right, in not very much longer Keydi-azda would be unable to affect her life. All she had to do was endure a few discomforts and soon it would end.

Keydi-azda would end.

Terazin sighed and slid out from under the bench. Any other thief would let it go. Wouldn't risk it. But as she'd told Poli, she wasn't any other thief. *I've never killed anyone and I'm not about to start now...*

Slipping on one of the dirty robes, she started down the stairs and cracked her forehead on the edge of a metal lamp bracket.

... which doesn't mean I'm not tempted.

ଓ ଓ ଓ

The altar had been carved from a solid piece of the local sandstone. It might have been hollow underneath but Terizan's instincts said otherwise. There was always the possibility that the priests had hired a wizard to sink the icons into the stone, but from what Terazin had overheard, she didn't think that had happened.

So they had to be hidden somewhere else.

Somewhere in the temple.

Somewhere that could be used to focus the power from the seven gods onto Cot'Dazur.

Hugging the shadows at the base of the walls, Terazin made her way toward the doors. In the combination of moon and starlight that spilled through the open windows, she could just barely make out the painting of the god.

Wet paint.

Cot'Dazur couldn't possibly be that new.

The collection boxes were lighter than she expected. She only hoped they'd hold her weight. When she had them stacked as high as her head, she made a bag out of the robe, tucked her sandals under her sash and climbed

carefully to the top of the pile. From there, she stepped onto the lintel of the door.

The plaster was still wet enough to cut with her longest lockpick. She sliced out a careful square, slipped it into the bag, and reached into the hole. Her fingers brushed the familiar cold curve of the Eye of Keydi-azda. Some of the other pieces were a little harder to find and by the time she'd finished, she'd destroyed most of the painting.

She was just about to step back onto the boxes, bag tied to her back, the Staff of Hamtazia shoved awkwardly through the knots, when she heard voices approaching from outside.

"I'm sure I left it up in the robing room. I'll only be a minute."

Oh crap. When they opened the door, the boxes would go flying. Balanced on the lintel, Terazin measured the distance to the closest window and realized she had no choice but to attempt it. If she couldn't go down...

Stretching her left arm out and up as far as she could, she drove her longest pick into the wall, swung out on it, kicked holes in the plaster, changed hands and did it again with her second longest pick. The Dagger of Sharidan, Guardian of the Fifth Gate, would have worked better but she couldn't take the time to dig it out. As she crab-climbed up and over toward the window, the returning acolytes pushed open the door.

The sound of collection boxes crashing to the floor, some of them bouncing, some of them smashing against the tile, covered her involuntary curse as the second longest pick proved too short and began to pull out of the wall. Desperately scrabbling for a toe hold, she ignored the shouting from below as the astonished acolytes stumbled over bits of broken wood demanding that somebody bring them a lamp.

Her fingertips caught the bottom edge of the window.

A new voice shouted from deep inside the temple.

Shit! I should've known there was a caretaker! She'd been incredibly lucky so far but unless she got out the window before the caretaker came with a light that wouldn't mean

much. Under better circumstances, she'd have used her grip on the window as an anchor and moved carefully around the corner onto the side wall. Under these particular circumstances, she jumped.

Her right hand gripped the ledge safely but lost its grip on the pick. As the steel spike began to fall, Terazin jerked her head forward and caught it in her mouth, somehow managing to hang on in spite of a split lip. Anything left behind could lead a wizard right to her.

Muscles straining, she got the upper half of her body over the window sill, wrestled the Staff of Hamtazia out the opening, and lowered herself onto the steeply angled roof. *If I can make it to the ground before they figure out which way I went,* she reasoned as she began to slide, *they'll never catch me.* Most roofs in Oreen were flat or domed — it wasn't until she noticed how fast the edge was approaching that she realized her danger.

That's a storey and a half drop! Flipping over onto her stomach she dug in fingers and toes but the clay tiles overlapped so smoothly there was nothing to grab. Then her legs were in the air. Her body began to tip while she tried grab a handful of roof.

Her hip hit a protrusion of some kind. Then the knotted robe slammed up under her chin and her left arm pit and she found herself hanging between two of the decorative wooden things that stuck out from under the edge of the roof, dangling half throttled from the jammed Staff of Hamtazia.

It's about time something went my way...

Since her hands were free, she quickly returned both picks to the seams of her trousers, pulled herself up enough to free the Staff, then dropped. By the time the hue and cry began, she'd lost herself in the shadows.

ભ ભ ભ

In the temple of Keydi-azda, the same three lamps burned unattended. Although Terazin half expected something to go wrong, the Eye fit back into the stone socket as easily as it had come out. The other six stolen icons, she

set carefully onto the shelves where they'd be found by those who needed them. Then she knelt, folded back the robe, and pulled out the last item it held. The first square of damp plaster she'd cut out of the wall — the face of Cot'Dazur, miraculously in one piece in spite of everything.

"I'm a thief," she told the watching Eye of Keydi-azda. "I'm not a judge, and I'm not an executioner. I've never killed anyone and I'm not about to start. If the priests of Cot'Dazur need their icon back, they can find it here with the rest."

The silence was absolute but Terazin hadn't expected an answer. She didn't need a god to tell her when she was doing the right thing. Brushing bits of plaster dust from her clothes, she left the Eye to keep watch alone.

ೞ ೞ ೞ

"So what did the Tribunal say?"

"What could they say?" Terazin bit into a cheese dumpling and sighed in contentment. "The priests of Cot'Dazur complained that the stolen icons had been stolen back and the Tribunal pointed out that they'd fulfilled their part of the contract and what happened to the icons after they were handed over was not their problem."

"But they don't have the contract."

"The priests don't know that. If they did, they'd cause trouble. So, as much as they'd like to come down on the thief with both feet, the Tribunal is not going to do anything that may push whoever took the contract into telling the priests that it no longer exists. Although they have nailed shut the trap door in the ceiling of the Sanctum."

Poli studied her from under darkened lashes. "So they suspect it was you?"

"They've never liked me much. They think I'm ambitious." Her grin pulled to one side by her swollen lip, her expression seemed more disdainful than amused. "You know, Poli, this whole thing was a set up from the start. The Tribunal had no reason to send me after the Eye, anyone could have done the job. But, even pinched and prodded by the god, no one else could have stolen the

contract out of the Sanctum or have got the icons back from Cot'Dazur."

Equal to the announcement, Poli nodded calmly. "Of course, the Tribunal planned on double crossing Cot'Dazur all the time."

"No, I don't think so. Had any other thief stolen the Eye, Cot'Dazur would, this minute, be absorbing the power of the small gods. I think I was their solution."

"You think you were the god's solution?" Poli reached across the table and patted her arm. "Think highly of yourself, don't you, sweetling."

"Actually, yes. But it's also the only explanation that makes sense. The way I work it out, seven gods owe me a favour. Eight if you consider that I didn't destroy that pretty picture of Cot'Dazur when I had the chance."

Poli sat back looking a little stunned. "Eight gods," he said at last. "All owing you a favour." He blinked twice then managed to recover his poise. "Well, I suppose that it's a good thing they're small gods."

Terazin flashed him a triumphant smile. The rash was gone, her bruises were healing, and the immediate future looked bright. "But there are eight of them."

"Should I be worried?"

"You? No." She took her time eating another dumpling, savoring the moment. As Tribune One had implied, there were a number of things about the guild that had never met with her approval. They were small things, for the most part, but it was, after all, the small things that made life worth living.

Bless Keydi-azda.

The Lions Of al'Kalamir

"Is it just me or are there more Kerbers in the city lately?"

"More Kerbers?" Terazin popped the last bit of bulgar-laden flatbread into her mouth and leaned back as she chewed. "I hadn't noticed."

Poli made a small moue of distaste. "Chew or talk, sweetling, not both at the same time."

"Sorry." She swallowed before continuing. "I only notice people who have something that might be worth stealing. Kerbers have nothing that's worth the risk."

"What about their weapons? I thought the Kerbers' blades were the best."

"They are but I don't think so highly of my skills that I'd try to take a weapon from a Kerber." As one of Poli's delicately arched brows arched even higher, Terazin grinned across the table at him. "Okay, maybe I do think that highly of my skills but I'm not completely crazy."

"So it's safe to assume that the Kerber advancing across the cantina toward us is not on vendetta?"

Terazin turned so quickly the bench rocked and the hulking figure sitting alone on the far end growled a wordless warning. Wrapped completely in voluminous, sand-coloured robes the advancing Kerber noted her attention with a nod and began moving a little faster.

"I don't like the way the robes hide their gender," Poli murmured.

"Since when does that matter?"

"It matters in the approach, sweetling. I know you don't get out much but men and women are not the same."

Terizan's response got lost in the Kerber's arrival.

"I have a message for you." The voice was a sexless whisper, barely emerging from behind the veils.

"For me?"

A gloved hand opened and a swan's feather dropped onto the table.

A message from Swan, the mercenary captain who'd helped Terazin get the better of the Thieves' Guild Tribunal. A message from Swan, who'd offered a thief a place in her company. A message from Swan, who'd... Terazin swallowed and managed to keep her voice nearly normal as she asked, "Should we go someplace private?"

"Someplace less likely to be overheard."

"My place?" Poli offered politely. When both heads turned toward him, he spread his hands. "Well, you clearly want to keep whatever it is you're doing under wraps. If you leave with Terazin people will assume you want her to steal something. If you leave with us both and we go to my rooms, people's assumptions will be confused."

The Kerber nodded. "Confused would be good."

"Confused will be an understatement," Terazin muttered as she stood.

લ લ લ

Two of the three brothels that had given the Street of Pleasures its name had moved out to the new city along with many of the independents. In remaining faithful to old Oreen, Poli was able to afford a pair of attractive rooms up on the third floor over a wig maker's shop.

"Good idea," Terazin said, gesturing toward the folds of colored gauze over the two tall windows in the sitting room. "A thief'd get tangled up in those."

"Well, yes," Poli admitted, "but that's not why I did it. It softens that harsh afternoon light, spreads the shadows, makes everyone look more beautiful. Beautiful people tip better." He turned to the Kerber and smiled. "Can I get you anything?"

"This isn't a social call, Poli." Turning to the Kerber, Terazin folded her arms. "I'd like to hear Swan's message now. What does she want?"

"You." A deft twist dropped the robes to one side and Terazin found herself caught up in a familiar embrace.

"That certainly looks like a social call to me," Poli commented dryly. "No wait, it's beginning to look like something I'd charge for."

Disengaging enough to catch her breath, Swan grinned down at the woman in her arms. "Actually, I have a job for you."

"My point exactly."

"Poli, shut up."

"I need the services of the best thief in Oreen to end a civil war."

ᘒ ᘒ ᘒ

"Prince Hasan al'Kalamir is dead. His two surviving sons are fighting over who should inherit. Essien, the elder by some seven minutes, hired the Wing."

"They're twins?"

Swan shook her head, the brilliant red-gold of her life braid swaying almost hypnotically with the motion. "No, different mothers. The Prince, may he rot in the Netherhells, raised both Essien and his half-brother Jameel to consider themselves the heir." One corner of her expressive mouth quirked upwards. "They can't stand each other but that's nothing to how they feel about him. Anyway, with the Wing's help, Essien defeated his brother — although didn't manage to actually kill him — and took the Palace."

"That sounds like the civil war is over," Terazin pointed out. She'd had to fight to hear Swan's story over the multitude of voices in her head calling out the mercenary captain's name — and one or two other more explicit suggestions.

"It would be over except for one small problem. The people of Kalazmir won't accept Essien as their Prince unless he has the regalia which is locked in a secret treasure room somewhere in the catacombs under the Palace. Unfortunately, Essien was a little quick to kill his father's old vizier who was the only other person — besides dear, dead, daddy — who knew where in the catacombs that treasure room was. Is."

"He's got an army he's not using now, why doesn't he send them down to look for it?"

"Because after the first one died, the rest wouldn't go. He tried sending captives, promising them a long and happy life if they bring out the regalia but they keep dying too. The old prince was rather remarkably paranoid and this place has traps up the ass."

"How painful," Poli murmured. "More beer?"

"Thanks. Anyway, the natives are getting restless and Essien's decided he has no time to waste. When he asked if I had any ideas, I immediately thought of you. You are the only supplicant to have ever made it all the way to the inner sanctum of the Thieves' Guild."

"True," Terazin acknowledged, slowly. "But while I'd do anything for you, I really prefer that anything didn't involve dying. Most of the traps in the guild house were non-lethal."

Swan snorted. "I imagine that most of the traps in the catacombs are usually non-lethal as well. The lot Essien's been sending below ground couldn't figure out how to dig a field latrine with detailed instructions. First one down sprang a pit trap you could see from the entrance."

That did seem to raise the odds a bit, Terazin thought. Then Swan smiled at her and she stopped thinking at all.

"Please, Terizan. I know you can do it."

Lost in Swan's smile, she heard Poli sigh.

"And I really want to get the Wing out of Kalazmir before the rains start," the mercenary captain continued.

"So the two of you will be leaving immediately?" Poli wondered.

Shooting him an exasperated glare — in spite of what Poli seemed to think, she wasn't quite ready to surrender to the inevitable — Terazin leaned forward and pinned Swan with her most businesslike expression. "Wouldn't it be simpler if this Essien just had the regalia copied?"

"He can't, it's god-touched. Even if he could afford to have it copied, the priests would immediately know it's a fake."

"All right, if I bring out this regalia; what's in it for me?"

"Anything else you can bring out of the treasure room."
She felt her jaw drop. "Anything?"

☙ ☙ ☙

"Anything," Essien agreed. Stroking his narrow mustache, he stared darkly down into the catacombs. "You have my word as al'Kalamir."

"Thank you." Although he wouldn't actually be al'Kalamir until she came out with the regalia, Terazin decided to let that slide. There were enough of the Wing around to see that he kept his word regardless of what he chose to call himself.

"Two things I can tell you for certain to beware of," Essien continued. "One, my father, may he rot in the Netherhells, paid a wizard for three spells but what the spells do, I have no idea. Two, beware the lions of al'Kalamir." As Swan stepped forward, frowning, he raised a ringed hand. "Given the conditions down there, I doubt they're real lions, Captain. It is merely something the vizier was fond of saying." Dark brows drew thoughtfully in. "In fact, it was the last thing vizier said; beware the lions of al'Ka..." The last word trailed off into a fair impersonation of a man choking on his own blood. A number of the soldiers standing around laughed but Terazin rolled her eyes. A little less killing and a little more questioning would have been a little more helpful from where she stood.

Settling her pack more comfortably on her shoulders, she moved to the top of the long flight of stone stairs. A slight smell of putrefaction wafted up from below.

"We can also tell you with some certainty that there's a pit trap under that first big blue tile," Swan said dryly passing over a lantern. "Pressure on the middle of the bottom step releases the support and..." Her gesture made the result quite clear. "It sounded deep," she added, somewhat unnecessarily in Terizan's opinion. Bending forward, the mercenary captain lightly kissed the top of the thief's head. "Be careful."

"I'm always careful," Terazin told her. Careless thieves ended up with their heads adorning the spikes of the

Crescent — or more specifically in this case, smashed open like a melon at the bottom of a pit.

∽ ∽ ∽

"So much for the easy part of the trip," Terazin murmured thoughtfully as she ducked under the trigger mechanism that would set a course of counterweighted blades swinging, their positions having been given away by the diced bits of body scattered down the corridor. The chopped bits of robe surprised her a little as Kerbers seldom got involved in anything but inter-tribal warfare, mostly because they were usually so pre-occupied with inter-tribal warfare. She wondered if Swan — who got her coloring and her right to wear the robes from a Kerber grandfather — had felt as though she'd been fighting on the wrong side. Probably not. Swan and her Wing were mercenaries and the right side was always and only the side paying the bills.

Like the other four traps set off by the unfortunate soldiers who'd gone into the catacombs, this one had automatically reset after having been sprung. She had to give the old prince credit, he'd been willing to pay for the best. Five soldiers, five traps. From this point on, there'd be no corpses to warn her.

"Which ought to improve the air quality, if nothing else."

So far there'd been no sign of the three spells although a faint feeling of unease had been licking up and down her spine ever since she'd stepped over that first, trapped tile. The sensitivity to magic that usually kept her from blundering into things she couldn't handle seemed to be reacting non-specifically to the entire place — which could mean any number of unpleasant things but since none of them were particularly helpful, Terazin ignored the feeling as much as she could and got on with it.

The next trap involved a large, and probably heavy, section of the ceiling. Terazin had no idea how it could possibly be reset but wasn't curious enough about it to risk being flattened. Another pit trap and the ubiquitous spring-loaded spears later, she reached a short corridor that seemed, at first inspection, to be trap free.

As a second inspection turned up the same result, she moved slowly forward, came to a T-junction, and paused. Not enough time had passed since the building of the catacombs for the correct path to have been worn into the stone and the webs of the few, small spiders who'd chosen to live in the dark seemed to show no preference. Lifting her lamp, she watched the flame flicker one way and then the other, the strangely equal breezes causing it to smoke slightly as it bent.

"All right, the odds are good the vizier, the old prince, and whoever actually designed the route to the treasure room were all right handed. Nine times out of ten, when given a simple choice between one direction and the other, right-handed people turn to the right."

When she reached her first dead end after three corners and two cross corridors, she retraced her way to back the T-junction.

"All right, so this is that one time out of ten they don't go to the right."

Except that heading left took her into an identical maze.

"Which isn't really surprising from a prince who raised both of his sons to think of themselves as heir," she muttered, scowling at nothing in particular.

About to retrace her steps yet again, she heard a sound that froze her in place. The prince's warning to beware the lions of al'Kalamir ringing in her ears, she'd actually taken two steps back when she realized that lions seldom sang and certainly weren't in the habit of adding new and salacious verses to Long-Legged Hazrah in a better than average baritone. When Hazrah stopped inspiring, the voice started in on The King's Menagerie. Although the echoes made it difficult to tell for certain, Terazin didn't think the singer had moved while she'd been listening.

Sighing, she pulled a monkey from her pocket and deftly flipped the coin up into the air. "Heads, I find him and make sure he isn't a threat. Tails, I ignore him and get on with the..."

Heads.

It took her longer to find him than she'd expected. He'd been standing at a dead end, probably inspecting the wall

for secret passageways when the floor underneath him had
given way, slanting suddenly downward. Her lamp resting
on the lip, Terazin squatted and stared down a slope too
slick and too steep to climb but angled with just enough
false promise that anyone caught would die trying.

The man in the hole had been silent since her light had
spilled into his prison.

"I can't pull you out," she said, setting her grappling
iron into the gap where the slope joined the floor and
dropping fifty feet of silk rope down into the hole, "so I
hope you can climb."

Her only answer was a tightening of the rope.

"Fine, be that way," she muttered. Pulling her dagger,
she laid the blade against the knot. If she didn't like what
she saw, she could always send him back into the pit and
have one of Essien's people retrieve him later. That he could
only be a fellow thief was not particularly reassuring —
in her experience thieves were not always the pleasantest
of people.

She could him breathing heavily — even with the rope
the climb wasn't an easy one. She heard him curse, heard
something, probably a knee, slam into the wall as he
slipped, then finally saw a hand come up into the light.
A second hand took a higher grip.

Not a thief. At least not a professional, the hands and
arms were far too large. And not a soldier, no soldier ever
wore that much jewelry — that much good jewelry, Terazin
amended, rapidly calculating the street value of each piece.
A heavy gold thumb ring set with a star sapphire flanked
by diamonds would buy her a few months' security even
after the Guild's commission. All right, not a thief, not a
soldier...

The top of his head came into the lantern light and
Terazin sucked air through her teeth. In this part of the
world, hair a brilliant red-gold meant only one thing.
Kerber. But Kerbers tended not to wear jewelry. So, like
Swan, he hadn't been raised in the tribes.

For Swan's sake, or maybe just for Swan's resemblance,
she couldn't send him back into the pit so, keeping her
dagger ready, she moved out of his way.

Concentrating on the climb, he didn't look up or speak until he was lying face down on the floor. He turned his head toward her, life braid sliding across his bare back, and wiped the sweat from his eyes with one shaking hand. "Who in the Netherhells are you?"

"You're welcome." Terazin shoved his leg aside and began to pull up her rope.

After a startled moment, he grinned and propped himself up on an elbow. "I do beg your pardon. Being down in a pit for two days does tend to wear at a man's manners. I am, indeed, most grateful for your rescue. And," he added, as a small bundle appeared wrapped in the last twenty-five feet or so of rope, "for retrieving my pitiful possessions. I left the robes down in the pit; after two days I'm sure you can understand why."

The bundle consisted of a flaccid waterskin and a pair of expensive sandals wrapped in a vest. Although plain, the vest's fabric had the heavy, fluid feel of high resale value. She tossed it to him and while he dressed, used the time to refill her lamp. When half the oil she carried was gone, she was leaving whether she'd found the treasure room or not.

"I don't suppose you're carrying food and water?" he asked at last.

"I might be." Although he sounded hopeful, not dangerous, she kept her gaze locked on his face, repacking rope and oilskin by touch. "But there's both waiting at the entrance."

"For you, perhaps, but not for me. If I show myself..."

"...your brother will kill you?"

One red-gold eyebrow rose and he smiled charmingly at her. "Have we met?"

Terazin ignored the charm and answered the question. "No, but there's only two people who want the regalia. I know you're not Essien so you have to be Jameel. Besides, you sound much the same when you talk. I expect that's why you didn't say anything until you were out of the pit."

"And you'd be right," Jameel admitted. "Although you must grant that I have the better singing voice."

"I wouldn't know," Terazin told him dryly. "I haven't heard your brother sing." He wore two long daggers in his belt. Probably Kerber steel although the bad light made it difficult to tell for certain.

Jameel tracked her gaze and spread both hands. "I'm not going to fight you for your supplies — that would be boorish in the extreme, considering you just saved my life."

"True."

"But as I'm not giving up my search for the treasure room nor going back down into that pit, it might be best if we work together."

He sounded so reasonable, she almost agreed. Then she remembered. "I'm working for your brother."

"It's a funny old world, isn't it? So am I."

Terazin snorted and stood.

"I tell you no lie, little thief." Jameel mirrored her action. "My brother has an army in the city, has secured the palace, and has hired the best mercenary troupe in the region. My army is scattered, I doubt I could even get my mother's family to fight for me again, and it's only a matter of time until I'm found and executed. It seemed to me that my only chance of survival is to be the one who presents the regalia to Essien."

"A peace offering?"

"Exactly."

It made sense. Terazin didn't care about the regalia, it was the treasure room's other contents she had plans for. "You'll swear you couldn't have done it without me? So I get paid?"

Jameel bowed, his life braid falling forward and lying like a line of fire along the crease of his neck. "I'll swear that I'd have died without you."

"Just remember that when we get out," Terazin muttered. She didn't trust him but it was hard not to like him although, besides the superficial resemblance he bore to Swan, she wasn't quite sure why. As he straightened, she threw him one of her waterskins. It made no sense to have saved him from the pit only to have him die of thirst. "The name's Terizan. And that's all the water you get," she warned him. "Ration yourself."

"My thanks, Terizan, for your generosity." He drank thirstily and, with an effort, re-corked the skin. Slinging it over his shoulder, he used the gesture to jauntily flick his lifebraid back. "Now what?"

A good question. Considering where she'd found him, it was a good bet the prince knew as little about the true path through the maze as she did. "It — or rather they — can't be classical mazes," she murmured, "too many thieves know the patterns. And yet it can't be too complex or no one would be able to remember the key."

"Only my father, may he rot in the Netherhells, and the grand vizier knew the key."

"Exactly..." Thinking of how long it had taken her to come this far, Terazin suddenly smiled. "We're going back."

"Back?"

"To the corridor leading to the maze entrances." She waved a hand toward the dead end. "Do you honestly think your father would put up with this sort of shit in order to get to something that belonged to him? The mazes are a distraction. There's another way."

"Brilliant."

"Thank you." Holding the lamp up to shoulder height at the first corner, she peered at the stone. "I've marked the..."

"Wall?" Jameel asked. His tone suggested this wasn't unexpected. "My father, may he rot in the Netherhells, had a wizard spell the maze," he explained as she whirled around to face him. "You can make as many marks as you want but the moment you stop looking at them, they disappear."

"So if I don't remember the way out?"

"Well, let's just say we're both going to get a lot thinner. And speaking of thinner," he added, gesturing at her pack. "You wouldn't have anything to eat in there would you?"

He looked so hopeful, she sighed and tossed him a bag of dates as they started down the corridor. "I don't suppose you know what the other two spells were?" she asked taking the first right.

"How do you know there's two more?"

"Essien told me there were three but he didn't know what they were."

"I know of one other besides the wall thing. My father, may he rot in the Netherhells, had a tapestry that had been magically woven to represent the catacombs. If a thief managed to get in, he could watch their progress. Watch them die."

"Lovely man."

"None lovelier." He licked his fingers clean and the red-gold brow rose again. "Are you sure this is the right way?"

Terazin turned left. "Yes. Where's the tapestry now?"

"The grand vizier used it as his shroud. It was wrapped around him when they lit the pyre."

"And the third spell?"

"I have no idea. I don't like to argue with a professional, Terizan, but I really think we need to go right here."

Terazin turned left again. "Why didn't your brother tell me about the walls and the tapestry?"

"I doubt he knew. He was always off learning to be a statesman or a swordsman, hoping our father, may he rot in the Netherhells, would approve of him."

"While you did what?"

"I hung around and sucked up, big time. Are you sure we're..."

"Yes." She turned right. "What about the lions of al'Kalamir?"

"Lions?" He had a pleasant laugh — or would have had, Terazin decided, had he not been laughing at her. "How could there be lions down here? It's too dark and there's nothing for them to eat. Present company excepted, of course."

"Of cour... shit on a stick!" They'd reached another dead end.

"You know, I did think that we should have turned right back there."

Spinning around, Terazin found her flat, unfriendly stare swamped by a well-I-did-mention-it-before sort of a smile. "Do you remember this part of the pattern from the tapestry?" she sighed.

Jameel spread his hands, rings winking in the lamplight. "I might."

Two rights, a left, and another dead end later, he added, as though no time had passed, "Or it might have been a lucky guess."

Terazin took a deep breath and exhaled slowly. Then she frowned and did it again, head lifted and turned back the way they'd come. "Here." She thrust the lamp into his hands. "Take this and stay here."

"Why?"

"Because I need to smell something other than lamp oil and you." She was out of the light by the time she reached the last corner. Eyes closed, she pivoted first to her left and then to her right. Now that she was taking the time to notice, she could smell, very faintly, the not entirely unpleasant aroma of rot.

ର ର ର

"How fortunate for us my brother didn't decide to hire you immediately."

"Not very fortunate for those soldiers," Terazin pointed out as they stepped out into the corridor connecting the two mazes.

"I expect they were mine, not his." He paused as they reached the t-junction and stared up toward the entrance to the catacombs. The angle hid the last body from view but all five were making their presence felt on the slight breeze. "I'll have to see what I can do about getting them out of here and burying them with full rights."

Bring a bucket, was Terizan's initial reaction but Jameel sounded so distressed she kept it, and other pertinent comments, to herself.

Now she knew what she was looking for, it took her no time at all to find the outline of the door in the stone wall. A few moments more and she uncovered the keyhole.

"I imagine you don't need the key?"

"That's right." Rummaging around in her pack, she brought out a package of dried figs. A strangled noise from Jameel made her look up.

"You're going to pick the lock with dried figs?"

"No." She handed him half. "We're going to eat while I refill the lamp."

He really did have a pleasant laugh.

☙ ☙ ☙

Behind the door, a flight of stairs lead down into a darkness too thick for Terizan's small light to make much of an impression. A dozen steps and the door closed behind them with a small, snick.

For a prince, Jameel knew a number of very creative profanities.

"Don't worry." Not even bothering to turn, Terazin took another two steps, wishing she could see just a little further than her own feet. "There's a latch on this side, I noticed it when we came through."

"You're sure?"

"Trust me. Neither your father nor the Grand Vizier had any more intention than I do of being trapped down here."

The stairs broadened as they descended. Level ground was a six foot wide corridor, tile not stone and judging from the small section they could see, probably beautiful.

"No turns," Terazin murmured.

"How can you tell?"

"The way the sound travels. Stay close." She'd counted forty-nine paces when something up ahead reflected back a glimmer of light. "Gold."

"That's it then." As Jameel surged past her, she heard a tiny click.

Sweeping his feet out from under him, she got him flat on the floor just in time.

They laid there for a few moments longer, staring up into the darkness. They could see neither the huge metal spike nor the mechanism that had swung it down out of the ceiling but it was a dominating presence never-the-less.

"Well." Jameel's voice bounced back off the ceiling. "It seems I owe you my life a second time."

Taking what seemed like her first breath in hours, Terazin turned her head toward him. "A third time. I also got us out of the maze."

Smiling, he shrugged as well as he was able given his position. "Sorry, you know what they say about the memories of princes."

Terazin snorted and rolled over onto her stomach. "Actually I do." Inching forward, pushing the lamp ahead, she pointed toward a slightly raised floor tile. "Look here. If you survived the way in, that one'll get you on the way back. Swan's right, your father was a very paranoid man."

"You have no idea."

"I'm beginning to."

A pair of shims jammed the trigger mechanisms although thief and prince both carefully stepped over the actual tile. It took them longer to cover the next eleven paces than it had to cover the first forty-nine but there were no more traps.

The double doors to the treasure room had been covered in beaten gold and the handles hung from the mouths of two beautifully crafted golden lions' heads.

"The lions of al'Kalamir."

"Don't touch them," Terazin warned. "They're probably the trigger to the third spell."

His fingertips a hair's breadth from the left lion, Jameel froze and slowly let his hand drop back to his side. "So what do we do?"

"You stand back while I pick the lock then we stuff something in the hole and use it to open the door."

"Very clever."

"Thank you." Pulling her two largest lockpicks from her trouser seams, she knelt, stared into the keyhole and shook her head. "The key must've been huge. I wonder where it is."

"I expect it went to the pyre with my father, may he rot in the Netherhells."

"Don't take this personally or anything but the vizier didn't seem to want either you or your brother to get hold of the regalia."

"Well, he didn't like us much." When pacing took him too quickly out of the light, he rocked back and forth, heel to toe. "You're an incredible person, you know that?"

"Why?" Terazin asked absently, most of her attention on the lock.

"Look what you've done. You've defeated my father, may he rot in the Netherhells, walked through his traps as though they weren't there, solved the puzzle of his maze, and saved me two — no, three — times."

Feeling slightly embarrassed by his enthusiasm, she pulled the last fig from her pocket, took a bite and chewed while she worked. "That doesn't make me an incredible person," she said at last and, using the larger of her two lockpicks, pulled the door open a few inches. "It merely makes me an incredible thief." Before she stood, she took a quick look at the mechanism. "Be careful, there's no latch on the inside of this, if the door closes while we're inside, we're stuck."

"So we'll be careful." He waited until she was standing beside him then flashed her a quick smile. "Shall we?"

The door was so perfectly balanced, it took almost no effort to swing it wide. From where they stood, the lamplight barely spilled over the threshold but that little bit refracted into a hundred sparkling stars. As they moved closer, the hundred stars became one until, blinking away afterimages, they stared down at the regalia of al'Kalamir. The crown rested in the circle of the pectoral, the two rings within the circle of the crown. Each section of the pectoral and both of the rings bore a piece of quartz the size of Terizan's thumbnail. Another piece over an inch across was centered in the front of the crown. Only the settings, a heavy red-gold almost the color of a Kerber life-braid, had any intrinsic value.

There was nothing else in the treasure room.

Taking a deep breath, Terazin set the lamp on the pedestal by the regalia. "Your brother is a pile of leprous baboon shit," she snarled.

"Granted," Jameel agreed, reaching out to touch the crown with a single finger. "Any particular reason you bring it up now?"

"I was to take my payment from the other items in the treasure room."

"And you think he knew there was nothing else in here?"

Mouth open to say just exactly what she thought, Terazin paused. It hadn't even occurred to her that he wouldn't have known.

"And you'd be right," Jameel continued. "We both knew. Father, may he rot in the Netherhells, made no secret of it."

"I didn't know," Terazin growled, "and he knew I didn't... What are you doing?"

Sapphire thumb ring tossed onto the pedestal, Jameel slid one of the regalia rings into its place. "Just trying things on. After all, this is my heritage as much as Essien's and this'll be my only chance." The second ring slid onto his other thumb. He laid the pectoral on around his neck without fastening the catch and settled the crown on his head. "Well, what do you think? Does it suit me?"

Even through her anger, she had to admit that it did. The gold of the crown almost disappeared in his hair so that the large piece of quartz seemed to float above his brow refracting far more light than it should have — more light, she suspected than was actually in the room. Had she not seen the regalia off Jameel, she'd have thought he was wearing a king's ransom in diamonds.

"It's the whole god-touched thing," he told her when she said as much, "but it only works when all the pieces are together and on a prince of Kalamir."

"You look better than Essien will," she muttered.

He laughed then suddenly sobered. "I'm sorry, Terizan."

"Why, because your brother is such a shit?"

"For that too."

It wasn't so much a blow as a hard shove into the back wall of the treasure room. Her head hit stone and, seeing stars, she slid to the floor. Jameel grabbed the lamp and stepped out into the corridor.

"I'm sorry," he said again, and closed the door.

All at once more tired than angry, Terazin got slowly to her feet, careful not to leave the definition of the wall.

The darkness was so complete, touch would be her only usable sense and she had no time to get lost, even in such small room. One hand against the back wall, she moved into a corner and halfway along the side. Jamming her left foot into the angle of floor and wall, she leaned out as far as she could and scooped Jameel's forgotten ring off the pedestal.

At least the trip isn't a total loss...

Straightening, she finished the side wall and reached the doors, pushing gently on the nearest. It swung silently open a handspan and she lightly touched the piece of dried fig she'd jammed into the mechanism. Getting in was only part of the problem, a good thief always made sure there was a way out.

She could see the lamp and realized Jameel had almost reached the stairs. There was a latch on the inside of that door but it wouldn't be easy to find. Still, it wouldn't hurt to slow him just a little bit more.

Not long before, she had stolen the Eye of Keydi-azda and ended up ensuring the continuing existence of eight small gods. Six of them still owed her for it. One of them had been Yallmaya, the Zephyr That Blows Trouble From the World. An emphatic prayer reminding Blessed Yallmaya of the debt — gods having much the same memory as princes — drew a gentle breeze past her cheek that grew to a gust of wind by the time it reached the other end of the corridor.

Terazin heard Jameel swear.

The lamp blew out.

His footsteps echoed in the corridor as he bounded up the stairs and under cover of the noise, Terazin walked eleven paces and squatted to check the trigger tiles. He'd taken the time to remove the shims. Clearly, he'd inherited some of his father's paranoia.

By the time she'd worked her way past the trap, Jameel was pounding on the inside of the door, not even searching for the latch, just trying to beat his way out. By the time she'd covered half of the forty-nine paces, his rising panic was beginning to make her regret blowing out the lamp. He'd spent two days, trapped in the dark, waiting to die

and she'd thrown him right back there again. His terror made it hard to remember that he'd left her to die in the treasure room.

By the time she reached the bottom of the stairs, she could hear only the sound of labored breathing from the top.

"You didn't pass the dead soldiers on the way in," she said softly, "or you'd have known they were yours. Two of them were Kerbers. You know another way into the catacombs and you'll use that to get out. You have no intention of taking the regalia to your brother and you never did."

"I locked you in." It was a token protest. It sounded more like he was saying, you're not really here. And saying it like he'd said it a hundred times before. Two days in complete darkness. Complete silence. Waiting to die.

"You thought you did."

"I reset the traps."

"So?"

Jameel laughed, a shaky sound but free of panic. "Oh yes, I forgot. You're very good at what you do. So, what happens now?"

He recovered quickly but she'd seen that before. He also moved very quietly for a large man — but not quietly enough.

"You go back up those two stairs," Terazin told him. "And we'll keep talking. You don't, I leave you alone in the dark."

"You can't get by me."

"Not as long as you stay by the door," she agreed. When she heard him return to the top of the stairs, she added, "We need each other to get out." Which wasn't entirely true. She could taunt him until he charged then easily slip by and have him bargain for his freedom with the regalia but she had as little intention of creating a powerful enemy as she did of leaving him in the catacombs to die. Thieves who never learned that the paths between people were as precarious as those along the edges of buildings, took fatal falls. "I suggest we go back to your original plan; you give the regalia to your brother in return for your life."

"No. I have as much right to rule as he does."

"Except that he's out there and you're in here and I was hired to get him that regalia."

"What do you care? Essien screwed you out of your payment!"

"Technically, no." In spite of everything, Terazin couldn't prevent a smile. After all, a similar technicality had gotten her into the Thieves' Guild. "Essien never said there was anything else in the treasure room. He's not responsible for my assumptions."

After a moment, Jameel sighed. "You're taking this rather well."

"Getting angry," she told him flatly, "doesn't change things. Now, are we going to stay here, in the dark, and argue about this or are we leaving?"

She heard him sigh again. "We're leaving."

"My way?"

"I can't stay down here."

"I know."

The third and final sigh had a reluctant smile shaping it. "Your way."

ഗ ഗ ഗ

Each piece of the regalia flared as Essien stroked it lightly with a reverent fingertip. Lifting his hand, he turned to the priests and curled his lip in what might have been a smile. "Satisfied?"

"We are satisfied, al'Kalamir." The priests looked so relieved Terazin had to wonder what would have happened to them had the regalia not been genuine. Removing the priests would certainly have removed any protests.

"Good." Continuing the turn so that the regalia was at his back, he allowed the smile to become genuine. "The coronation will be this afternoon. You'll all stay of course."

Terazin looked to Swan who shrugged and nodded.

"Good," Essien said again. "And afterwards, I'd be happy to have you witness the execution of my brother."

Jameel began to move but the guards who'd been flanking him grabbed his arms before he took his third step and forced him to his knees.

"My last bit of unfinished business," Essien murmured, patting his brother's cheek.

Ignoring instincts that told her not to get involved, Terizan's fingers clenched into fists. "He brought you the regalia!"

"There are two answers to that, little thief. The first is that, for reasons of your own which I do not need to know, you allowed him to carry the regalia out of the catacombs. Jameel may have handed it to me, but only through your efforts. The second response is a little more succinct." He spread his hands. "So?"

And that second response was impossible to argue with. One part of her mind watched Jameel struggle — his lifebraid, so like Swan's whipping back and forth as though it would be free on its own — and the other part tried to think of something, anything she could do. She felt Swan's hand close around her shoulder but she shrugged it off and stepped forward.

"What about my payment?"

Essien's dark brows rose. "I thought you said the treasure room was empty of everything but the regalia?"

"It was, but you said I could have anything I brought out." She nodded toward the struggling prince. "I want him."

Jameel stopped struggling.

"By your own words, I brought him out so by your word as al'Kalamir, he's mine."

"My word as al'Kalamir," Essien repeated. He walked around the small table so he could stare at his brother and the thief over the regalia.

The silence stretched and lengthened. Terazin could hear nothing from Swan and those of the Wing who were behind her. The Wing would take their cue from Swan and Swan seemed willing to let her play this out.

"My word as al'Kalamir," Essien repeated again. Glancing down at the regalia he frowned thoughtfully. "And you have made me al'Kalamir." When he glanced up again, he'd clearly come to a decision. "Very well, he's yours. But the next time I catch him..."

"He's on his own."

⊂℞ ⊂℞ ⊂℞

"That's four times you saved my life."

"It won't happen again," Terazin reassured him. "You're going back to your mother's people. And I'm going home."

One hand holding the flapping end of his veil, Jameel grinned down at her from the saddle. "Maybe I'll find myself a wife and settle down. Put all this behind me."

Terazin snorted. "Good luck."

⊂℞ ⊂℞ ⊂℞

"So, what happened between you and Jameel down in those catacombs?" Had Swan not been so well armed, Terazin might have attempted to exploit that suspicious tone with a little teasing. As it was..." I saved his life three times and the pile of leprous baboon shit tried to lock me into the treasure room."

"So you saved his life a fourth time?" The mercenary captain snorted.

"It seemed like the thing to do." She'd managed to block out most of her memories of their ride from Oreen to Kalamir. Everything except the nights with Swan had been hot, sandy, and painful. Horses were too far off the ground, saddles were not made for comfort, and Swan, while a surprisingly considerate lover, was a less than patient riding instructor. Now, once more in the saddle, it was all coming back to her. "He kept reminding me of you."

"Why?" Suspicion had made its move into jealousy.

"The life-braid. You have one just like it."

"Oh."

Terazin smiled at the tone and tried not to fall off her horse.

"So, did you ever find out about the lions?"

"Find out? I put one in charge and saved the other's life. The lions of al'Kalamir," she prodded when Swan looked blank. "al'Kalamir is the prince's title. Jameel and Essien were the lions."

"But why beware...."

"Jameel said the vizier didn't like them much. Since Essien killed him, his dislike seems to have been well founded."

"I'm sorry I got you into this."

"Why?"

Swan shrugged. "Beware the lions of al'Kalamir and all that. One of them cheated you and one of them tried to kill you after you saved his life four times."

"Only three times at the time."

"Still. I'd have been furious. In fact, I was furious for you."

Clinging to the saddle with both hands, Terazin smiled. "I don't get angry. Instead, I stole one of the regalia rings and I slipped it into Jameel's pocket when I said good-bye."

The mercenary captain sucked air through her teeth. "Essien's going to know it was you. You've left a powerful enemy back there."

"No. Jameel forgot a thumb ring in the treasure room. I grabbed it and left it in the missing ring's place."

"Essien will think Jameel took it."

"Uh huh."

"And I thought I brought you from Oreen to end a civil war."

"The war's over. They had to bring in mercenaries and Kerbers to fight this one. You were paid off when Essien got the regalia and the Kerbers have lost interest. Now, it's personal. Essien will never feel secure on the throne as long as a piece of the regalia is missing and Jameel will never feel secure knowing Essien's people will be coming after him."

They rode in companionable silence for a few minutes, wrapped in the noises of the Wing on the move.

"You know," Swan mused, "they could have lived happily ever after if you hadn't done this."

Terazin smiled over at her lover. "One of them cheated me and one of them tried to kill me after I saved his life four times."

"Three." Swan pointed out.

"Still..."

"Do you know what I think?"

"That beer is better than wine. That everything tastes better with enough dried chilies to kill a normal woman. That sex in a tent with a couple of dozen mercenaries listening in is perfectly normal. And..." Terazin winced as her horse changed his gait, the saddle rubbing against her inner thigh , "...that in spite of evidence to contrary, saddles are not instruments of torture."

"No... well, yes, but also that the lions of al'Kalamir should have been told to beware of you."

Even perched as precariously she was, it was difficult not to look smug. "Oh yeah. That too."

Sometimes, Just Because

"Was it something I said?"

Tribune Two paused, pale eyes narrowing, one hand raised to indicate the target on the map of Oreen.

Tribune Three snickered in what could, in no way, be considered a reassuring manner, amusement sending oily drops of sweat dancing down the smooth rolls of his neck.

Tribune One lifted a sardonic brow; as much, it seemed at her companions as at the thief facing them. "Why do you ask?"

"First you want me to steal from gods; now wizards." Terizan scratched at a flea bite on her forearm. "If I didn't know better, I'd think you were trying to get rid of me."

"Get rid of you?" One asked, eyebrows moving from sardonic to exaggerated shock. "The only thief to ever make it all the way to the Sanctuary?"

"The thief who can bring Swan and her Wing of mercenaries to heel?" Two added.

Three rolled his eyes heavenward. "The thief who dares to steal from the gods themselves and in such a way she benefits from the theft?"

"The thief who holds the debt of the al'Kalamir for bringing his regalia out of a trapped and enchanted treasure room?"

"The thief whose current investments with the Guild have reached close to record levels in a record amount of time?"

"Why would you think the Guild would want to get rid of you?"

Terizan shrugged, the movement causing a dribble of moisture to run down her sides, making her cotton tunic less comfortable and even more fragrant. "Just a feeling."

"Besides," One amended with an aristocratic snort, "it's only one wizard."

"Right."

"And even were you not the best we have, your sensitivity to magic would make you the logical choice."

"Uh huh. Usually, my sensitivity allows me to avoid magic. Breaking into a wizard's tower and stealing a curse..."

"A curse anchor," Three offered helpfully when she paused.

Terizan nodded her thanks. "...is not avoiding. It's st..." Suddenly realizing that the Thieves Guild Tribunal might think she was calling them stupid instead of the concept and fully aware that the consequences of such a misunderstanding would likely not be in her favor, she forced her tongue around a different combination of letters. "...range. Strange to think I could even get into a wizard's tower."

"Strange but not impossible," One replied, the twist in her lips a fair indication she'd actually heard the original word but was content to ignore it for now. "The Council has given us full plans of not only the grounds around the wizard's tower but of the interior of the tower itself with all known spells and enchantments marked."

"The wizard's servant was most forthcoming," Three added, smiling broadly.

"Tortured?" Terizan asked.

"Bribed." From the tone, she assumed Tribune Two would have preferred the former. "The woman came to the Council when it became clear that this recent heat was the wizard's doing."

"Gee, since she's frying too I'm surprised she didn't offer the information from the goodness of her heart." Raising a hand between her and the three nearly identical expressions facing her, Terizan sighed. "Sorry. Kidding. Go on."

"Besides your percentage of the rather sizable fee the Council is paying us to steal this anchor, you will of course be able to remove anything else that takes your fancy."

Take anything else she fancied from a wizard's tower? They really were trying to get rid of her.

Something of the thought must have shown on her face as Two leaned forward, map crinkling under damp palms. "Of course, if you refuse the job, we'll only have to send someone else."

Someone less likely to succeed.

One and Three looked at her and smiled.

Someone less likely to survive.

It was a bitch being the best.

ов ов ов

"Okay. Let me see if I got this straight." Balthazar leaned against the doorjamb, arms folded, brow furrowed. "The wizard's pissed at Council for telling him to cut down that big thorny hedge so he makes it hot. His servant goes to Council and tells them the wizard is making it hot and for a price, she'll tell how to stop it. Council comes here and tells the Tribunal they'll pay them to steal the thing the wizard's using to make it hot. The Tribunal gives you the job so you're going to steal an anchor from the wizard?"

"Essentially, yes." Terizan tested the grip of a grappling hook, tossed it back in the basket, and pulled out another.

"Ain't anchors kinda big?"

"It's not that kind of an anchor. It's just a small item the wizard is using to focus the curse."

"Oh." He stuffed his hand into his armpit and scratched vigorously. "You get all the good jobs."

"Balthazar, do you remember what wizards do to thieves they catch?" Crossing the storeroom, she ran questing fingertips over the ropes sorted onto a row of brass hooks by length and weight.

"Sure. They turn them into mice then set the cat on them."

"I don't want to be a mouse."

"I wouldn't mind."

As she turned toward him, an eyebrow rose in a conscious imitation of Tribune One.

"Right. Bare feet shuffled against the tile. "But you won't get caught, you're the best."

Right. And that was working out so well for her. Gods. Wizards...

"You never get caught," he added mournfully.

He'd been caught twice. Once more and the guild would ground him — Magistrates were expensive in Oreen and the guild wouldn't pay out indefinitely.

It was, if possible, hotter in the storeroom than it had been in the Inner Sanctum. Hotter and dustier. Wiping her face on her tunic left a grey/brown smear across the fabric. One more thing and she could head for the relative cool of the streets.

"What happened to your stuff?" the older thief wondered as she sorted through the lock picks for a set that felt right in her hand.

"Nothing."

"Then what's with the shopping spree?"

"Items you use frequently become imprinted with your... essence."

"Scent?"

"Close enough." Terizan tossed the set of picks that felt the least wrong into her pack. "I'm not taking anything into that tower that might tell the wizard who I am."

ରେ ରେ ରେ

"Sweetling, wizards are not exactly in my line of work. They're reclusive, every last one of them. They have no interest in the pleasures of the flesh, they're only interested in the pursuit of obscure knowledge and their only indulgence is arcane ritual." Poli frowned at her in the mirror, a minimalist expression that wouldn't disturb his cosmetics. "What?"

Grinning, Terizan waved a hand at the bottle, jars, and brushes. "Arcane ritual?"

"Don't be ridiculous; this is skill, not magic." A touch of oil on his lower lip and he turned to face her, looking stylized and beautiful.

"Looks like magic to me," she told him fondly. Poli in cosmetics looked more like himself. If she'd tried to apply an equivalent amount of paint and powder, she'd have looked like one of the priests of Busoo, the God of Laughter. "So if you have no first hand knowledge..." She handed him his robe as he stood. "...have you heard anything?"

Eventually, the whores heard everything.

"Sweetling, you're not listening — wizards don't use the services of my guild."

"People who work for wizards do. Don't they?"

"No." He narrowed kohled eyes and sighed. "Terizan, have you agreed to steal something from the wizard's tower?"

"You know I can't answer that."

"Wonderful. So, sharing your bed with an insane mercenary captain isn't enough to satisfy this sudden death wish of yours? Now, you want to be turned into cat food?"

"One." Terizan flicked a calloused finger into the air. "Swan isn't insane, she's just really, really good at what she does which happens, incidentally, to be mayhem. Two." A second finger followed the first. "I don't have a death wish, I have a reputation as the best thief in the city and that brings with it certain unavoidable responsibilities but I have every intention of surviving the experience. And three." She folded the first finger down.

"You can't afford me, Sweetling."

આ આ આ

The oldest of the storytellers throwing words into the air on the Street of Tales insisted there were once three wizard towers in Old Oreen. A non-descript neighborhood of middle-class shops and houses had grown up over the ruin of one, the squalid hovels and tenements of the Sink covered another, and the third stood alone. Had stood alone for as long as anyone could remember.

According to the storyteller, that middle-class neighborhood produced more than its share of priests and artists and the totally insane. And the Sink — well, every city had a cesspool, the Sink was the cesspool of Old Oreen.

"Do the stories say how those two towers were destroyed?"

"They do." The storyteller sucked her teeth and waited, right arm raised so she wore her cupped hand like a hat, the bowl of her palm facing the sky. Or at least the awning over her square of pavement.

Terizan sighed and dropped a monkey into the old woman's hand. She waited patiently while the brass coin vanished into the folds of a grimy robe and a little less patiently as a small leather bottle was consulted.

"It was a dark and stormy night," the storyteller began at last, adding, as Terizan's brows rose, "No, really, it was. A dark and stormy night..." She cleared her throat. "...thunder, lightening, hail. A night that cleared the streets of all the good citizens of Oreen — as few as they were within the walls in those dark days. When the ground beneath the city shook and the air filled with the scent of burning hair and the screams of tormented souls rode on the backs of howling winds, no one dared to turn an eye to the cause. No one but one small boy," she added hurriedly as Terizan opened her mouth to protest. "A small boy who swore he saw ribbons of red spiraling from one tower, ribbons of blue from another, and bands of white around the third. In the morning there was but one tower remaining and blasted, empty, cursed ground where the other two had stood."

"Two of them fought, the third shielded himself."

"So it seems." Her hand rose once more to lie against her head and Terizan sighed.

"That wasn't worth another monkey. What was said of the remaining wizard?"

"Ah, young one, the stories I could tell you..."

Terizan twirled the coin between her fingers. "Give me the high points without embellishing and this is yours."

"Embellishing." Rheumy eyes narrowed. "A large word for one in your profession."

A second coin joined the first. "A large fee for one in yours."

"True enough, times being what they are."

Terizan didn't ask how times were. It would only lead to more stories and a higher expected payment.

"They say that the wizard remains in that tower to this day, extending his life by fell magics. That he is secretive, even for a wizard. That young women enter his tower and emerge as old women a lifetime later with no memory of their service. They say he lives on moonlight and dew. That those who try to breach his solitude meet a grisly doom." She snatched the tossed coins out of the air with the ease of long practice. "You know about the whole thief-mouse-cat thing?" When Terizan nodded, her face refolded itself into a new pattern of contemplative wrinkles. "Your guild must value your talents highly."

"Yeah, that's what they keep telling me..."

ℭ ℭ ℭ

Although space was at a premium in Old Oreen, no one had attempted to build up against the wall that defined the triangular grounds surrounding the wizard's tower — which was more than a little annoying since it meant Terizan would have to cross a broad, open street in full view of the tower's upper windows no matter which part of the wall she approached. On the bright side, the neighboring houses had turned their backs to the wizard, presenting no windows and therefore no likelihood that she'd be seen and the Guard called.

"Because there's nothing like worrying about being arrested when you should be worried about becoming a mouse," Terizan muttered. Torches in iron brackets jutted from the top of the wall not quite close enough together to prevent narrow bands of shadow between them — thieves' paths. The trick would be reaching one.

Hidden in the darkness where the back of one house joined another, she ticked off items on her mental copy of the servant's list.

"The gate and the path from the gate to the tower are heavily warded. Step on it and my master will know everything there is to know about you."

No problem. She hadn't planned on taking either the gate or the path.

"The thorn hedge that grows around the inside of the wall is not magical but it is deadly. You must move slowly, methodically to defeat it."

Defeat it? Terizan had no intention of fighting with it.

"The only safe way to enter the tower is from above. My master keeps pigeons and has no desire to know everything there is to know about them but they will act as an alarm if you're not careful."

Pigeons. Flying rats. The thief who didn't plan for their presence on every rooftop in Old Oreen had a short career.

"I'll leave the trapdoor unbarred."

Once inside the tower things got... complicated but she'd worry about that later.

The crescent moon slid behind a cloud.

Wiping sweaty palms against her thighs, Terizan took a deep breath, locked her gaze on the path she planned to use, and raced forward. Time had worn a handy ladder of hand and foot holds in the wall. At the top, her body pressed against the capstones, the sandstone still warm from the heat of the day, she turned in place, and slowly — very, very slowly — began to climb down between the thorns and the wall.

Fortunately, the thorns were attached to big bushes rather than any kind of clinging vine and the space between bushes and wall, although not exactly generous, was almost wide enough to slide through unscathed. As long as she kept herself from snatching punctured body parts away, she was reasonably sure she could avoid attracting further attention from the bush.

Attracting attention from a bush. This is why I hate stealing from wizards.

One of the reasons anyway. That whole thief/mouse/cat thing didn't thrill her.

When her feet touched the ground, she shuffled them sideways until she lay in the angle between earth and wall

staring out between twisted trunks as big around as her arm at a grassy lawn. Two body lengths, maybe two and a half, and she'd be in the clear. Crawling forward on fingers and toes, she tried to ignore the debris mixed into the leaf litter and the heated, heavy smell of rot. Things impaled on the thorns eventually fell. Instincts very nearly had her claim a heavy gold ring, but a hint of brass changed her mind. Moving on, she left it — and the finger bone that wore it — where it lay.

Should the wizard happen to look out the right windows, he'd see her on the lawn. All the hair lifting off the back of her neck, Terizan unhooked the crossbow from across her chest and fired the grappling hooks toward the roof, fully intending to be off the lawn as quickly as possible. A faint hiss of metal against stone and two of the padded edges caught.

By the time she reached the roof, any pigeons startled by the appearance of the grapple had gone back to sleep. Shadow silent, Terizan coiled her rope, replaced the grapple in her pack and slipped past the coop.

The trap door was locked.

It wasn't supposed to be locked.

Isn't it fortunate I have trust issues. She hadn't become the best by leaving things to chance. Or disgruntled servants. After screwing a hook into the center of the wooden door, she carefully slid a metal tube from the thieves pocket in the wide seam of her trousers, ran a fingernail through the wax seal, unscrewed the metal stopper, and outlined a rough square out about two inches from the edge of the door. She had no idea what the liquid was but the alchemist had assured her it would get rid of problem tree stumps. He'd also warned her that it was highly illegal to use on anything but problem tree stumps and had winked broadly while pocketing his extremely high fee.

The wood dissolved.

Terizan lifted out the square and found herself staring down into the emerald gaze of a plump calico cat sitting on the topmost landing of a spiral staircase.

Tossing a cotton square stuffed with dried catmint down the stairs - thief/mouse/cat implied there would be a cat

somewhere in the tower — she dropped quickly to the landing as the cat disappeared.

The room she wanted was on the next landing down.

There was a wizard globe outside the door. She waited until her eyes adjusted to the light, checked for traps, and pushed open the door finger-tips touching only the random pattern of wood not imprinted with magic.

The wizard's workroom looked exactly the way Terizan expected a wizard's workroom to look, crowded with books and scrolls and a confused jumble of a hundred arcane objects — although she hadn't expected the wizard's servant to be pacing back and forth in front of a full length mirror. The two women stared at each other for a long moment.

"The trap door was barred," the servant said at last, crossing her arms over a plump bosom.

Terizan shrugged. "I noticed."

"A final test." She nodded toward the room's only window. As far as Terizan could tell from her position by the door, it looked out on the darker, less exposed side of the tower. "I was watching for you."

"I came up the other side."

"But that side…"

"Wasn't being watched," Terizan pointed out. Good thieves learned early on that the way less traveled usually had more guards on it. "As long as you're here, where's the anchor?"

Nothing stood out. If she had to find it on her own in this mess, she'd be here for hours.

"The what?"

"The thing the wizard's anchoring the heat to!"

"Oh, that."

"Oh that?" For someone who'd allegedly gone to the Council, with the information - who'd been paid a great deal of money for the information - she sounded as if this was the first she'd heard of either anchor or, for that matter, heat. The general, all purpose, what-kind-of-an-idiot-steals-from-a-wizard bad feeling Terizan had had since her meeting with the Tribunal, began to grow more specific.

A sound on the landing outside the workroom took her from stool, to table's edge, to bookshelf, to balanced on the top of the thick, open door. When the wizard - Who else would be on the landing in a wizard's tower outside a wizard's workroom? — came into the room, she'd drop down behind him and make a run for it.

Thief-mouse-cat. Not going to happen.

Glaring down at the wizard's servant, she laid a silencing finger against her mouth just as the calico cat stalked into the room.

"My master isn't here," the servant sighed. "That's why you are."

"What?"

"He's been stolen."

"What?"

"I need you to steal him back."

Terizan opened her mouth and closed it again. Carefully avoiding the cat - all things considered, staying on the cat's good side seemed smart — she jumped down off the top of the door. "The wizard's been stolen?"

"Yes."

"Don't you mean kidnapped?"

"No, stolen. Turned into a doll, and then stolen right from this room."

"By who?"

She glanced over her shoulder at her reflection. "Something from the mirror."

Something? That didn't sound good. "Another wizard?"

"I don't know. The mirror showed me what happened but not the form of my master's enemy."

Terizan glanced at the mirror but saw only the reflected servant and workroom. "And you want me to steal him back?"

"Yes."

"From the something in the mirror?"

"Yes."

"Go into the mirror, and steal him back?"

"Yes."

"Are you nuts?"

"No."

She sounded so matter-of-fact that Terizan frowned. "Is there some sort of spell on this place that kicks in if he's not back by a certain time? Something that would destroy the city?"

"Goodness, no!"

"Then why would I agree to steal him back from something inside a mirror?"

"Because you're the best."

"Oh for…" Throwing up her hands, Terizan pivoted on one heel, took two steps out onto the landing, pivoted again and took two steps back. "First, how do you know that?"

"You're here."

Okay. Terizan had to admit that was fairly solid evidence.

"The Council went to the Tribunal," the wizard's servant continued, "and the Tribunal chose you. They wouldn't have chosen anyone but their best - that's why I went to them, why I told them the story I did. I couldn't risk not having the best."

"So the wizard isn't causing the heat?"

"It's summer. It's always hot in the summer and people always seem to forget that."

"It's hotter than usual. And for longer."

The servant shook her head. "No, it isn't. What was your second point?"

"My what?"

"You said first. That implies a second."

Wondering why she didn't just walk away, Terizan reversed the conversation far enough to remember what her second point had been. "What does my being the best have to do with agreeing to steal the wizard back? Wouldn't you assume that, as the best, I'd be too smart to do something so stupid?"

"I assumed that, as the best, you would rise to the challenge."

Terizan found the urge to slap the smug smile off the older woman's face almost impossible to resist. The only thing that stopped her was the knowledge that she'd heard

the plan, that nothing was preventing her from leaving, and she was still standing in the wizard's workroom. "What's in it for me? And if you're about to say, the challenge..." Arms folded, Terizan curled a lip and put on her best street tough expression. "...think again. I'm a thief, not a hero."

"When he is safely returned to his tower, my master will reward you. My master has many, many treasures. Gold. Jewels."

"Your master is a doll."

"Not once you return him here and I put this around his neck." The bronze amulet dangling from the servant's hand wouldn't have been worth more than a monkey on the street, maybe another monkey for the chain. "This protects him from magical attack. Had he been wearing it at the time, he would never have been changed and taken."

"Why wasn't he?"

"It turns his neck green." Sighing deeply, she dropped it into her apron pocket. "Every now and then, he takes it off to bathe."

"Right."

Gold.

Jewels.

No other thief in the guild could claim to have stolen a wizard back from inside a magic mirror.

Oh no. Don't even think that. You are not... Terizan caught sight of the expression on the servant's face and sighed. *Oh crap. Yes, you are and she knows it too.* "All right, you win. What do I have to do?"

"Just walk into the mirror."

"And he'll be right there?"

"If I expected it to be that easy," the older woman sighed, "would I need the services of the best thief in Oreen?"

Good point.

Her gaze locked on her reflection - which didn't look happy - Terizan crossed the workroom, tripped over a box of scrolls, and only just managed to stop herself from hitting the floor by grabbing a handful of apron.

"You're not filling me with confidence, here." She slapped Terizan's hands away from the bunched fabric and straightened it herself.

"You want confident?" Terizan muttered stepping forward. "How's this: if this is a trick and I find myself with my nose mashed against the glass and you laughing, I'll kick your..."

"...ass."

Her body sizzling in reaction, she found herself standing alone in a reflected version of the wizard's workroom. Heart pounding, she spun around to face the mirror and discovered her reflection had not crossed over with her. A hand against the glass found only that — glass.

It seemed that she needed the wizard in order to get home.

"Oh goody." The words echoed slightly. "Incentive."

CR CR CR

A quick search determined that the doll-wizard was not in the tower. In fact there were no magical items of any kind - every thing was show without substance. And speaking of show... Terizan walked to the window and looked out over a city that was almost but not quite Oreen. Like the workroom, like the tower, everything had been reversed - mirror imaged - but that wasn't the most disturbing change. Oreen never slept. The streets were never empty of people. The air was never still and quiet.

This Oreen looked and sounded abandoned.

No. Never lived in.

It was nearly midnight on the other side of the mirror, a dark night with a cloud covered crescent of moon. A thieves' night. On this side, a cold grey sky shed a cold grey light and a thief would have to be very good indeed to move through the city un-remarked.

According to the story-teller, there had once been three towers in Old Oreen.

If she had to search Oreen for the wizard doll, the logical place to start would on the site of one of those two towers.

Which tower, though? Which of the defeated wizards seemed the most pissed off about it? On the ruins of one - a middle class neighborhood. On the ruins of the other — the Sink.

Personal prejudices suggested she should head towards the middle class neighborhood. Fortunately, she was merely prejudiced, not delusional.

One problem: this was not the Oreen the towers had disappeared from, this was her Oreen, a copy of the city on the other side of the mirror and in her Oreen there was only one tower. She could see the Sink. She couldn't see the tower.

Maybe when she was closer.

How do you get to the Sink?

You slide in on shit of your own making.

Street wisdom aside, there were a number of ways into the Sink.

Taking the direct route, she could walk down the middle of the street unimpeded by people or dogs or mountebanks or constables or priests. It would be the fastest and the simplest route, it would shorten the length of time she'd have to spend inside the mirror - definitely a plus — and, as she'd told the wizard's servant, those were the routes that were seldom watched.

Seldom. Not never.

The hair lifting off the back of her neck convinced her to stay out of sight.

By the time she reached the Street of Tears - a road that had once lead between a long demolished jail and the executioner's block in the Crescent and that now marked the edge of the Sink - she knew she wasn't alone even though she'd seen and heard nothing. As a rule, her instincts were good and she was willing to give them the benefit of the doubt.

Might have been nice if they'd stopped me from walking into the mirror in the first place, though. Or if they'd made some noise during that whole 'here's a challenge you can't resist' thing.

If she knew the 'something' was there then the odds were good the 'something' knew she was there as well even

if didn't know exactly where. Slipping into the Sink, she worked harder to stay hidden.

"But you won't get caught, you're the best."

Her gut told her this would be the worst possible time to disprove Balthazar's statement. Caught on this side of the mirror, there'd be no guild to buy her freedom.

The air was so still she could feel it move past her and the silence left her no masking noises to hide behind. On the bright side, the filth and decay that usually choked the Sink's narrow streets had form but no substance. On the other hand, she was beginning to see teeth in the shadows.

Given a choice, she'd have taken the filth and decay no matter how hard it was on the sandals.

About a third of the way in, she could feel the tower although the way its presence danced against her skin like a thousand invisible ants kept her from being really happy about it. She still couldn't see it though, and that would make breaking into it just a little more difficult than usual.

Crouched on a roof between a crumbling chimney and a pile of debris, Terizan peered at the space she knew the tower filled and wondered what in the names of the small Gods was she supposed to do now. How did a thief, even the best of thieves, break into a feel...

She froze. Held her breath. Tried to stop her heart from beating so loudly inside her chest. She wasn't alone on the roof.

It was behind her. Whether it was tracking her or had merely found her was irrelevant - it was there. And coming closer. Hunting her.

What does a good thief do when the situation can't be salvaged?

They steal away.

All things considered, not very helpful.

Running like all seven Hell's however, that sounded like an option.

Breaking cover, Terizan sprinted for the edge of the roof and flung herself across the gap between the buildings. She'd leapt greater distances a hundred times - one of the nice things about the Sink was how close together the

buildings were. And one of the unfortunate things was how structurally unsound those buildings were. Under normal circumstances, she'd have never jumped without being certain of where she was going to land.

Not normal circumstances.

The Hunter landed in the space she'd just vacated sending a frisson of terror through blood and bone. It was close enough now for her to feel more than just 'something'.

Hunger.

As her feet slammed down on the ancient yellow bricks, they began to crumble. Throwing herself forward did little good with nothing solid underfoot to push off from.

Terizan had originally joined the thieves' guild because a cornice had crumbled and she'd fallen a story and a half to the ground. Fingers scrabbling for purchase on disintegrating brick, she realized through the building panic that this fall was going to be a whole lot worse. The last time, there'd been nothing waiting for her when she hit the ground.

Closing her eyes, she silently cursed all wizards, their servants, and their stupid invisible towers!

Thick sod cushioned her impact with the ground, leaving her winded but essentially unharmed.

Sod? Her eyes snapped open. She'd been expecting cracked cobblestones, a cracked skull, and rending teeth not the well manicured lawn surrounding what had to be the second wizard's tower. A quick roll tucked her under the cover of a garden bench. She lay there unmoving, counting her heartbeats, until it became clear no one had seen her.

Or they had seen her and were waiting for her to further commit herself.

I should be committed. Looking on the bright side, the Hunter hadn't followed her over the wall. It probably knows that I'm in enough trouble without it. Although, considerate invisible monsters were of dubious comfort right now.

Crawling forward on elbows and toes, Terizan peered out of her sanctuary. Living in the middle of an empty city, this wizard had no need for thorn bushes to discourage

visitors. Even in the real Oreen, being invisible would probably be defense enough - although she knew a number of people it wouldn't discourage.

The second tower looked a lot like the first. The biggest difference was in the number and design of the windows - there were more of them and they all boasted decorative stonework on lintels and sills creating a thieves stair right to the roof. The whole place pulsed with magic. The last thing Terizan wanted to do was spend more time than she had to inside but if the wizard's workshop was in the same place, and the wizard wasn't in the workshop, she could be in and out the open window in two shakes of a cat's tail.

And what if the wizard was in the workshop?

What if the doll-wizard wasn't?

Telling herself firmly to stop borrowing trouble, Terizan started her climb.

At least I don't have to worry about being spotted by someone outside the tower grounds. Did outside the tower grounds even exist? High enough to see over the wall, she balanced securely on top of a protruding lintel, jammed her fingers into the space between two bricks, twisted her gaze back over her shoulder, and nearly fell. The city both did and didn't exist - rippling in and out of sight like a desert mirage behind a curtain of heat.

More wizardry!

Stifling a snort, she started to climb again. At this point in the game there wasn't going to be less wizardry.

Below the edge of the uppermost window, she paused, and listened. The silence was so overwhelming she feared for a moment that she'd gone deaf and lightly rubbed her fingers against the ledge of dressed stone just to hear the soft shrk shrk.

Not deaf then. Good.

Her breathing shallow and as quiet as she could make it, Terizan adjusted her grip and peered over the edge of the window ledge.

The workshop looked so much like the one she'd first broken into that she wasted half a heartbeat wondering if she'd gotten turned around and was at the wrong tower.

Then she started noticing the differences. No mirror - magic or otherwise — dominated an inside wall. More scrolls were piled haphazardly than shelved. And in a space hurriedly cleared by shoving a jumble of odds and ends aside - where one of the odds was an emerald as big Terizan's thumbnail and one of the ends a string of tiny gold skulls — stood an eleven inch doll wearing not particularly well-carved wizard's robes.

No sign of the second wizard.

Unless it had been the wizard chasing her through the city...

Do not go there!

Because if it had been the wizard, there was no way this could end well.

She pulled herself up and into the room, pausing for a moment crouched under the window to make sure her entry had gone unnoticed. No point in moving away from an exit she might have to suddenly use.

When no alarms sounded and no magical flares went off, she hurried across the room to the doll. It didn't look like much. It certainly didn't look it had once been alive. It looked... well, it looked kind of skinny and ineffectual, if truth be told.

Now she'd found what she'd been sent for, time was of the essence. Terizan didn't know where the other wizard was — in bed, in the kitchen, in the privy - and it didn't matter, she had to be back on the other side of the mirror before the wizard returned to the work room and noticed the doll was missing.

Grappling hooks pulled out of chest pack, doll shoved in, hooks set, rope dropped out the window, and a quick slide to the ground. She shook down her gear, sprinted across the lawn, climbed to the top of the wall and...

Oreen continued to pulse in and out of sight. Sprawled along the capstone, she fought the urge to puke as she closed her eyes and rolled off the wall. Considering how she'd gotten into the tower grounds, there seemed to be only one logical way to get out.

Ow!

Cobblestones.

Her shoulder blades were hard against the nearest building before her eyes were fully open. Bruises could be inventoried later; right now it was more important to get out of sight. The Hunter could be...

Something between a sound and a feeling drew her gaze upward. She could see only crumbling yellow brick and above it a pale grey sky but she knew the Hunter was perched on the roof of the building directly above her, staring down at her. Terizan froze, expecting it to pounce, knowing she couldn't move fast enough to avoid it.

No pounce.

It seemed to be moving back from the edge.

Heading for the stairs...

A terrifying supernatural hunter that had to take the stairs? That cranked the terrifying down a notch or two, releasing her from her paralysis and lending speed to her feet. Maybe it hadn't followed her over the tower wall because it couldn't make the jump between the buildings, not because of magics designed to keep it out. If she took the high road across the city, the thieves' path that used the spaces between the buildings as much as the buildings themselves, maybe it wouldn't be able to follow her.

If she could just reach the other tower - the first tower — she'd be safe.

Unfortunately, as she dropped down into the angle where the back of one house joined another, the copy of the hiding place she'd used to study the wizard's wall back when the night was new, she felt the Hunter's presence in front of her. It had apparently also realized that if she reached the first tower she'd be safe.

Muscles trembling, joints aching, Terizan slumped to the ground and fought to keep her labored breathing from giving her away. Her chosen craft tended toward intense moments of specific exercise rather than marathon exertions. Between the climbing of two towers and the crossing and re-crossing of half of Oreen, she was exhausted. She had no energy left to fight the Hunter even if she'd had any idea of how to fight it.

And the next time someone feeds you a line of crap about how you're the only thief good enough to steal an enchanted wizard back from inside a mirror, what are you going to say?

Terizan, you're an idiot.

Harsh, but true.

The doll looked no worse for its trip across the city. Reaching deep into her thieves' pocket, Terizan pulled out the brass amulet the servant had said would return the wizard to his human form. She'd stolen it from the servant's apron during her bit of pre-mirror stumbling. A good thief realized that getting in was usually the lesser part of the job - getting out again with the goods, that was the tricky bit and it sometimes helped to have a little leverage.

The Hunter brushed against the edge of her senses.

Of course, it also helped to be alive.

Amulet poised to drop over the doll's head, Terizan hesitated.

If she brought the wizard back here, in the angle with her, he'd demand an explanation. Before she'd have a chance to give one, the Hunter would be upon them and with the wizard's attention on her, they'd be doomed. So he had to come back with his full attention on the Hunter.

Setting the doll so that it faced the broad street between the houses and the tower, Terizan threw herself up the narrow end of the angle until she perched between the two walls a long body-length from the ground. All she had to do now was drop the amulet over the doll's head.

Which would be a lot easier if her hands would stop shaking.

Okay on three.

One.

She could feel the Hunter approaching, moving fast and with the kind of purpose that suggested it knew exactly where she was.

Oh screw it.

She dropped the amulet.

No flash of light, no colored smoke - just a doll one moment and a wizard the next. And the moment after that...

"Oh dear!"

Which, as an initial observation concerning the Hunter, didn't sound very martial. Or very wizard-like for that matter. Terizan had to admit she'd been expecting something more along the lines of "Be gone foul fiend!" Or maybe an instant flare of eldritch fire.

Cowering. That can't be good!

Fortunately, the eldritch fire came an instant after the cowering and, as the after images faded, Terizan realized she could no longer feel the Hunter. Skinny, the wizard definitely was. Ineffectual, apparently not.

Body language suggesting confusion more than victory, he began to turn when a poof of displaced air announced the arrival of the second wizard. Appearing in the alcove behind his former captive, he was clearly counting on the element of surprise. As his hands came up and the air began to crackle, Terizan adjusted her grip on a protruding brick, briefly considered the Guild's position on non-violence, and kicked him in the head.

He dropped like a rock.

She lifted her gaze from the crumpled body to find the first wizard, the doll-wizard, staring up at her.

"Do I know you?"

"No." How much should she tell him? How much would it be safe to tell him? How safe would it be to lie to him considering that even if she could get the amulet off him, he wouldn't become a doll and she needed him to get back through the mirror? "I'm the thief your servant hired to steal you back."

The wizard blinked; the movement slow and deliberate enough that Terizan tensed for magic. "Ahmalayz hired a thief?"

No magic. Just a puzzled question. "It's a long story."

"I'm sure it must be. I wasn't aware you could hire thieves. The same way you hire a... a gardener?"

Her fingers were starting to cramp. "Something like that."

"Oh." He glanced down at the other wizard then back up at her. "You're very thorough."

"Yeah, well..." She shrugged as much as her position allowed. "I'm the best."

"I see. I guess you'd have to be, though, wouldn't you?" They stared at each other for a long moment then the wizard gestured toward his tower. "We'd better be going before Zafran wakes up."

"You're not going to turn him into something unpleasant?"

Pale grey eyes blinked again. "Should I?"

"He turned you into a doll."

"Yes, well I sent him…" Another gesture, this one taking in their immediate surroundings. "…here. Things even out don't they?" Without waiting for an answer, he turned started along the road toward the gate.

Figuring that Zafran still had a way to go before he settled the score, Terizan dropped to the ground and hurried to catch up.

"So, this is what Oreen looks like." His tone was conversational, mildly curious; they might have been walking home from the market.

"You live in Oreen."

"I don't get out much."

According to the stories, he didn't go out at all. "How did that other wizard…"

"Zafran?"

"Yeah, him." Terizan might be fool enough to think she could steal a wizard-doll from inside a magic mirror but she wasn't fool enough to make free with a wizard's name. Names had power. "If he's been here for so long, how does he know how Oreen looks?"

"He doesn't. Zafran's landscaping runs to nothingness and fog. This seeming of the city came from your mind."

"My mind?" Suppressing a shudder, she glanced around at the reflection of home and protested, "My mind doesn't like an empty Oreen."

"Oh, this place can't do people. People have substance."

"But the Hunter…"

"The thing I destroyed?" He smiled down at her. "The Hunter, that's a good name for it." His voice did everything but pat her on the head. Terizan found herself wanting to slap him which was probably not a good idea all things considered. "The Hunter was created over the years

from Zafran's anger. He'll be glad it's gone." A soft, con-descending clucking of his tongue. "He always did have trouble controlling his anger."

They were at the gate, almost to safety. Terizan glanced back over her shoulder and nearly tread on the edge of the wizard's robe as she followed him through the gap in the wall. "What about the third wizard? What happened to him?"

"Her." His expression contained only gentle admon-ishment. "You're very curious. You do know what curi-osity killed?"

"Yeah, but I thought you liked cats."

Thief-mouse-cat.

"That's right, I do."

∾ ∾ ∾

They stepped through the mirror together.

Ahmalayz clutched at her apron pocket with one hand and jabbed an indignant finger toward Terizan with the other. "You stole the amulet!"

Terizan shrugged. It seemed pointless to deny it with the proof draped around the wizard's neck.

"You stole my amulet?"

Stealing from wizards. Not a good thing. Getting caught stealing from wizards. A worse thing. She walked over to the window, trying to look as though the possibility of going out it hadn't even begun to cross her mind. "If I hadn't stolen the amulet, we wouldn't have made it back. The Hunger would have taken me and... the other guy would have re-taken you."

"But your intent..."

"Was to get us both out of the mirror in one piece."

"You're not lying to me." He sounded pleasantly sur-prised. "All right then. How much do I owe you for... stealing me from Zafran."

She stared out the window, comforted by the sounds rising up from the city. "You don't. I did it for the chal-lenge."

"She's the best thief in Oreen." Ahmalayz had a sneer in her voice, but the wizard only nodded.

"Then because debts are an uncomfortable thing to have hanging about, let me give you a bit of advice in exchange for your rescue. My rescue. The rescue."

With one last look at the cloud cover between her and the stars, Terizan turned to find the pale grey eyes locked on hers. The sweat running suddenly down her sides had nothing to do with the oppressive heat.

"Zafran was believed to be the best wizard in Oreen."

ର ର ର

"You didn't get it? I thought you were the best?" Two sneered.

Terizan shrugged.

"Council won't pay for your failure!" Three snapped. "We'll have to send someone else to get the anchor."

About to point out that no one else stood even half a chance at success - or she'd have never gone in the first place - Terizan found her words drowned out by a sudden crash of thunder. It echoed down the long, narrow stairs that connected the inner Sanctum with the world above, it vibrated in the shelves of scrolls and it brought with it a cool breeze and the sound of rain.

One steepled her fingers and frowned. "It seems the spell has been removed regardless."

"We could tell them our thief was successful, thus the rain."

Terizan frowned Did Tribune Three just say thus?

"No." Jowls wobbling, he continued, negating his own suggestion. "The Council wanted the artifact themselves. They have a minor spell caster on staff; she was going to test it."

"Then we could…"

Terizan left them to their arguing. In the end they'd tell the council that they'd been unable to complete the job because, in the end, thieves couldn't also be liars or the whole system fell apart.

It wouldn't be long before the rest of the guild knew she'd failed. She hadn't been caught but neither had she stolen the item she'd been sent to steal.

That the item didn't exist was irrelevant; only two people knew that and Ahmalayze wasn't going to tell or the wizard would find out that she'd laid out his tower defenses. For the same reason, the servant would tell that she'd broken into the tower. The wizard didn't get out much. He had no idea how Oreen worked.

Terizan could have asked for something from the wizard's workroom, something the Council would have believed was the anchor but then the Council would have assumed things could be stolen from the wizard and the next time they thought he was interfering they'd come to the Guild again. And the guild would come to her.

Now they wouldn't because they knew it couldn't be done.

From the speculative glances that followed her across the common room, the whispers of her failure had already begun.

After a nap, she'd console herself with some shopping having stopped on her way back to the Guild House and fenced the string of gold skulls for tidy sum. By now, the skulls had been melted down. By tonight they'd just be part of some jeweler's inventory on the Street of Glass.

"Zafran was believed to be the best wizard in Oreen."

And look where he ended up.

Sometimes, Terizan stole to make a point. Sometimes to right a wrong. Sometimes because she really hated to be dicked around.

And sometimes just because she was the best thief in Oreen.

Even if only she and Zafran knew it.

Author's Afterword

This collection includes THIRD TIME LUCKY, the very first story I ever sold. I wrote it back in the early eighties while on vacation in Cuba, rewrote bits of it at the insistence of a couple of friends (primarily Bruce Schneier if I remember correctly, although Maia Cowan did move all the commas one word to the left), sent it off to Gardner Dozois at Asimov's who didn't want it (although he may have seen the pre-Bruce and Maia version), then sent it to George Scithers at Amazing who did. Given publishing schedules, the second story I sold (WHAT LITTLE GIRLS ARE MADE OF for Magic in Ithkar III) came out first but THIRD TIME LUCKY started the whole thing.

Sixteen novels and twenty-four short stories later, I still think it's a pretty good story.

Once I'd created the most powerful wizard in the world it was impossible to leave her alone; it was just too much fun to write about someone so cheerfully lecherous and unabashedly lazy who almost incidentally happens to be incredibly powerful. The fine people at Tesseract Books have set the Magdelene stories in as close to chronological order as is possible given the vague time markers within the stories but checking the dates on the copyright page will give you the order they were written in. The first is the order of Magdelene's life, the second of mine. I like to think the later stories show a matured writing ability. I like to think that, it may or may not be true.

If I could be any of my characters, I think I'd like to be Magdelene.

Terizan? Well, Terazin grew out of the punch line of SWAN'S BRAID which obviously needed a thief to pull it off. In many ways she is the antithesis of Magdelene — driven, competitive, emotions tightly under control. Terizan's stories are a little less lighthearted than Magdelene's; not being the most powerful wizard in the world, she's forced to be more involved in the world around her. But there's still room for a few laughs.

Will there be more Magdelene and/or Terazin stories? Probably.

There should always be room for a few laughs.

Author's addendum 2005

I wrote WE TWO MAY MEET, the new Magdelene story in this revised collection, for the DAW 30th anniversary anthology. Because the due date was September 30th, 2001, most of us were trying to write our stories in the weeks directly after 9/11. A number of people were having some trouble getting any work done and I mentioned on a couple of occasions that I was glad I was writing a Magdelene story since it was unlikely to be effected by the event. Then I discovered I was writing a story about survivor guilt.

Writing never happens in a vacuum.

Publication Credits

Our titles are available at major book stores
and local independent resellers who support
Science Fiction and Fantasy readers like you.

Apparition Trail, The by Lisa Smedman - (tp) - ISBN:1-894063-22-8
Black Chalice by Marie Jakober - (hb) - ISBN:1-894063-00-7
Blue Apes by Phyllis Gotlieb (pb) - ISBN:1-895836-13-1
Blue Apes by Phyllis Gotlieb (hb) - ISBN:1-895836-14-X
Children of Atwar, The by Heather Spears (pb) - ISBN:0-888783-35-3
Claus Effect by David Nickle & Karl Schroeder, The (pb) - ISBN:1-895836-34-4
Claus Effect by David Nickle & Karl Schroeder, The (hb) - ISBN:1-895836-35-2
Courtesan Prince, The by Lynda Williams (tp) - 1-894063-28-7
Dark Earth Dreams by Candas Dorsey & Roger Deegan (comes with a CD) -
    ISBN:1-895836-05-0
Distant Signals by Andrew Weiner (tp) - ISBN:0-888782-84-5
Dreams of an Unseen Planet by Teresa Plowright (tp) - ISBN:0-888782-82-9
Dreams of the Sea by Élisabeth Vonarburg (tp) - ISBN:1-895836-96-4
Dreams of the Sea by Élisabeth Vonarburg (hb) - ISBN:1-895836-98-0
Eclipse by K. A. Bedford - (tp) - ISBN:978-1-894063-30-2
Even The Stones by Marie Jakober - (tp) - ISBN:1-894063-18-X
Fires of the Kindred by Robin Skelton (tp) - ISBN:0-888782-71-3
Game of Perfection, A by Élisabeth Vonarburg (tp) - ISBN:978-1-894063-32-6
Green Music by Ursula Pflug (tp) - ISBN:1-895836-75-1
Green Music by Ursula Pflug (hb) - ISBN:1895836-77-8
Healer, The by Amber Hayward (tp) - ISBN:1-895836-89-1
Healer, The by Amber Hayward (hb) - ISBN:1-895836-91-3
Jackal Bird by Michael Barley (pb) - ISBN:1-895836-07-7
Jackal Bird by Michael Barley (hb) - ISBN:1-895836-11-5
Keaen by Till Noever - (tp) - ISBN:1-894063-08-2
Land/Space edited by Candas Jane Dorsey and Judy McCrosky (tp)
    - ISBN:1-895836-90-5
Land/Space edited by Candas Jane Dorsey and Judy McCrosky (hb)
    - ISBN:1-895836-92-1
Lyskarion: The Song of the Wind by J.A. Cullum - (tp) - ISBN:1-894063-02-3
Machine Sex and other stories by Candas Jane Dorsey (tp) - ISBN:0-888782-78-0
Maërlande Chronicles, The by Élisabeth Vonarburg (pb) - ISBN:0-888782-94-2
Moonfall by Heather Spears (pb) - ISBN:0-888783-06-X
On Spec: The First Five Years edited by On Spec (pb) - ISBN:1-895836-08-5
On Spec: The First Five Years edited by On Spec (hb) - ISBN:1-895836-12-3
Orbital Burn by K. A. Bedford - (tp) - ISBN:1-894063-10-4
Orbital Burn by K. A. Bedford - (hb) - ISBN:1-894063-12-0
Pallahaxi Tide by Michael Coney (pb) - ISBN:0-888782-93-4
Passion Play by Sean Stewart (pb) - ISBN:0-888783-14-0
Plague Saint by Rita Donovan, The - (tp) - ISBN:1-895836-28-X
Plague Saint by Rita Donovan, The - (hb) - ISBN:1-895836-29-8
Reluctant Voyagers by Élisabeth Vonarburg (pb) - ISBN:1-895836-09-3
Reluctant Voyagers by Élisabeth Vonarburg (hb) - ISBN:1-895836-15-8
Resisting Adonis by Timothy J. Anderson (tp) - ISBN:1-895836-84-0
Resisting Adonis by Timothy J. Anderson (hb) - ISBN:1-895836-83-2

Silent City, The by Élisabeth Vonarburg (tp) - ISBN:0-888782-77-2
Slow Engines of Time, The by Élisabeth Vonarburg (tp) - ISBN:1-895836-30-1
Slow Engines of Time, The by Élisabeth Vonarburg (hb) - ISBN:1-895836-31-X
Stealing Magic (expanded edition) by Tanya Huff (tp) - ISBN:978-1-894063-34-0
Stealing Magic by Tanya Huff (hb) - ISBN:1-895836-64-6
Strange Attractors by Tom Henighan (pb) - ISBN:0-888783-12-4
Taming, The by Heather Spears (pb) - ISBN:1-895836-23-9
Taming, The by Heather Spears (hb) - ISBN:1-895836-24-7
Ten Monkeys, Ten Minutes by Peter Watts (tp) - ISBN:1-895836-74-3
Ten Monkeys, Ten Minutes by Peter Watts (hb) - ISBN:1-895836-76-X
Tesseracts 1 edited by Judith Merril (pb) - ISBN:0-888782-79-9
Tesseracts 2 edited by Phyllis Gotlieb & Douglas Barbour (pb) - ISBN:0-888782-70-5
Tesseracts 3 edited by Candas Jane Dorsey & Gerry Truscott (pb) - ISBN:0-888782-90-X
Tesseracts 4 edited by Lorna Toolis & Michael Skeet (pb) - ISBN:0-888783-22-1
Tesseracts 5 edited by Robert Runté & Yves Maynard (pb) - ISBN:1-895836-25-5
Tesseracts 5 edited by Robert Runté & Yves Maynard (hb) - ISBN:1-895836-26-3
Tesseracts 6 edited by Robert J. Sawyer & Carolyn Clink (pb) - ISBN:1-895836-32-8
Tesseracts 6 edited by Robert J. Sawyer & Carolyn Clink (hb) - ISBN:1-895836-33-6
Tesseracts 7 edited by Paula Johanson & Jean-Louis Trudel (tp) - ISBN:1-895836-58-1
Tesseracts 7 edited by Paula Johanson & Jean-Louis Trudel (hb) - ISBN:1-895836-59-X
Tesseracts 8 edited by John Clute & Candas Jane Dorsey (tp) - ISBN:1-895836-61-1
Tesseracts 8 edited by John Clute & Candas Jane Dorsey (hb) - ISBN:1-895836-62-X
Tesseracts 9 edited by Nalo Hopkinson and Geoff Ryman (tp) - ISBN:1-894063-26-0
TesseractsQ edited by Élisabeth Vonarburg & Jane Brierley (pb) - ISBN:1-895836-21-2
TesseractsQ edited by Élisabeth Vonarburg & Jane Brierley (hb) - ISBN:1-895836-22-0
Throne Price by Lynda Williams and Alison Sinclair - (tp) - ISBN:1-894063-06-6

EDGE

EDGE Science Fiction and Fantasy Publishing
P. O. Box 1714, Calgary, AB, Canada, T2P 2L7
www.edgewebsite.com
403-2545-0160 (voice)
403-254-0456 (fax)

Speculative Fiction Short Stories

Science Fiction Space Opera

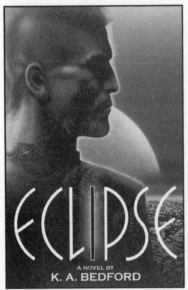

Science Fiction
Psychological Thriller

Speculative Fiction

Alternate History

High Fantasy

Fantasy

Science Fiction

Alternate History

High Fantasy

Fantasy

Science Fiction

WHAT SHOULD I READ NEXT?

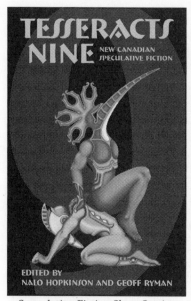

Speculative Fiction Short Stories

Science Fiction Space Opera

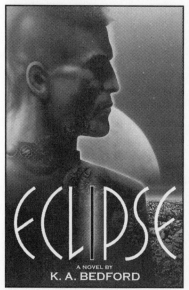

Science Fiction
Psychological Thriller

Speculative Fiction

EDGE

EDGE Science Fiction and Fantasy Publishing
P. O. Box 1714, Calgary, AB, Canada, T2P 2L7
www.edgewebsite.com
403-2545-0160 (voice)
403-254-0456 (fax)

Our titles are available at major book stores
and local independent resellers who support
Science Fiction and Fantasy readers like you.